Infallible

INFALLIBLE

Wait... The Holy Father Said What???

Howard Siegel

Right Angle Books
Johns Island, South Carolina

Infallible Copyright © by Howard Siegel. All Rights Reserved.

Contents

Books by Howard Siegel
xi

In Memoriam
xii

Preface
xiii

The Jesus of Thomas Jefferson
xiv

Prologue
xv

Chapter 1.
Savior Land
1

Chapter 2.
Roland Jaspers
6

Chapter 3.
When All Hell Broke Loose in The Vatican
17

Chapter 4.
The Infallible Pope Meets Precious Darling, the Suicide Dog
22

Chapter 5.
Marching to the Beat of a Different Drummer Boy
30

Chapter 6.
Call Me Tom
42

Chapter 7.
Back in Business
48

Chapter 8.
The Butt is Buttered
58

Chapter 9.
It's a Gift from God
64

Chapter 10.
The Albino Option
70

Chapter 11.
Reality TV
79

Chapter 12.
Holy Shit Times Infinity
88

Chapter 13.
Let's make a deal
92

Chapter 14.
The Tom in My Cell, Part 1
100

Chapter 15.
The Tom in My Cell, Part 2 (The Tale of the Toms)
110

Chapter 16.
Lightning Hath Struck the Shithouse
117

Chapter 17.
The Deacon of Doubt
121

Chapter 18.
The Straitjacket Plan
129

Chapter 19.
All Rithe
133

Chapter 20.
The Wisdom of Mike Tyson
142

Chapter 21.
Plan B
147

Chapter 22.
Jesus!
152

Chapter 23.
The Resurrection
161

Chapter 24.
The Making of a Sow's Ear
168

Chapter 25.
It's A Good Book
174

Chapter 26.
2 Thessalonians Walked Into a Bar
181

Chapter 27.
ShalamaKorabaniRendoshalaZabarenuTalamende
185

Chapter 28.
Jihads and Crusades
191

Chapter 29.
Finding the Ether
196

Chapter 30.
Truck Stop Mary and the Twelve Opossums
203

Chapter 31.
[Lepers and Lourdes](#)
211

Chapter 32.
[The Day of the Mildly Injured](#)
217

Chapter 33.
[Br'er Rabbit Redux](#)
222

Chapter 34.
[All The World is a Stage](#)
227

Chapter 35.
[Faith](#)
230

Chapter 36.
[God is Great!](#)
234

Chapter 37.
[Just One More Thing](#)
239

Chapter 38.
[Hey, Y'all... Watch This!](#)
242

Chapter 39.
[Oh Shit!](#)
247

Chapter 40.
[Opening Statements](#)
251

Chapter 41.
[Mary and The Demiurge](#)
258

Chapter 42.
[Epilogue](#)
263

About the Author

Books by Howard Siegel

The First Thing We Do is Kill All the Isms
(Critical thinking in the age of ideology and religiosity)

The Beast and the Light in the Garden of Eden
(Making sense of Genesis and animal suffering)

Ordinary Beasts
(Hunting and Cultural Psychopathy)

Donald Trump is President of the United States
(Are You Shitting Me)

Everything that Lives and Moves
(A Confrontation with the Origin of Natural Evil)
www.howardsiegel.com

In Memoriam

For Eleanor and Sandy Orr, who somehow taught me how to think outside the box that the box came in at a time when I thought I was not at all interested in thinking about anything other than the opposite sex.

INFALLIBLE XIII

Preface

I began writing *Infallible* a couple of decades ago. It was originally called *The Blasphemer* for reasons that will become obvious as you read on. I decided to update and finish it a year or so ago, having abandoned it to move on to matters I considered more pressing, such as the modest goal of trying to rid the world of its addiction to willful stupidity.

For those of you who read my last novel, *Everything That Lives and Moves*, you will meet Pope Thomas again. He was originally inspired by the fictional Ukranian Pope Kiril I, in Morris West's 1963 novel, *The Shoes of the Fisherman*. So, while it may seem as though I borrowed Pope Thomas from my previous novel, the truth is that I borrowed him for *Everything that Lives and Moves* from the book you are reading. I hoped that life might have possibly imitated art when Pope Francis was elected in 2013. Try and imagine Pope Francis on mind-expanding drugs or after a head injury with sense knocked *into* him, and you will begin to get the idea.

Anyway, I had great fun writing this one. I hope that you have fun reading it.

I almost forgot. All the characters in this book come from my imagination, and any similarity with real people is purely coincidental — except for the references to Donald Trump, who is a real person and who, in real life, has been, and always will be, a flaming asshole.

Howard Siegel
February 12, 2024

The Jesus of Thomas Jefferson

"I hold the precepts of Jesus as delivered by Himself, to be the most pure, benevolent and sublime which have ever been preached to man."

"Among the sayings and discourses imputed to him (i.e. Jesus) by his biographers, I find many passages of fine imagination, correct morality, and of the most lovely benevolence; and others again of so much ignorance, so much absurdity, so much untruth, charlatanism, and imposture, as to pronounce it impossible that such contradictions should have proceeded from the same being"

"The clergy converted the simple teachings of Jesus into an engine for enslaving mankind and adulterated by artificial constructions into a contrivance to filch wealth and power to themselves...these clergy, in fact, constitute the real Anti-Christ."

On Revelation... "merely the ravings of a maniac, no more worthy nor capable of explanation than the incoherences of our own nightly dreams"

"Ridicule is the only weapon which can be used against unintelligible propositions."

Prologue

You are probably reading this book because you, like much of the world, wonder how Pope Thomas I came to be put on trial for crimes of disorderly conduct, trespassing, blasphemy, destruction of property, and littering. And how did it happen to begin on the 100th anniversary of the Scopes Monkey Trial in Dayton, Tennessee?

You may also wonder why he chose me to write an account of these events. The answer to the first question is a long one. Hence, this book. The answer to the second question begins here.

When the New York Times wrote the story titled WHY DID POPE THOMAS I CHOOSE A HOMELESS ALCOHOLIC EX-HISTORY PROFESSOR AS HIS OFFICIAL CHRONICLER? I thought it was a fair question. There has been much speculation about the fortuity of my connection to H.L. Mencken, who covered the original Scopes trial, and whether my involvement in Scopes II was a coincidence or a carefully orchestrated choice. The answer is that it was neither. I want to address the seemingly unlikely convergence issue here. The question asked (and mostly unanswered) by the *New York Times* article will involve telling the story.

How could it have possibly come about that a man who was educated by virtue of a trust set up by the H.L. Mencken became intimately involved and was selected by the Pontiff to recount the events of Scopes II?

Read on.

Here is what you need to know about me. My mother named me Henry Lewis (H.L.) Jefferson. I am a descendant of slaves, so our family name, Jefferson, is evident. The Henry Lewis moniker is another story. My grandmother, Sarah Laverne Jefferson, was a housekeeper in Baltimore for most of her life. She worked for H.L. Mencken, the famous *Baltimore Sun* journalist, satirist, and critic of American culture and democracy who accurately predicted, a hundred years before the election of Donald Trump, "As democracy is perfected, the office of the president represents, more and more closely, the inner soul of the people. We move toward a lofty ideal. On some great and glorious day, the plain folks of the land will reach their heart's desire at last, and the White House will be adorned by a downright moron."

Much has been written about H.L. Mencken's racism, elitism, and antisemitism. The truth is that he laid waste to much of the human condition, which happens to include everyone. He was an irascible ass who woke up every day wondering who he could take a shot at. But he was a great writer who had a soft spot for my grandmother and created our family education endowment that helped put twelve of us through college.

I read everything he wrote before I graduated from high school. Twenty years later, I went on a sabbatical from my tenured professor of American history position at Vanderbilt to research and write a comprehensive history of the 1925 Scopes trial originally reported to the world and immortalized by my benefactor. That is how I came to be in Dayton when the Pontiff was arrested. I will explain how I became his cellmate in the Rhea County Detention Center in a few chapters of this book. So, you see, if my connection to H.L.Mencken and my involvement in Scopes II strikes you as either an improbable coincidence or serendipity – well, like many events that initially make our eyebrows go up and we find it difficult to believe – it is all quite easily explained.

In the week before William Jennings Bryan and Clarence Darrow gave their opening statements to the jury, Mencken wrote of Dayton, "The town was plagued by its population of *yokels, hillbillies, and the lower orders,* and *ignorant, dishonest, cowardly, ignoble,* and *immortal vermin.*"

When I arrived, those characters were no longer at plague levels, but they were undoubtedly present, and I will do my best to tell you about them. History repeats itself, sometimes due to ignorance and sometimes because it serves a common purpose to do it again. On one level, the Scopes Monkey trial was a sham and a carefully orchestrated farce. I suppose it will be argued that Scopes II fits that same bill. But both trials still have much to tell us about the human condition. I hope I do them justice.

Henry Lewis Jefferson July 10, 2025

xviii   Howard Siegel

1

Savior Land

Two miles west of Dayton, Tennessee, on Highway 27, about twenty miles east of Chattanooga, sat Savior Land, where for $14.95, the faithful could visit a monstrous indoor mall, a museum of religious curiosities, and a Jesus-themed amusement park. The museum was designed with an elaborate dinosaur hall that included one exhibit showing a cave boy riding a raptor engaged in what appeared to be a game of dino-polo and another with a blonde cavewoman, who bore a striking resemblance to Marjorie Taylor Greene, behind a plow hitched up to a smiling, happy-go-lucky triceratops.

The mall had the largest indoor ride in the world, called The Holy Roller Coaster, and an indoor-outdoor John the Baptist Water Slide Park (Requires Separate Admission: $10.95 plus $4 for a towel and locker) where all the water had been blessed by the mall minister, Reverend Allister Conogher (*Bless you folks. Enjoy your purchases, Praise Jesus, and come back and see us real soon!)* This attraction allowed for wholesome aquatic family fun combined with an upbeat baptism ceremony in the *Pool of Our Lord* for an additional $13.95 (10.95 for seniors and children under twelve and $17.95 on Christmas and Easter Sunday.) The acclaimed indoor ice rink hosted the minor league Tennessee Crusaders Hockey Team in season and a *Christ on Ice* musical extravaganza during the rest of the year.

But the crowd favorite was the gondola ride around the dreaded Lake of Fire. Contrary to the condescending reviews in the New York Times, the Savior Land Lake of Fire exhibit was not a representation of hell. It was more of a preview of the coming attractions for hell as described in Revelation. A red neon sign above the entrance menacingly warned, *But for the cowardly and unbelieving and the abominable and murderers and immoral persons and sorcerers and idolaters and all liars, their part will be in the lake that burns with fire and brimstone, which is the second death. Revelation 21:8.* In his Sunday sermon, Savior Land Reverend Conogher had taken pains to explain to the congregation that although Donald Trump possibly told an occasional fib, he would be exempted from the liar's fate set forth in *Revelation* due to his courageous pro-life stance regardless of whether, as rumored, he had paid for three abortions. After all, King David was in heaven, and he had sent Uriah, the soldier-husband of Bathsheba, with whom he was having an adulterous relationship, off to serve in the front lines, where, exactly as the king had hoped, the poor cuckolded warrior had been sliced and diced by three accommodating Philistines clearing the king's path to Bathsheba's earthly garden delights.

There were unwritten exceptions to every holy rule.

The Savior Land faithful treated the gruesome fiery

events foretold in *Revelation* as a wondrous celestially sanctioned 4th of July type celebration and a signal that Jesus had returned to bless the righteous with rapture. More importantly, he would roast the non-believers like Hebrew National hot dogs. The Lake of Fire exhibit consisted of a four Olympic swimming pool-sized artificial lake filled with the most advanced pyrotechnics and was fueled by five underground 60,000-gallon propane tanks. On the sides of the lake were robotic men with carefully sculpted hooked noses who could have been either Jews, Muslims, or Italians – robot women, who were dressed in low-cut revealing tube-tops and Daisy Duke shorts, and children who were all dead ringers for the horror movie star doll Chucky or his twin sister. They were cast *en masse* into the flaming lake as if propelled by grenade launchers and immediately appeared to be roasted into a burnt marshmallow-like substance. Blood-curdling screams and laments were pumped in from above using the latest Dolby Surround Mega Sound System 12.4. The Lake was in the middle of a small island encircled by a moat with twenty gondolas manufactured by the same company that made the boats for the equally ridiculous *Canals of Venice* ride at the opulent Venetian Hotel and Casino in Las Vegas. The ride was thought to be a bargain at $11.95. Cheering from the gondolas was encouraged when the liars and non-believing men, women, and children were cast into the fire. The original theme for the attraction called for allowing visitors to help push the heathens into the flaming hell pit for a slight extra charge, but it was nixed as potentially too controversial.

There was no lack of controversy surrounding the Wrath of God Gun Exchange, the largest year-round "private" gun show in the world where any lunatic who swore allegiance to the United States of America and Jesus Christ Our Lord and Savior, would be admitted for $10 and was then free to purchase a variety of military-grade weapons which could be used to hold off the Chinese atheist communists when the yellow hordes came storming across the Mexican border intent on defiling and gang raping the nations privately owned fleet of pick-up trucks. Every admittee received a free *Build the Wall* and *Stop the Vermin From Poisoning Our Blood* bumper sticker.

A discrimination suit had been filed in the United States District Court for the Southern District of Tennessee brought by one Fareed Ali Atwa, a devout Muslim and leading Midwestern frozen falafel distributor who refused to take the patriotic and religious pledge and was denied admission. The suit was terminated (the legal term is *dismissed with prejudice*) when Mr. Atwa's bullet-riddled body was found in the parking lot of Fareed's Frozen Falafel plant in Nashville.

Harlan Whitestone, the police detective investigating the case, had fought in the Iraq war and had sustained a disfiguring injury when a sniper had shot off half of his right ear while he was beating a local street vendor whom he suspected of being an Arab. As a community, Nashville had more than its share of hard-working Middle Eastern immigrants who were rarely in trouble. "That's terrific," Harlan had said when his wife confronted him with the FBI crime statistics, "but we can only guess what those camel fuckers are doing when we aren't watching." At the scene of Atwa's murder, he remarked to his partner that the eleven bullet wounds meant foul play could not be ruled out. The culprits were never apprehended even though a Ford F-150 with a Confederate Flag decal and a bumper sticker that said, *Biden Sucks, Pelosi Swallows* was seen leaving the area at a high rate of speed.

No further discrimination suits were filed against the Wrath of God Gun Exchange.

At the entrance to the enormous gun show exhibit hall was a 24-foot by 24-foot oil painting that looked like it might have been painted by Leroy Neiman after ingesting a double dose of LSD and meth, showing Charlton Heston with a musket held above his head. Above the painting in giant gold leaf letters were the inscriptions: WHEN THEY PRY IT FROM MY COLD DEAD HANDS and BE PREPARED TO DEFEND THE LORD WHEN THEY COME. It was unclear exactly who "they" were. Charlton Heston had passed on to the great armory in the sky in 2008. The official cause of death was reported as "natural causes," but it was known that the famous actor and former president of the National Rifle Association suffered from Alzheimer's. The rumor was that Carlos, his certified nursing assistant, was, ironically, struggling to pry the icon's favorite assault rifle out of his hands when it went off. It missed him, but his heart gave out, putting an unfortunate firearms-related end to an otherwise glorious and delusional life spent believing that he was God's gun messenger.

For over a decade, Savior Land ranked in the top five malls in the United States. And then things took a disastrous downturn. The mall's owner, Roland Jaspers, feared things were headed straight to hell.

2

Roland Jaspers

Savior Land was the brainchild of Roland Jaspers, a Dallas, Texas, born-again former asbestos mogul who got out with a cool billion before all the nasty asbestos litigation began and was now heavily invested in shopping malls and tobacco companies. (*People are gonna shop, and those oriental types love a good smoke. Plus, there's a shitload of them, and they ain't allowed to sue us if their lungs get yellower from the cancer.*)

Jaspers claimed to have been born again after he had been saved from almost certain choking death while attending an award gathering sponsored by the Evangelical Business Achievers in Branson, Missouri. At the dinner banquet, while he was eating and staring at the ample cleavage of the Miracle Glue CEO's escort, a large portion of his not-so-petite filet mignon (which was actually a rump cut of Wyoming quarter horse) became lodged in his throat. Fortunately, he was seated next to Pastor Rick Hawkins, who commanded a Christian financial empire, the estimated net worth of which Forbes reported to be over 650 million. Reverend Rick was the King of the TV Evangelicals, and his "prosperity church" was prosperous indeed. His book, *Jesus Wants You to Be Totally Richer than the Non-Believers*, was an Amazon best seller. Reverend Rick, a former Trinidad and Tobago Condo timeshare charlatan, had amassed a personal fortune convincing the faithful that if they prayed hard enough, watched his show regularly, and sent in significant portions of their savings and social security checks to aid him in bringing the "good news" to the masses, they would get a return on their faith investment that would have them living in heaven on earth. Rick already lived in heaven on earth by virtue of his acquisition of six multi-million dollar homes around the world, two G-5s, thirteen exotic cars, and a virtually unlimited supply of porn stars, so there could be no denying that the system worked as advertised.

When Roland Jaspers began to gag and turn a shade of blue reminiscent of the azure cover of *Trinidad-Tobago Timeshares*, Reverend Rick muttered, "Oh fuck me," under his breath, got up after hesitating long enough to see if anyone else at the table would hopefully beat him to the role of CPR savior, and when no one did, he administered a half-assed Heimlich maneuver that, as luck would have it, praise be to Jesus, worked well enough to get Roland Jaspers to expel the fraudulent cut of horse derrière which went flying across the table and landed in a glass of pinot noir being held by Margaret Farnsworth, heiress to the Captain Finnegan Fried Fish fast-food fortune. Mrs. Farnsworth asked her waiter for a fresh glass just before commenting on how relieved she was that Roland Jaspers seemed to be on the road to recovery.

Jaspers and Hawkins became fast friends, and Jaspers was both impressed and amazed at the stunning fortune amassed by the pastor in the business end of faith in the Lord. In the weeks that followed, Jaspers extrapolated that (1) Hawkins and his religious cohorts were essentially selling air and nothing of value at deliciously obscene markups, (2) the fundamentalists-born-again segment of the Christian population were dumber than lemmings and much easier to lead over the cliff, and (3) there were bushel baskets full of them just begging to hand over their money for the promise that it was going into Jesus's coffers or at least going to a first-string member of the Jesus team. And that was the exact moment when Roland Jaspers decided to be born again.

Jaspers split his time between managing his financial empire and keeping tabs on the medical research he funded at the Bryan –as in William Jennings Bryan — Baptist University. At age sixty-seven, Jaspers weighed slightly under two hundred and seventy pounds and stood only five feet, five inches with lifts that he had put in every pair of shoes and his bedroom slippers. In a particularly unflattering Rolling Stone profile, he was described as "... a sawed-off version of Zero Mostel devoid of anything resembling jocularity."

Roland Jaspers was acutely aware that he had been in the money-making line when the Lord was handing out good looks, but the additional curse of a severe case of early onset psoriasis was a cross he felt he should not have had to bear.

It had started on his ankles and elbows as rough annoying, slightly itchy patches and then appeared suddenly with a vengeance in the sensitive area between his ample butt cheeks just north of his rectum. He had tried everything and seen the best dermatologists at the Mayo Clinic. Still, they all left him essentially where they found him complaining that their creams were like putting hydrocortisone on a goddamn chigger bite. Chiggers have been heard to yell in unison, *Bring it!* when a hapless victim is about to apply any anti-itch salve to an affected area. No matter what they prescribed, it did not help. And there was simply no surreptitious way to scratch between one's butt cheeks. He had lamented to the Chief of Dermatology at the Mayo Clinic, "*Look Doc, when it comes to scratching your balls, you can get away with it by pretending you are looking for loose change or a pocket watch. Try scratching your ass at a board meeting. There's just no fucking way to pretend you are doing something else. It ain't like you can pretend you are looking for your fucking cell phone. Who keeps a cell phone up his ass?*"

The doctors agreed this was the first reported case of intergluteal cleft psoriasis. They were baffled by the condition's location and resistance to the strongest topical steroid ointments they prescribed. The condition periodically got so bad that Jaspers had resorted to inserting a sheet of P280 grit designation sandpaper between his butt cheeks. By shifting in his seat, he could obtain temporary relief, but the price he paid was an ass that resembled the color and texture of steak tartar. It was at those times that he tried to figure out which was worse; an ass that felt like it had been beset by a bevy of hungry chiggers (the bites of which are often described by Tennessee country folks as "itching like a motherfucker"), or a backside that had been placed on a fire ant mound. It was a classic Hobson choice, and it led him to give a two million dollar grant to the BBU natural medicine program to be used exclusively to find a cure for what he called "the skin condition from hell."

Psoriasis is an autoimmune condition. As such, the chances of finding a cure were roughly equivalent to the Bryan University Lions' lily-white-boy basketball team winning the NCAA Division I Championship. Nevertheless, the research went on, and Department Chairman, Dr. Chip Wentworth, whose previous claim to dermatological research fame was a treatment for solar lentigo, that scourge of the septuagenarian, also known as the "liver spot." Dr. Wentworth's miracle liver spot cream had been sent to Pfizer and was currently subject to meticulous double-blind testing. Preliminary in-house results equated the cream's efficacy with Mary Kay's "Cover-it-up."

Dr. Wentworth had made zero progress in two years of research on the curse of ass-crack psoriasis, but he had completed three trips to the Amazon rainforest to investigate promising native botanical salves. The truth be known, he never made it off the beaches and resorts of Rio, which were technically adjacent to the rainforests, where he was able to nail down, once and for all, the truth of the legends of the best string bikini bodies in the world. The stories were true. Dr. Wentworth always took Roland Jasper's calls and assured him he was working on "something really promising."

But nothing inflamed Roland Jasper's ass more than losing money, and lately, he had been losing shit-tons of it. Several unforeseeable trends had conspired to threaten his financial empire. During the disastrous economic turndown of 2008-9, Americans had begun to break their addiction to malls. Roland, of course, blamed Obama (*Look boys, I can abide by a nice colored feller as much as the next guy, but when I see that Muslim doing his jigaboo dancing and singing and jump shooting in the White House... well, by God and Jesus Christ, there are limits!*) But the truth was that shopping malls became passé overnight. Part of that was because the markets had crashed, and unemployment was at record highs. Part of it was due to a growing dissatisfaction with the mall's "atmosphere" such as it was. The same stores and the same Gap crap were everywhere. One economist described the shopping exodus as a hundredth monkey phenomenon, a curious and seemingly unexplainable form of group behavior described by a British crackpot scientist who reported as a fact that monkeys on one island in Japan could read the thoughts of and learn behavior from monkeys on another island. The hundredth monkey phenomena turned out to be complete horseshit, and even if it were true, it is doubtful that the collective consciousness of the American mall goer was as cosmically in tune as the average Japanese macaca fuscata.

The slow and ignominious death of the American mall was brought about by the good folks at Amazon.com. They did it better and cheaper because, in the jargon of the smoothie unemployed commercial real estate broker, they didn't have to pay for "bricks." Join Amazon Prime, and you didn't even have to pay for deliveries. Returns were a snap; they even credited your account before returning the merchandise. Shopping choices seemed infinite. If Amazon didn't have it in one of their warehouses, they had a link that brought whatever you craved to your doorstep. Virtual shopping was another variation of instant gratification on the internet for the lazy masses. The malls became to shopping what the 8-track was to music. Unnecessary, and so last year. Yes, many folks still liked to shop by the touch-and-feel method, but they were a dying breed. Shoppers had simply tired of dealing with driving, parking, crime, and little fuckwads on skateboards who never bought anything. And the only people who would even consider working at the mall stores were the girlfriends of the little skateboarding fuckwads, the curdled cream of the American workforce (*Like, I think this stuff is on sale, but I'm like totally not totally sure...*) The handwriting was on the bathroom wall and the great American mall seemed doomed.

The steady decline in the ranks of religious fundamentalists hadn't helped Savior Land's business either. The believers were still out there in formidable numbers and still able to influence elections in much of the country by expressing their support for the men God had chosen as leaders, like Donald Trump. Still, the tide was turning, and there were times when it seemed like the only publicity about Jesus involved ministers, priests, and pastors caught up in sexual perversion stings, embezzlement of parishioner donations, and extravagant lifestyles that made rock stars blush. To make matters worse, predictions of the highly anticipated End of Days never seemed to pan out as promised. Bill Maher, Jimmy Kimmel, and Trever Noah had legions of godless joke writers who would turn to the religious scandal of the day for the can't-miss punchline *de jour.*

Savior Land and Roland Jaspers had been parodied so often that the mere mention of the place made audiences belly-laugh. When a treacherous medical records clerk who had been fired from Savior Land after a security search of her locker uncovered a copy of *Fifty Shades of Gray*, leaked details of Roland Jasper's intergluteal cleft psoriasis in clear violation of HIPPA, 45 CFR Part 160 and

Part 164 it seemed as if the former asbestos mogul was smack dab in the middle of a 21st-century follow-up to the *Book of Job*.

Things went from bad to worse with the Jesus Loves You Dating Site (*Motto: Find the Romance that Our Savior has in mind for you!*) fiasco. The Jasper's Enterprises Christian version of Match.com was going like gangbusters until it was successfully hacked by cynical pranksters who linked the entire membership up with flaminghotpussy.com. All members were given their choice of watching free *Sex Starved Bang Sluts, Womb Raider, Romancing the Bone, White Men Can't Hump,* or *Saturday Night Beaver*. The introductory offer was signed by a forged Roland Jaspers signature and photo and contained what was claimed to be an authentic picture of his inflamed ass at the bottom with the promise that he would be starring in the upcoming sequel to *Sorest Rump*. While short-term membership increased dramatically, the site had to be closed indefinitely until the *Jesus Loves You* IT department could erect effective firewalls. In the meantime, some members were spooked at the turn of events and the distinct possibility that their lingering moments watching *Womb Raider* would become a matter of a hacked public record. It seemed much safer to migrate to ChristianMingle.com, where "God's match" was claimed to be waiting and flaminghotpussy.com had been successfully firewalled.

The public perception of American religious fundamentalists as dolts began in earnest with Congresswoman Michelle Bachman, who brazenly asserted that the swine flu epidemic surfaced under President Obama, a known and unrepentant Muslim democrat, and Jimmy Carter, another notorious socialist.

She seemed to be arguing that there was a causal connection between liberals and loathsome diseases. She remained unfazed when a member of the press corps pointed out that the "Obama swine flu epidemic" (1) did not even qualify as a notable event and (2) that it was Gerald Ford, a Republican, who was in the White House when the disease had surfaced. Bachmann's fictitious and ludicrous proclamation was followed and one-upped by Georgia Representative Paul Broun, who held a seat on, of all places, The House Science Committee, announcing definitively that evolution and the Big Bang theory were "lies straight from the pit of hell meant to convince people that they do not need a savior." The idea was that Darwin was sitting around one day with Thomas Huxley, trying to think of a way to discredit the Savior idea. "I've got it," said Huxley. "Why don't you spend five years traveling around the world on the HMS Beagle, and when you come back, write a book about the origin of species, and everyone will read it and run out in the streets shouting *We don't need no Savior!*"

Then, there was Oklahoma Senator James Inhofe, who sat on the Senate Science Committee. Senator Inhofe — also a dedicated conspiracy theorist — claimed that climate change was a monstrous hoax perpetrated by socialists who were hell-bent on *regulating* Americans' lives. Regulation, according to the Senator, was the moral equivalent of handcuffing and defiling virgins. Inhofe offered the following reasoning as definitive proof of the climate change hoax. "The hoax is that there are some people who are so arrogant to think they are so powerful they can change the climate. Man can't change the climate. My point is God's still up there. The arrogance of people to think that we, human beings, would be able to change what He is doing in the climate is to me outrageous," God apparently did not make mistakes regardless of what people thought about the dinosaur's rule of the planet for 165 million years only to be the victim of a calamitous cosmic do-over. Some speculated that Inhofe and Broun had been dropped on their heads by the same father as children. The truth was that they were simply morons.

No one appreciated these public displays of stupidity of Broun and Inhofe more than Congressman Hank Johnson, a Democrat whose unwanted stranglehold on the title of "dumbest man or woman ever to hold office anywhere on the planet" was won when he was cross-examining a General about the troop buildup on Guam. Johnson had done his homework and, with the cameras rolling, asked the general about a disastrous potential scenario that only he had been astute enough to foresee. "My fear, General, is that the whole island will become so overly populated that it will tip over and capsize."

None of this was good for the image of Roland Jasper's fundamentalist-Christian-based businesses. Profits from Savior Land were down 24%, and the Jesus Loves You Dating Site was effectively out of business. However, flaminghotpussy.com became one of the leading porn sites in the industry.

Roland Jaspers was in a foul mood when he met with his CFO, Morris Greenberg. Morris had brought him up to date on the downturn in revenue the last quarter. He tried to cheer him up with the good news that The Jesus Ouija Board was selling like gangbusters at the Lake of Fire and on Amazon.

"Oh, fuck me and everyone who looks like me," Jasper's said in the tone of a man who has just been diagnosed with a malignant prostate tumor the size of a bagel. Morris

Greenberg thought very few humans looked like Roland Jaspers (thank God), and even fewer would want to take him up on his offer.

"Mr. Jaspers, things have been trending this way for the last five years, and I just don't see it turning around any time soon."

"Anytime soon?! How about any motherfuckingtime ever? I swear to God, Morris, if it started raining pussy, I'd catch one that already had a dick in it."

"Well, I'm not sure about a long-range forecast of that magnitude. The mall is still a vacation destination for a large population segment that mainstream American retailers virtually ignore. There are still 26 million people who identify themselves as deeply religious Christians. Those are our people."

Jaspers snickered out loud, thinking about his Jewish CFO (I tell you, those people can work miracles with numbers...) talking about the legions of devout Jesus-loving Christians as "our people."

"Morris, what we need is a drastic change in how we market this thing. That or a motherfucking miracle."

That same day about 1000 miles away, Pope Thomas, the spiritual leader of over a billion Catholic souls, tripped over a little brown dog in the White House, and Roland Jaspers' motherfucking miracle had begun.

3

When All Hell Broke Loose in The Vatican

There was concern and curiosity among the Cardinals when the Vicar of Christ began to resist wearing the traditional red shoes. Panic did not set in until much later.

Cardinal Battista and Cardinal Calcagno had tea every morning in the Domus Sanctae Marthae dining room. Cardinal Battista was the first to address The Pope's secretive visits to the Apostolic Archives.

"Has he spoken to you about what he has found that is so interesting? Every morning for a month. I wonder if such behavior has ever been observed by a pontiff."

"It is impossible to know," said Cardinal Calcagno. "I am often asked about his likes, dislikes, and personal habits by people outside the Vatican. I think it is for the best that the personal interests of pontiffs are not documented and are rarely even discussed."

So began the discussion of The Pope's personal habits, likes and dislikes.

"Their privacy has, as you are well aware, been protected at a transcendent level. I did ask him if he was finding his research rewarding. He told me that rewarding would not be an accurate way to say it. He looked concerned to me and said simply that it was necessary... You know that no one goes in there with him."

"He doesn't need anyone. He is fluent in Greek and Aramaic."

The Vatican Apostolic Archives is the repository that houses every document produced by the Holy See. The Pope has complete control and ownership of what is popularly known as The Secret Archives. That ownership is passed on to succeeding Popes. Pope Paul V separated The Secret Archives from the Vatican Library in 1614. In the 19th century, it was opened to scholars approved for research by the Vatican. Each petitioning scholar undergoes an extensive background check. There is one super secure room within what has been called the most secure archival building in the world, and no one but the pope has ever been allowed to enter. The room's existence was not known until 1933, and wild rumors have continuously circulated about its contents. Books have been written speculating about magical Indiana Jones-type artifacts, records of exorcisms, real-life encounters with Satan, records documenting visits by ancient aliens, and of course, the inevitable salacious tales about papal orgies and all kinds of depravity.

Papal orgies might have caused far less concern among the faithful than what was actually in that room.

The Pope's time spent in the Secret Archives was not, however, the cause of the concern circulating at the Vatican. Imagine the CEO of Exxon-Mobile commencing the annual shareholders' meeting by making a speech about corporate responsibility for climate change and suggesting that they donate half of their annual profits to green energy research and the rest to housing for the homeless. Then he announces he is supporting a Bernie Sanders protégé for the presidency. Now imagine the other members of the board, who had no idea that the CEO was about to engage in fossil fuel blasphemy, reacting to the blindside change in corporate direction. The first joint gasp and coffee being shot out of multiple noses might be followed by the universal rhetorical query that comes out of men's mouths at times like this. The assembled might even cry out in unison;

"*What the fuck?!*"

Then, they would wonder whether the death penalty was available as a remedy.

And *what the fuck?* (or *quid autem irrumab?* in Latin) might have been the first utterance of Cardinal Battista and the assembled upon learning that the Pope had decided to call into question the Church's official positions on birth control and the priesthood being the exclusive domain of men. But such expressions are frowned upon even as a reaction to the unthinkable amongst Cardinals and Bishops. Those men do not even say *Oh My God!* It is impossible to know, however, if *what the fuck?* is what they were really thinking or perhaps suppressing the same way they might try to self-exorcise thoughts that cause unwanted sexual arousal when conducting an official review of an internet porn site to declare it off-limits. There are visceral human reactions that even the holiest of men cannot deny or control.

For two weeks now, Cardinals Battista and Calcagno had been exchanging *sub-silentio What-the-fucks*, unable to contain at least some level of indelicateness in their reactions.

"My dear Cardinal... who, may I ask, is he sequestered with now? "Asked Giovanni Battista, ranking member of the Pontifical Commission for the Vatican City State.

Cardinal Domenico Calcagno, President of the Commission, sighed the resigned sigh of the hopelessly defeated. It was as if all the air was out of him before he responded, and his response was offered in the drone of a man who had not been sleeping well.

"Professor Nathan Markowitz, the American biophysicist."

"He sounds very Jewish," said Giovanni.

"He is, but when pressed, he describes himself as a pantheist of the Spinoza school, whatever that is," replied Domenico

"Ah... he sounds very much like an atheist of the scientific persuasion," said Cardinal Giovanni, sighing again and gesturing to the heavens for help that he had every reason to doubt was coming.

"Holy Mother of Jesus. What are we going to do?"

That question had been bouncing around the Vatican for two of the longest weeks in the Church's two-thousand-year history. As one observer had put it, not so delicately, all hell was breaking loose in Vatican City. It had finally come to pass. The unimaginable hypothetical disaster that had been hiding in the doctrine of papal infallibility since its inception.

Was the infallible Pope still infallible if he suddenly lost his mind?

4

The Infallible Pope Meets Precious Darling, the Suicide Dog

⁂

The Vatican has seen its share of scandals and aberrant Papal behavior. There was a Pope who had engaged in every kind of sexual deviancy imaginable and a few acts that were not. Popes who squandered the Churches' fortunes on lavish and garish excesses that would have made Donald Trump's wives gasp, almost bankrupting the Vatican. Popes who had ruthlessly ordered their political enemies murdered, Popes who had sanctioned the torture of those who voiced any criticism of the institution or its occasional excesses, Popes who had started holy wars where millions were slaughtered, and, of course, Popes who had covered up the plague of rampant sexual abuse of children by priests that stretched back to the first century.

Cardinal Calcagno thought celestial misdemeanors compared to this mess. There was simply no precedent for the unthinkable. And worse, no way out. The Catholic Church – the House that Peter built – was in danger of cracking at its foundation, and the irony was that it was about to be hoisted by its recent adoption of a new and unnecessary sacrosanct dogma. The Church had erected a seemingly impenetrable epistemological fortress that had lasted for two millennia, only to discover that they had neglected to include a back door. A fortress without an emergency exit door is a death trap once a fire starts. The very doctrine that they had invented to be the foundation of papal stability was about to bring the whole edifice crashing to earth. And "*Oops, we may have screwed the pooch on this one, so we'd better rethink this...*" was not an available response.

Papal infallibility is a doctrine that appears nowhere in the New Testament. Neither does celibacy for priests or specific admonitions against birth control. And it is doubtful that Jesus envisioned a Church that ran a financial empire that controlled a staggering amount of cash, real estate, jewels, and art and happily did business with the world's largest moneylenders. Jesus might have been shocked to witness an institution spearheaded by Popes who wore expensive white robes and red shoes who would speak on His behalf, demand total spiritual obedience, scare the bejesus out of 1.2 billion followers with tales of hell, damnation, and demonic possession, and protect legions of pedophiles in its ranks. It is doubtful that Jesus envisioned a church in any sense that we think of today.

The doctrine of papal infallibility states that when it comes to formal beliefs of the Catholic Church, the Pope is *a priori* protected from the possibility of *ever* committing a mistake. The Pope's word on matters of scripture is, in effect, the word of God who speaks through him. God, however, changes his mind and thinks up amendments, footnotes, and clarifications of his policies from time to time and must make his new positions known through the Pope. Hence, the evolution of Catholic dogma from the Council of Nicene in 362 to today.

Infallibility was not formally adopted as official Catholic dogma until the First Vatican Council of 1869 –1870 and was, therefore, a very recent theological construct. It seems to have taken that long for God to decide the matter. No one ever asks why he changed his mind. It isn't important. The great dinosaur and the comet fiasco are a case in point that is rarely brought up. The only caveat to the doctrine is that the infallible teachings of the Pope must be germane to sacred scripture.

A caustic blog by science writer and professional skeptic Sean Patterson, who had personal issues with the Church, summarized the doctrine's implications.

It had always been assumed that the Pope was 'the man' when it came to matters of biblical interpretation. But the First Vatican Council left no doubt and no room for argument. "Because he said so!" became the be-all and end-all for inquiring Catholic minds. The Pope is always right, and that is the end of that. So, for example, if the Pope were to interpret what has always been accepted as a clear biblical admonition against homosexuality, which states, "a man who lies with another man shall be stoned," to mean that gay men should do a J before engaging in sexual relations, that would be the correct interpretation ipso facto and a billion Catholics would just have to learn to live with it. And he could so proclaim because it pertains to matters of scripture.

A common misconception is that the doctrine means the Pope is infallible about everything. This is not the case. If the Pope suddenly issued a papal bull declaring, Hey diddle, diddle, the cat played the fiddle, the cow jumped over the moon, he would be expressing an opinion on a matter not contained or referenced in scripture, and the faithful would be free to doubt whether a cow could actually jump over the moon or whether a cat could play a fiddle. The whole diddling issue, however, was a matter of formal scripture and, therefore, fair game.

In the case of Pope Paul V, who forbade Christians from reading Galileo or believing his theory that the earth revolved around the sun, things became somewhat muddled. Such a heretical assertion would have conflicted with the biblical account of Joshua stopping the sun and the moon so that he could have an extra day to complete his genocide festivities against the Canaanites. This line of reasoning would become a foundational premise of the modern flat earth movement. Hybrid examples of papal infallibility coming in conflict with science are resolved relatively quickly; we are told by apologists (who, in reality, are never actually sorry for any illogical or moronic argument they put forth) because Pope Paul V was pontificating about the movement of celestial bodies before the doctrine of infallibility was formally adopted in 1870. There are numerous other rationales that apologists put forth and write long, tortured explanations about that nobody reads except the professors who teach logic in college courses who routinely blow milk out of their noses when they read them.

Science is not the bailiwick of the New Testament. Neither is math. So, if the Pope declared that trigonometry was heretical and should not be taught in schools, the faithful could presumably ignore it and assume he was having a bad day without the risk that they would be roasted in hell for eternity. That fate is argued to be reserved for children who are born in the wilds of the Amazon jungle and never get the opportunity to believe in Jesus—Revelation 21:8. And, of course, for Jews, Buddhists, Muslims, and humanists.

There is admittedly some confusion regarding extra-biblical proclamations, but upon which there has been consensus for centuries. So when Pope Thomas mused that there should be room in heaven for dogs after tripping over and squashing a Pomeranian belonging to President Robert Lancaster while attending a dinner at the White House, there was a veritable explosion of disagreement amongst the wise men at the Vatican about whether good dogs could get through the pearly gates. Were all dogs now permitted to enter or only "good dogs?" It was a thorny problem.

It was hard to believe that the whole mess had started with a nine-pound fluffy tan dog whose existence was proof positive that man should not tamper with the natural forces of evolution. The American Kennel Club describes the Pomeranian as follows: "The tiny Pomeranian, long a favorite of royals and commoners alike, has been called the ideal companion. The glorious coat, smiling, foxy face, and vivacious personality have helped make the Pom one of the world's most popular toy breeds." Of course, the real poop on these dogs is that they were bred with one and only one thing in mind; elderly women who have or would like to retire to Jupiter, Florida. The Pomeranian is the perfect condo dog. They do nothing aside from sitting on elderly ladies' laps, insist upon the most expensive gourmet dog food, and occasionally use their hysterical falsetto warning barks to threaten an oldster in a passing Cadillac or Buick the size of an aircraft carrier. During walks on rainy days, they will refuse to poop until they are damn ready or wait until they get back and drop a load under the dining room table on the oriental rug, where Mildred Worthington will step on it during the weekly mahjong game. Approximately 65% of them are named "Precious." The males of the breed are compulsive oriental carpet pissers and cannot be broken from their penchant to mark their territory against the genuine danger of an invading Shih-Tzu. Pomeranians are responsible for funneling obscene amounts of elder income to unscrupulous veterinarians (*I'm not certain, Mrs. Goldberg, but I fear it could be residual long-haul Lyme disease*) and dog groomers, who make more than Florida cardiologists.

You have probably seen a Pom being walked by some pathetic-looking octogenarian husband who has the forlorn expression of a man whom his wife has whipped for half a century. Men usually loathe the little dogs but are required to do most of the Pom walking for some inexplicable reason. Even more pitiable than an old guy who has to use a walker to get the mail is an old guy wearing stretch jeans hiked up to his sagging pectorals with a pink sequined leash in one hand and pooper-scooper in the other, picking up the foul excrement of a creature wearing a Ralph Lauren sweater and a Swarovski crystal festooned collar. It has been reported anecdotally that Florida husband-retirees have intentionally slipped in the bathroom and broken hips (*Help! I've fallen, and I can't get up to walk Precious!*) to get out of Pom walking/poop-scooping chores.

If you admire the symmetry of the predator-prey relationship in the evolutionary scheme of things, the Pom has become the favorite snack food of Florida alligators. The dogs are so unfathomably stupid when it comes to survival skills that they will happily wander up to a nine-foot gator, lift their legs to pee on the reptile's head, and promptly disappear. Mildred Lipshitz of Boca Raton is said to hold the Florida State lost "Precious" record and is reportedly on Precious #7, the first six having mysteriously vanished while sniffing for deer droppings (Pomeranian Raisinets) in her backyard that backed up to artificial algae and scum-covered pond that qualified her condo as waterfront property. Few fish were in this ugly mosquito breeding hole, but alligators do not have to eat often. This pond was the exclusive hunting ground of a resourceful alligator named Snickers, who made an excellent living ingesting lap dogs.

It certainly could not be thought of as the Pope's fault. Shortly after peeing on the Oval Office rug, the cheerful little presidential dog, Precious Darling Lancaster, came silently bounding down the steps while the Pope descended the staircase to the White House dining room. Little dogs must get anywhere they believe they must go ahead of everyone else lest they miss something important. And they never expect collisions. They assume other creatures will get out of the way. In nature, living things rarely collide by accident. So when the First Pom became entangled in the Pope's white satin robe, both of them went tumbling down ten stairs, and when the robes were cleared, the Holy Father Vicar of Christ had squashed Precious Darling and hit his head on a decorative bronze statue of John Adams. First Lady

Barbara Lancaster shrieked and then immediately collapsed.

The White House flag was lowered to half-mast.

Pope Thomas had lost consciousness for only a few minutes and appeared to have recovered his faculties before the first lady. Out of an abundance of caution, he had been rushed to George Washington Hospital Center, where the chiefs of the neurology and neurosurgical departments were waiting to conduct every diagnostic test and examination that medical science offered. After 24 hours of observation, a CT Scan, and an MRI, His Holiness was declared to have suffered a mild frontal lobe concussion and released. First Lady Lancaster was revived and advised to increase her dose of Xanax by an extra half pill as needed. The following morning, she asked her social secretary to begin an immediate search on www.pom.com for a replacement Precious Darling.

Tucker Carlson promised that he would soon be revealing irrefutable evidence that Precious Darling Lancaster may have been raised by a coven of Islamic extremist pro-open-border liberals with suspicious ties to the Democrat party and that the seemingly harmless little yapper had been carefully trained since birth as a suicide dog.

5

Marching to the Beat of a Different Drummer Boy

～∞～

The first sign that something may have been amiss happened shortly after Pope Thomas returned to his residence in the Vatican. His Holiness was being briefed at a Curia of The Pontifical Council of the Family. The subject was the thorny problem of contraception. He gently interrupted a presentation being made by Camerlengo Giuseppe Angiollati on the lack of progress of the Church in Uganda with their well-intentioned abstinence campaign. HIV was spreading at an alarming rate, and new cases were being recorded in record numbers

"I think..." the Pope said and paused. Everyone in the room noted his use of the pronoun "I." Every Pope since Peter had referred to themselves as "We" because the Pope spoke not just for himself but for Jesus Christ, God, and the entire Catholic Church. The plural pronoun was mandatory. So when the Pope said, "I think..." instead of "we think," it did not slip by unnoticed. Eyebrows were collectively raised, and before the Cardinals even had time to digest the cosmic significance of the alarmingly humble choice of the pronoun "I," the Pope made it clear that this was no slip of the pontifical tongue.

"I think..." he went on and repeated with unmistakable emphasis on "I" just in case any of them missed the first one, "that we... and by "we" I mean "us" the assembled ... need to reexamine *our* ... and from now on when I use the term "our" I will be referring to all those present for these Curia ... reexamine *our* position on this entire matter. Camerlengo Angiollati. Refresh my recollection of the scriptural basis for our 2000 years of admonitions to our flock against failing in their duty to God to overpopulate the earth."

The oxygen in the room decreased alarmingly when those present gasped in unison. Camerlengo Angiollati, his eyes the size of 1968 Buick Electra hubcaps, attempted to compose himself. It immediately occurred to the Camerlengo that His Holiness might somehow have become the victim of demonic possession. His second thought was that he was in the middle of a horrible dream sent to test his faith. His third thought was, "*Holy shit!*" followed closely by five self-imposed silent Hail Marys.

"M... M... Most Holy Father," the Camerlengo

stammered. "Our position on birth control dates back to Genesis 1:28 when God said to Adam and mankind, "Be fruitful, and multiply, and replenish the earth..." and, of course, the story of Onan in Genesis 38:8. Our view on this matter is as old and as unwavering as our faith in..."

"Yes, yes..." the Pope jumped in, raising his hand to signal that he would speak. "But correct me if I am wrong, my dear Camerlengo. It does not say, multiply like rabbits until there is no room left on the planet, does it?"

"Well... no, Your Holiness, but..."

"And it certainly does not give any guidance on exactly *how* fruitful the faithful are required to be. What if I were to tell you that I was reading that exact line of scripture about being fruitful, multiplying, and replenishing the earth last night, and it occurred to me that we may have been reading it all wrong? What if being fruitful and multiplying means we should plant apple trees and study mathematics?

"Just kidding. I was joking. I am allowed to joke, am I not?" There were a few perfunctory, nervous smiles.

Joking? thought Camerlengo Angiollati. *Is the Vicar of Christ joking about the Book of Genesis?* A Tourette's-like *"holy shit"* entered his mind for the second time, and he tried to figure out where all this could be coming from. Had Lucifer finally found his way into the Vatican? The Cardinal hesitated, so the Pope continued.

"Camerlengo Angiollati. Are you familiar with the work of Thomas Malthus?"

This time, all of the Cardinals crossed themselves in almost perfect unison. Malthus was an English cleric who led Darwin down the evolution path that many argued took God out of the creation business, forcing the church into acknowledging that perhaps the seven-day creation story was not literally accurate and that God created everything through the wonderous process of survival of the fittest and killing the less fortunate who were, through no fault of their own, less fit. Everyone knew that God worked in mysterious ways, so what exactly was the problem? It had turned out to be a big problem.

"Allow me to refresh your recollection. Over two centuries ago, Malthus argued convincingly that all living things' populations tend to multiply geometrically. At the same time, food supplies increase arithmetically, and land, as we know, doesn't reproduce at all, absent the occasional super volcano. Hence, populations of living things routinely outstrip food supplies, leading to mass starvation. And only the fittest survive in the competition for limited resources. It seems to me that common sense leads to the rather unassailable conclusion that if we – and here I mean humankind – not we the assembled – if *we* keep multiplying like rabbits in a land without a sufficient number of rabbit eaters, we will eventually devour the planet. Do you know how many people occupied our beloved planet in 1950?"

The Camerlengo did not know. The Pope looked around the room and was not surprised that none of his Cardinals were ready to volunteer an answer.

"Two and a half billion. And today? Anyone?"

Some of them knew the answer, but no one was anxious to play the role of straight man for the Pontiff.

"Approaching eight billion. Six billion people in sixty-five years. Think about it."

None of them seemed in a hurry to think about it. Several of them were thinking instead that they were witnessing the beginning of the End of Days. This wasn't how the Apocalypse was supposed to start. Revelation nowhere mentions the Vicar of Christ going crazy.

"And Onan?" the Pope continued. "As I recall, Onan's brother Er was killed by God because, we are told, he was evil. That is all it says. That is the entire biblical explanation. I think it would have been better if we were given some guidance regarding the nature of his evildoing. But let us leave that aside for the moment. As you know, Er left behind a wife named Tamar, who was childless. Now, as I recall, in those days, there was a tribal obligation that required the brother-in-law of a childless widow to assist his sister-in-law in multiplying. Onan apparently did not mind engaging in this multiplication exercise with Tamar. Still, for some reason about which the Bible is completely silent, Onan withdrew just before delivering his seed and spilled it on the ground in the first and only incidental biblical reference to contraception. After this episode of seed spilling, God killed him. That is all we are told. Am I correct? Have I left anything out?"

No one replied. Pope Thomas could recite the entire Bible from memory, and they all knew it.

"So it seems to me to be a reasonable interpretation that God punished Onan, not so much for his act of birth control in and of itself. It would seem that he punished Onan for failing to deliver his spilled seed to Tamar, thereby failing to fulfill his traditional tribal impregnation obligation to *Er and Tamar*. My reasoning is based partially upon the ancient practice known as levirate marriage, in which a dead man's closest unmarried male relation was required to marry the widow to produce an heir for the deceased. This duty was set forth very specifically in Deuteronomy 25:5-10, and its purpose was to preserve tribal inheritance rights. For all we know, seed spilling may have been rampant in those days. Do any of you seriously think that Onan was the world's first and only sinful seed spiller? And while I am on the subject, is there today an obligation to impregnate one's widowed sister-in-law? When, may I ask, was that rule amended or repealed? It hasn't been, has it? And would such a rule be an exception to the admonition against adultery? It's all very perplexing."

Several Cardinals shifted nervously in their seats.

"Perhaps the adultery commandment ended the ancient tribal obligation, but then there is the matter of Deuteronomy 25:5-10. Perhaps God changed his mind about carnal relations with one's sister-in-law. We don't know now, do we? Am I missing anything? No, my dear Cardinals. I think it is high time that we rethought this whole contraception issue. Replenish does not mean defile and devour. HIV is rampant in Africa, and our proscription against the use of condoms condemns countless innocents to the ravages of this terrible disease. Additionally, my thinking about this subject leads me to believe that it is likely that our interpretation of scripture in this regard had its origin in my predecessors' desire to increase the ranks of our faithful at a time when pagans vastly outnumbered us so we could spread the word of our Lord to the furthest corners of the planet. We needed soldiers to spread the good news about Jesus, and there was only one way to make new soldiers. In any event, that is my judgment, and I am, in these matters, infallible. Is it not so? I think it is quite nice to be infallible. It dispenses with so many disagreements, don't you think?"

They did not so think as Camerlengo Angiollati demonstrated by fainting.

Nothing like this had ever happened before. It was not

just the radical departure from 2000 years of Church dogma. It was the way that Pope Thomas delivered his thoughts: the unthinkable Socratic informality and the reference to *joking*. No one could recall a Pope having ever *joked* about a matter in the Curia. In the days that followed, there was Vatican speculation and rampant gossip about everything from the work of Beelzebub to a brain tumor.

The theory that seemed to make the most sense was put forth to a select few by the Vatican's chief physician, Dr. Salvatore Girone, a specialist in cardiology and neurology, who briefed three Cardinals on the phenomena of post-concussion frontal and temporal lobe syndrome, which was known to cause moderate to severe personality changes, impulsivity, mood dysregulation, impaired social judgment, the inability to appreciate the effects of one's behavior or remarks on others and occasional uncharacteristic lewdness. It was also called post-traumatic Tourette's syndrome. What if His Holiness were to – God forbid – start using profanity? The phenomenon was known to have happened in similar situations.

There had been a surprising number of reported cases, including Mary Lee Osborne, wife of former Ambassador to China, Carlton Osborne III. Mrs. Osborne suffered what seemed like an insignificant bump when she lost her balance after four pre-dinner martinis at a state dinner while bowing to the Chinese Secretary General of the Politburo Standing Committee and fell face first onto a Ming dynasty ornamental table, knocking over and breaking a priceless 6th Century vase. She was hammered but had enough of her faculties to have been mortified. A lifelong student of Chinese history and culture, fluent in Mandarin, she was the best thing the ambassador had going for him aside from his law school whoring days with

President Lancaster. The embassy physician was called, examined her, pronounced her fit, and told her to keep an ice pack on her forehead and call him if she had any symptoms such as blackouts. She seemed fine in the days that followed. A few weeks later, when the Ambassador and Mrs. Osborne reciprocated and had the Secretary-General and his wife to the Embassy for dinner while the guests were enjoying a lovely desert of pineapple rum flambé, Mrs. Osborne quite casually asked the Secretary-General if it were true that Chinese men had balls the size of miniature lychee nuts? Then for some inexplicable reason, she called him a little cocksucker. It did not help that she delivered the insult in flawless Mandarin. In the following weeks, Mrs. Osborne used the term "cocksucker" in virtually every conversation and was eventually diagnosed with PTT. Luckily, the condition proved transient and completely vanished four months later as quickly as it had appeared. The infamous "lychee nut confrontation," as it later became known, did not result in a nuclear exchange, but relations between the two countries were strained for months afterward.

Almost all cases of PTT were resolved with time. It was Dr. Girone's opinion that the Pope's new and alarming personality transformation would likewise clear up at some point. When asked how long it would take, Dr. Girone said it would take a few days to six months. No one wanted to consider how much damage Pope Thomas could do in six months.

And not a single person in the Vatican aware of the Pope's sudden metamorphosis hazarded a guess that he might simply have begun to look at things differently.

Shortly after his election, there were signs that this Pope might not be cut from the same sackcloth as any previous

Pope. The first was his refusal to wear the traditional red shoes worn by every Pope dating back to 1566. The shoes were thought to symbolize the blood of Christian martyrs and were kept as part of the traditional papal red attire until Pope Pius V made the important historical fashion decision to change the papal vestment from red to white. However, Pius V is remembered to this day by Vatican fashionistas for his decision that the Pope's cap, cape, and shoes would henceforth remain red. Previous Popes had worn red loafers adorned with a gold cross so that the faithful might be in touch with the spirit of Christ when kissing the pontiff's feet. Pope Paul VI kept the red shoes but did away with the foot-kissing tradition. Pope Thomas decided to do away with the red shoes as part of his official wardrobe using the ecclesiastical rationale that they "looked ridiculous." Salvatore Ferragamo III, the official Vatican footwear designer/consultant, was reportedly devastated.

This Pope seemed to be a brilliant choice after the sudden death of Pope Benedict II. South America, Africa, and Asia accounted for 52% of the world's faithful, and everyone in the Vatican recognized that the time had come for a non-European pontiff. An American Pope was out of the question. Americans were too modern, too liberal, too powerful, and too wealthy. They also had adopted the pesky national proclivity for allowing and even encouraging lawsuits being brought against the Church for every act of sexual abuse since the beginning of time. Give the Americans a Pope and the third-world resentment would be at a fever pitch. Mahmoud Ahmadinejad would have stood an even chance against an American Cardinal. There was a battle going on for third-world souls and Islam was pulling ahead with almost 1.7

billion of the faithful and they were proving to be angry as of late. So, a Pope from the pet country of the Great Satan was unthinkable. The third world was the future of the Catholic Church. Additionally, it was hard to ignore the fact that Europeans and Americans were turning more secular every day.

Pope Thomas, formally the Brazilian Cardinal Rolando Garrincha, had it all. The most creative Hollywood scriptwriter could not have invented a candidate for the Pope with more going for him. Brazil is home to over 100 million Catholics and is the largest Catholic country in the world. 66.4% of Brazilian whites and 58.2% of Brazilian Africans identify as Catholic. Cardinal Garrincha was a mixture of races that appeared to be heaven-sent. The son of a Portuguese-African father and a Filipino mother, he immediately covered three continents. The papal trifecta. And the Philippines accounted for another eighty million Catholics.

Cardinal Garrincha was respected as a decent, compassionate, and thoughtful man who spent hands-on time at free medical clinics in the worst slums of São Paulo with Brazil's poorest souls. He was fluent in six languages, educated as a physician, and held advanced degrees in theology, philosophy, and psychology. His election was met with enthusiastic and universal approval.

The press fawned over the new Pope, and the people adored a man loved by the press. His multiracial ethnic background earned him the nickname Pobama; some even called him the Tiger Woods of the Holy See. He reached rock star status almost overnight. His choice of the papal name Thomas was thought to be in honor of St. Thomas Aquinas, but in time, some would speculate that he may have had the doubting one in mind. Truth be told, it was neither.

The old guard at the Vatican had cringed when the Pontiff had spoken to a huge crowd gathered in Vatican Square in early December and urged them to resist buying sweaters, cell phones, and video games and instead take their children to soup kitchens and into the slums to show compassion for the less fortunate. He said Christmas had deteriorated into a commercial shopping greed festival and had nothing to do with Jesus. Walmart, Amazon, and Costco stock dropped alarmingly the next day.

Then there was the incident with the little girl and the kitten in Gdansk. He had been mingling with the crowd in the city square when an angelic little Polish girl asked him about her recently deceased kitten, who had been killed by a speeding Vespa. She wanted to know if the kitten was in heaven. The Pope reassured the child, telling her she would see her beloved kitten one day and that "paradise is open to all of God's creatures."

It seemed innocent enough and a compassionate reassurance for a pontiff to give to a grieving little girl. But the theological implications were unthinkable, and the upper-echelon theologians at the Vatican were scrambling and back peddling as if they were moonwalking. Because it was axiomatic that heaven most decidedly was *not* open to all of God's creatures. Before the Pope's afterlife *faux pas*, the Vatican had issued an official opinion on the subject that clearly stated that "...if the word 'soul' is used to refer to an immortal soul that one day will inhabit heaven or hell, then no, animals may not be said to possess a soul. This is the only conclusion that can be drawn, respecting the instruction on the subject found within the Word of God." And "no soul" equaled no heaven. It, therefore, seemed clear as filtered Evian holy water that whatever wonderful things people had to look forward to when they arrived in heaven, stroking Mr. Wiggles the cat or Precious the Pomeranian, was not in the celestial cards. The term "dead dog" meant that death was the end. Period.

The Pope's remark was widely reported, and the Vatican special ops *faux pas* control unit began immediate damage control reminiscent of the one after Mitt Romney's campaign disaster when the governor had told a gathering of rich people the equivalent of saying that 47% of all Americans were deadbeats who were going to vote for President Obama.

The Vatican press secretary clarified the Pope's remarks by saying that heaven held the promise of memories as real as the material earth and that pets would be available to those in heaven in that sense. No one knew exactly what that meant or how they could know what happened in heaven. Pope Thomas was not required to clarify the matter further as no Pope had ever held a press conference.

In hindsight, some would argue that these were clear warning signs that predated the Pomeranian-induced papal concussion. Some would say that this Pope had always marched to the beat of a different little drummer boy.

6

Call Me Tom

"Good morning," the lawyer said to the nondescript old man in the attorney conference room of the Rhea County Detention Center. "What is your name?"

All he knew at that point was that this was the old guy who had been arrested at Savior Land for a plethora of misdemeanors. The lawyer guessed he had been summoned by higher powers and was there asking the man's name because of his national reputation for causing trouble and annoying powerful people. Evidently, some very powerful people wanted him to meet with this old man.

Connor Kerrigan had received a mysterious call while playing the fourth hole of The Cassique Course on Kiawah Island, South Carolina. Members were not permitted to carry cell phones, so the pro shop would send a cart boy out with a message and a club cell phone in an emergency. On the other end of this call was the administrative assistant for Secretary of State Lawrence Hamilton, who politely introduced herself and asked him to hold for the Secretary. The next morning at 8:00 a.m., a G-4 was waiting to pick him up at the Charleston County Executive Airport about ten miles up River Road from his home on Kiawah Island.

Connor had no connection to anyone in Washington, and the closest he had ever come to the Secretary of State was the last time he had his passport renewed. Lawrence Hamilton explained that an important foreign ambassador was requesting that Connor fly to Chattanooga, Tennessee, to consult with one of their citizens who had been arrested and was currently incarcerated in the Rhea County Detention Center in Dayton, Tennessee. Connor explained that he wasn't a criminal lawyer, had no interest in becoming one at this stage of his career, and suggested that he call Butler Yates, a famous southern showboat and FOX news talking head who was widely recognized as a narcissistic, pontificating asshole. He didn't articulate the last part but didn't have to. Yates was the Donald Trump of trial lawyers. Secretary of State Hamilton patiently explained that the prospective client's advisers had carefully vetted Connor and that he, likewise, honestly had no idea why they had chosen him. His country was officially requesting his cooperation.

"Okay, Connor asked, "Tell me what this is really about."

"That is all I can tell you right now. You are simply going to have to trust me." He sounded like a dead ringer for the mission-impossible voice on the recording that self-destructs.

"Mr. Secretary, the last time I used the old *you-simply-*

have-to-trust-me line was in the 12th grade when I was trying to get laid for the first time," said Connor.

"We have reached a common ground. I remember using the same line."

Connor softened. There was a moment of silence. He sensed that he had broken through the pomp and circumstance barrier. Having established that they were both guys, Hamilton followed up on that theme.

"What'd you shoot on the front?"

"A 13. I just finished number 4 when you declared a national emergency. I three-putted two greens."

"I always felt that a three-putt after hitting a green was like losing a good hard-on on the paradise stroke."

"I'll try and keep that image in reserve the next time I am standing over a 3-footer for par."

And so on. Hamilton was no stuffed shirt mannequin. You don't get to be Secretary of State unless you have a certain amount of charm, a healthy dollop of bullshit, and an ability to shift gears on the fly. It also helps if you assisted the President in carrying Ohio.

The Citation CJ3 was waiting for him at 8:00 a.m. the following day. The trip to Chattanooga took less than an hour, and a limo was waiting on the tarmac to take him to the Rhea County Detention Center. *En route*, a big blond guy riding shotgun who reminded him of the young Robert Shaw in *From Russia with Love* handed him a clipping from *The Chattanooga Times and Free Press* regional section.

MAN DESECRATES HOLY BIBLE AT JESUS LAND
> *An unidentified man, who police said appeared to be in his seventies, was arrested today at Savior Land after he interrupted a performance of Jesus's Sermon on the Mount and began lecturing the crowd on what he said*

was "our moral imperative to rethink the Bible." Witnesses described a scene where the crowd initially thought the man was part of the performance until he began ripping pages from the Bible and scattering them into the wind. The man started with Revelation and called it "a biblical abomination conceived to frighten people into obedience and described it as lunatic ravings of a madman on a par with Hitler's Mien Kampf." Security was called, and witnesses described a scene of near bedlam when the crowd started to close in on the man. One witness said that someone shouted, "Kill the Antichrist," and the crowd began to surge forward. Savior Land security held the man until the Rhea County Sheriff's deputies arrived and took him into custody. Deputy Emit Regal said that the man refused to give his name and was not carrying any form of identification. He was charged with disorderly conduct, trespassing, blasphemy, and littering, destruction of property and transported to the Rhea County Detention Center, where he is being held after being unwilling to post a one-hundred-dollar bond. Sources at the jail say that a psychiatric evaluation is likely.

"This is the guy I've been flown here to meet?" Connor asked his driver. "A lunatic who invaded a holy roller theme park and tried to start a fundamentalist riot? Are you shitting me?"

The big blond guy turned his head around slightly and spoke for the first time.

"Sir, similar lunatic observations were probably made when Jesus appeared at the temple and confronted the money changers... And, you are correct that I shit you not."

Connor thought about that one, and it occurred to him

that his prospective client could not possibly be a run-of-the-mill lunatic. The Secretary of State, the Citation, the limo. This guy had to be an important lunatic. But who was he?

Connor handed the desk deputy his Attorney at Law card and his South Carolina Driver's license and was asked who he was there to see. He handed over the newspaper clipping.

"I'm sorry, but believe it or not, I don't know the guy's name."

"That's okay, said the deputy. Neither do we."

The desk deputy buzzed him through and directed him down the hall to the inmate visitors' waiting room. Another deputy met him and explained that his guy was in jail because he had refused to post the $100 bond placed on him by the magistrate even though he had $340 in his pocket when he was searched at intake. And they couldn't *make him* post bail. It was like the guy *wanted* to be in jail. The deputy put Connor in the attorney interview room, where he waited for ten minutes before the door opened and his prospective client was ushered in. The old man wasn't wearing a prison uniform and didn't have cuffs on. That might have had something to do with the fact that littering and disorderly conduct are not exactly considered high crimes where the accused is thought of as an imminent danger to himself or others. And if he had skipped out on the charges, nobody would have cared. This old guy was a criminal who had skipped *in* on the charges.

"Tom," he replied. "Call me Tom. Or Thomas. Whatever is easier."

INFALLIBLE 47

7

Back in Business

~~~

"Good to meet you, Tom. My name is Connor. Connor Kerrigan."

"Yes, I know. Thank you for coming."

Connor detected a hint of an accent. It could have been from anywhere. They shook hands. Tom could have been the poster boy for nondescriptness. Medium height, slender, smallish steel-rimmed round glasses, a slightly larger than average nose, receding gray hairline, and what was left was thin and wispy. He wore a pair of loose-fitting khakis and a somewhat wrinkled off-white shirt that perfectly complimented his ordinary look. If Connor were playing the "what does he do for a living" game, he would have guessed that Tom compiled statistics for the State of Iowa Department of Roads and Traffic. This, he would later realize, went a long way toward explaining how he was able to make it from the Vatican to Savior Land and Savior Land to jail without anyone taking notice of who he was. A Pope without a beanie, flowing robes, and red shoes is like a queen in a terrycloth bathrobe stepping out of a Holiday Inn bathroom after a shower.

"Tom. Do you have a last name?"

"Well..." He looked like he was thinking about it. "I think that Tom kind of is my last name."

"Did it come with a first name?"

He smiled a wry smile. "Sort of. More of a title."

Connor opened both palms facing upward in the international gesture for "I'll bite."

"Pope. I guess you could say that Pope is what comes first, so it is sort of like a first name."

It took a very long second for it to register. Connor looked like one of those idiots on *Wheel of Fortune*. *P_P_ T_ _ _ _ S. Let me think. PEPE TORRES! No... Pope Thomas. That's it. Pope Thomas. Holy shit! POPE THOMAS!*

"Pope Thomas? You're..." he hesitated. "...His Holiness?" And then it all made sense. Or absolutely no sense. He couldn't decide. He looked at him again. Yes. It was him. He had never seen the man in civilian clothes. There were new guys he played golf with that he would run into in a store and see something vaguely familiar about them, but without the golf hat, they were seriously incognito.

Connor could not decide how he was supposed to address him. Dissing the Secretary of State was one thing. But this guy was The Pope. Connor would have readily admitted to being a lifelong asshole with authority figures, but there were still lines he just didn't feel comfortable crossing. And it did not seem to matter that he had not been to Church since he was fifteen.

He considered himself to be either an atheist or a level nine agnostic. He wasn't sure. It's all very confusing when you declare your unbelief. It always struck him as intrinsically silly to declare yourself as part of a movement that religiously adheres to a negative proposition. It would be like forming a club comprised of people who steadfastly cling to the notion that the dark side of the moon is not made of green cheese and chanting, "No dairy products in space!" When he had been cornered by the press or in a heated debate with Warren Donovan, the president of the Catholic Anti-Defamation League, it took far too much time to explain his position in the time customarily allotted to a sound bite. So he would sigh the sigh of the haughtily indifferent, confess his sins, and say something like, "If by that you mean do I believe in Santa Claus or some other guy with a beard in the sky who puts yummy apples in front of defenseless women and tells them not to partake because he said so... and if it makes you happy to call such a person an atheist, an agnostic, or an apostate, I would not think it worth my time to argue with you about your choice of words."

Connor loved debating Donovan. The guy started as Irish-red-in-the-face when he woke up in the morning, and Connor took a perverse delight in imagining him with a blood pressure cuff and watching the digital systolic readout climb above 200.

"It really will be easier for both of us if you call me Tom," he suggested for the second time. The Vicar of Christ was *Tom*. That was the way it was going to be.

"Tom? Are you sure?"

"Yes. I'm sure."

He thought about it for a few seconds. He liked this guy.

Then again, he had liked him since shortly after he was elected Pope.

"Tom, it is. And you can call me Connor."

They shared a simultaneous smile.

"So, Tom. Why are we here? Why are you here? Why am I here?"

"I am here because I caused a... well... I guess you would call it a ruckus or something. You are here because you are very good at making people question their assumptions, and I want you to be my lawyer."

"Thank you. I'm honored. But some would say that I have done more to damage our church than the Protestant Reformation. Warren Donovan once said I could make the Antichrist blush."

Pope Thomas chuckled. "I heard that. Warren likes to think of himself as a self-anointed lawyer for Jesus and the papacy. Or, I should say, he used to before I came along. I make him uncomfortable, and he is rather excitable. Then again, Connor, you do seem to have a way about you. You have a God-given knack for getting people excited."

"I can be annoying," he admitted.

"Such modesty."

They shared another smile.

Connor Kerrigan had made a good living off the Catholic Church. The truth was that he had become embarrassingly wealthy, suing the bejesus out of the Holy See, representing victims of duly ordained pedophiles.

He began his career as a pedophile bounty hunter, the same way most trial lawyers pick up a specialty – by chance. He was a young, struggling Boston sole practitioner, which meant his grades at Northeastern Law School weren't good enough to get him an entry-level associate's position at a blue-blood Boston firm. That's the working definition of a sole practitioner. Regardless of what he told the women in the bars about how he got to where he was – about independence and refusing to become part of an hourly billing seventy-hour-a-week factory, he was where he was because there was no place else for him to go. Almost every young lawyer jumped at the opportunity to bag a six-figure starting salary, drive a BMW 3 series, and bang as many Boston girls as he could. Connor used the same lone wolf iconoclast line on any girl who asked. And it was sort of true. But so was the fact that he finished about two-thirds of the way down the list in law school, so it was hard to say whether the lone wolf way of life decision was made before or after he graduated with a 2.8 accumulative average. Law Review to Connor was pulling an all-nighter before the con-law final.

It all started one day when he was playing *World of Warcraft* in his $500-a-month sublet office that he rented from Marv Applestien, a shameless ambulance chaser and whiplash specialist. Marv proudly described himself as "Counsel to the uninjured." Connor paused the game and went online to research how long he could live in Costa Rica and surf on five thousand dollars when he got the call from a social worker at the Boston Juvenile Justice Foundation asking if he would go see a kid named Jimmy Reilly at the Manville Juvenile Detention Center. He sighed. He didn't relish working with juvies, but it paid the rent (barely, at $50 an hour), so he said sure and drove to see his new client. Jimmy Reilly was fourteen years old and had been caught shoplifting at Walmart. It was his fifth shoplifting beef, so he was detained rather than sent home pending a court date. "Home" was The Saint Joseph Home for Children. Jimmy and Connor got off to a somewhat rocky start. It had something to do with how Connor responded when Jimmy walked into the room and greeted his counselor with "Who the fuck are you?"

"Your court-appointed lawyer, twitwad, and I'm the only one you are going to get, so save your tough guy act for the boys who want to make your rear end their personal dick garage, and maybe I can help you."

A hint of a smile.

"What's a twitwad?"

Connor thought about it briefly before admitting, "I'm not really sure."

They both started laughing. It didn't take long for the kid to mention that he had some experience with asshole stretching at Saint Joseph's when he was younger. When he got big enough to fight back and inflict some pain, the problem went away.

"The older boys?"

"Yeah. And the guy who runs the place. Father O'Grady."

"Father Timothy O'Grady?" Connor sat up.

"Yeah, you know the creep?"

He knew the creep. O'Grady had been his parish priest at Gate of Heaven Catholic Church and had taken a shot at him on a camping weekend at Acadia National Park. He was twelve then and just old enough to realize that he wasn't buying into life as an obedient Catholic. He wasn't receptive to O'Grady's lets-be-close-pals overture when the priest came into his tent on their third night in the park. All of the boys knew about his reputation.

"Go away, or I will go straight to the police when this trip is over." He did go away, and Connor decided that guys like O'Grady would be the focus of reverse exorcisms where the demon gets the priest out of the kid. He never went back to church for anything except an occasional wedding.

The wheels started turning. O'Grady? In charge of a school for children? How could that be? People *knew*. They had to have known. They knew in the same way that people know a functional alcoholic or a cocaine abuser.

Connor wasn't the first attorney to go after a pedophile priest or the Church that enabled them. It's just that Connor was one of the flashiest. He sued O'Grady on behalf of Jimmy Reilly. During discovery, he was able to identify 117 children whom O'Grady had abused over the years. That led to a class action against O'Grady, which Connor later expanded to the Archdiocese of Boston. The more he learned about how the Church had protected O'Grady and moved him around, the more enraged he became. This led to him publicly demanding that Cardinal Robert Murphy be indicted for aiding and abetting in the sexual abuse of 117 minors by putting O'Grady in charge of a children's home when the Cardinal knew that the son-of-a-bitch was a pedophile. Cardinal Murphy was called to Rome while the Suffolk County District Attorney's Office was trying to figure out what to do with this can of unholy worms. Murphy was given some lower level position on the Counsel on Third World Nutrition and as a citizen of the Vatican, could not easily be prosecuted in the United States. It just wasn't worth the effort. Connor was so pissed off that he sued the Pope. That, of course, went nowhere fast. The State Department intervened to let the Court know that the Pope had the same immunity as any head of state or member of a diplomatic mission. Connor did, however, get a shitload of great publicity and appeared on talk and news shows on every network. It didn't hurt his career when he got a 650 million dollar verdict against

O'Grady, Murphy, and the Arch Diocese of Boston, forcing them close to bankruptcy and eventually liquidating about three-quarters of their assets.

Along the way, Connor learned quite a bit about the Church he had left and even more about pedophiles. Experts in the disorder will tell you that it is a hardwiring issue. Pedophiles are hard-wired sexually toward children the same way that people are hardwired toward heterosexuality or to be LBGT. Except pedophilia is considered to be highly compulsive. Which implies that they cannot control their urges. This, in turn, implies they are somehow *less* culpable for what they do to children. To which Connor came up with the following thought experiment while cross-examining the Church's expert psychiatric witness/apologist: *Take your grade 5 compulsive pedophile. Put him in a room with a little boy of seven who is wearing only his underpants. Add to this grouping a big burley Boston cop with a baseball bat and whatever kind of paring knife they use to remove hog testicles. How uncontrollably compulsive do you think your patient's behavior will be then, Doctor?*

End of free will discussion. Immediate unpleasant consequences trump compulsive behavior every time.

Connor learned the Catholic Church was in on it, and responsibility went to the steps of the Vatican. They facilitated these monsters by moving them around and giving them access to children everywhere. It wasn't like they were informally approving of it, but they might as well have. They covered up, they denied, and they lied. When it came to the pedophile priest problem, they were every bit as corrupt as the Mafia, and it had been going on since the first century. Until the first honest, decent, and incorruptible Pope was elected. That would be the guy who insisted he be called Tom, sitting across from him in the Rhea County Detention Center.

O'Grady served seven years in prison. He became known as the Hannibal Lecter of pedophile priests. When he was released from jail, he went to Ireland and tried to live an obscure life. The Vatican authorized an annuity that paid him $67,000 a year. That was to shut him up. Pope Thomas put an end to that. He then proceeded to clean the House that Peter built. This house cleaning wasn't a cursory dust and vacuum job. This was a strip-it-down to the original hardwood floorboard-type cleaning. The House of the Lord was built on hallowed grounds, and if what was needed was a complete teardown and rebuild, Pope Thomas was just the man to see that it was done. In the quarter of a century before Pope Thomas was elected, seventeen priests were defrocked for sexual abuse offenses. Of those seventeen, none were excommunicated. One year after he assumed his place as the Vicar of Christ, 1743 priests were defrocked, and every one of them was excommunicated. Pope Thomas made it clear that the purge would not stop until the Church was rid of this two-millennia-old disease. Zero tolerance coupled with one strike and you are out was the law of the land.

When Pope Thomas showed his hand two weeks after being elected, Connor knew his work was done. He had made more money than he knew what to do with, and the problem was now in good hands. As far as Connor could see, it was in the best hands.

"So, Tom," he asked. "What's the plan?"

It didn't take long to figure out that Tom had one. And it turned out to be a dandy. After all these years, the man who said Connor should call him Tom was about to bring him back into the fold. He started Connor out with a passage from Matthew 12:44: "I will return to my house from which I came; and when I come, I will find it unoccupied, swept, and put in order."

Three hours later, Connor left the Rhea County Detention Center grinning like a butcher's dog. He was not only back in the fold. He was back in business.

8

The Butt is Buttered

━━━━━━━━━━

The State's Attorney position for Rhea County is a part-time position. It's about as part-time as part-time can get. One former elected prosecutor described the job: "I work from 12:00 till 1:00 and take an hour for lunch." There are only 30,000 people in the entire county. There is crime, but it is not enough to justify a full-time State's Attorney's office. When Pope Thomas was arrested, the Rhea County State's Attorney was a fellow named Angus Ravenel, who, as fate would have it, was the great-nephew of William Jennings Bryan, his lineage traceable back on his mother's side. His resemblance to Bryan – balding, patrician nose, and ironically a somewhat simian forehead and oversized ears – was startling, and he successfully milked it into a local political career.

Ravenel spent five days a month cutting plea deals for

the County's assorted lowlife population when they were arrested for DWIs, crystal meth possession, wife beatings, burglaries, and various traffic offenses. Trials were rare. The rest of his time he handled any non-criminal matter that came through his private office door in Dayton. His position as State's Attorney for Rhea County meant that he was far and away the busiest private practitioner in the county, which did not make him rich by any measure but allowed him to lead a comfortable, low-stress country practitioner's life.   ANGUS RAVENEL

He also served as the deacon of the Dayton First Church of Christ, where one of his bi-weekly responsibilities was to post a clever aphorism on the Church marquee. This week, "Partaking of Forbidden Fruit Can Get You In a Real Jam!" replaced "This Church is Prayer Conditioned." Almost all of the members of the congregation who weren't having extramarital affairs agreed that the fruit-to-jam message was a real knee-slapper.

Angus was a biblical literalist. He graduated from Bryan University with a B.A. in Biblical Studies. He went on to attend Trinity Baptist Law School, whose motto is: *At its core, our community is shaped by our commitment to the Gospel – the life, death, and resurrection of Jesus. We exist to serve Christ by championing a biblical view of human law and government through our students, graduates, faculty, and staff.* Angus was editor of the Trinity Law Review and received acclaim for his article, *Separation of Church and State: An Anathema to Strict Constructionism and the True Intention of the Founding Fathers*. Although he would have never said it out loud, he had a certain grudging admiration for the Islamic fundamentalists who had successfully established caliphates in the Middle East, where Sharia Law was the law of the land. *Those boys got the right idea. It's just that they're on the wrong team.* Someday, this great country would lead the final crusade against those heathen goatfuckers, but first, there was much work to do against the country's secular heathen bastards.

Angus's most important non-criminal clients were Roland Jaspers, Savior Land, and Dayton Mayor James Ingersall. The Mayor's manufacturing plant, Couch Potato Overstuffed Sofa Company – Motto: *If you're gonna' lay around, lay around on us* – was the largest employer in the County after Savior Land.

Connor Kerrigan had done his homework when he went to see Ravenel to discuss the charges against his client. Everything he needed to know was in a file compiled by Pope Thomas's remaining loyal research priests at the Vatican. Connor had to keep reminding himself that the guy who looked like a Motor Vehicles Administration driver's license renewal clerk was the head of a tiny country with enormous assets.

"Hello, Mr. Ravenel." They shook hands. "I'm Connor Kerrigan. I represent the fellow who caused the commotion at Savior Land the other day."

"Yes, yes. I heard all about that. The guy had to be nuttier than a Christmas fruit cake."

"Have you ever thought," Connor responded, "Fruitier would work just as well?"

"Huh? – Oh, yes, I imagine it would." Angus prided himself in being a master of the cliché. "So, what brings a hot shot like you to our little town of Dayton? I took the liberty of doing the Google thing after you called me this morning. What in tarnation would cause you to represent a man charged with nothin' more than a few itty bitty misdemeanors?"

"I sort of had a calling."

"A call or a calling?"

"Well, actually, both."

The State's Attorney rubbed his chin thoughtfully. "I have to say, I admire the work you did against those Catholic pederasts. Too bad you couldn't bankrupt the whole evil empire."

"Well, it wasn't for lack of trying."

"Ha! I'll bet that's the good Lord's truth."

The State's Attorney's candor about his lack of love for the Catholic Church was not terribly surprising. Rhea County's demographics have the local Catholic population at 1.2%, putting them just slightly ahead of the Jewish, Islamic, Hindu, Buddhist, Jainist, and Hari Krishna populations, whose combined numbers added up to zero.

The origins of Southern anti-Catholicism in the United States can be traced back to the Reformation. A century before the Declaration of Independence, laws in the colonies commonly contained bans against Roman Catholics having any political power. In the 20th century, there was a still widespread belief that Catholicism was incompatible with loyalty to the United States and the notion of democracy. A man could simply not pledge allegiance to two masters, and the prevailing assumption among many Protestants was that Catholic loyalty would always rest first with the Roman Pope, who was most decidedly a foreigner. Before JFK, the only Catholic to ever win the nomination for president was Governor Alfred E. Smith of New York. Smith's 1928 campaign faced opposition from the QAnon-style lunatic fringe of his day, who claimed that he was planning on building a tunnel connecting the White House and the Vatican and that he harbored a secret agenda to make Catholicism the nation's established religion. MAGA-type gullibility bordering on mass insanity is hardly a new phenomenon in American politics. Smith was crushed in the presidential election of 1928 by Republican Herbert Hoover, who ran on the indisputable strength of the booming 1920s economy exactly a year before the stock market crash of 1929.

Parochial schools were thought to be indoctrination breeding grounds for slavish devotion to the Vatican. Catholicism was the only major religion that had a supreme leader, and he was viewed as a dictator by much of the Protestant world. The Ku Klux Klan would have just as happily burned a cross on the lawn of a Catholic Church as it would on a Black church.

Connor thought of himself as Catholic in the same way that other people think of themselves as Russian or French. There was still much about Catholic culture and traditions culture that he identified with. It was the religious part that caused an early divorce. His very public war with his church was a war with men and their abuse of power, not their beliefs. His battle with beliefs was a private one.

"What's his story?" Ravenel resumed. "I understand we don't even know his name. Do you think we should have him evaluated by the funny farm folks in Chattanooga? Who is this guy, anyway?"

"His given name is Rolando Garrincha."

"A Mexican, huh? Is he legal? We don't get many transient illegal Mexicans around here."

"Actually, he is Brazilian by birth."

"I've never met a Brazilian. We are simple country folk. Most people around here think a Brazilian is a number that comes after a million."

Connor smiled and paused for subtle dramatic effect. He was a master of subtle and occasionally not-so-subtle dramatic effects. He called it his about-to-pounce-Cheshire-cat technique. The District Attorney picked up on it and looked at him intently for the first time, and Connor could almost hear him thinking, *what's this Irish Yankee son of a bitch up to?*

"Mr. Ravenel..." he paused again. *No one, he thought, should be allowed to have this much fun.* "The Man you have incarcerated in the Rhea County Detention Center is Pope Thomas I, the spiritual leader of a population of approximately a billion Catholics."

"Is this some kind of a..." He stopped in mid-sentence. He suddenly realized this was no joke. He knew who Connor was, and it was beginning to make at least a modicum of sense.

"Wait a minute. Are you serious? You're telling me that the Pope of Rome is in a jail cell in Rhea County?"

"Serious as a heart attack. And I have much more to tell you. How would you like to become the most famous prosecutor in the United States?"

"Well, butter my butt and call me a biscuit. Counselor Kerrigan... I'm all ears."

And indeed he was, Connor thought while noting a pair of ears that would have made Dumbo envious.

9

It's a Gift from God

※

"Of course, I heard about it," said Roland Jaspers. Ravenel had shown up without an appointment and interrupted a meeting between Jaspers and his CFO. "Some crazy old son of a bitch nearly caused a riot. Tearing up the Bible, accusing us of being worse than the money changers in the temple, and raving about some new Bible. I heard he went on for twenty minutes before security took him away. Our closed-circuit park cameras caught it all. Our Jesus performer – a young man who used to appear on – what's that show, Morris? ..."

"The Vampire Diaries."

"Right. *The Vampire Diaries.* He played a level-two vampire or something. Anyway, the boy's a natural-born Jesus. Dead ringer. He does our Sermon on the Mount performance at 10, 12, 2, and 4. It's an abridged version as time only permits him to do a highlights speech—kind of a Cliff Notes version. Plus, most of the park visitors do not have what you'd call a gargantuan attention span, and well, there are so many other important things to see. This one isn't as popular as some of our other attractions. The Lake of Fire gondola ride is still the number one draw. Anyway, we had this special mount built and a small theater in the round with surround sound and everything. Well, here comes this old guy who walks right up on the stage and asks our vampire boy for the mic, and for some reason, I can't begin to understand; the idiot *gives it to him*. The old guy tells him to go sit down and prepare to learn something besides his pre-packaged lines, and then he starts to preach. The crowd thought it was all part of the performance at first."

Roland Jaspers could not figure out why the lawyer he referred to as "my State's Attorney" had called for a meeting "about something really earth-shattering" and what it could possibly have to do with some batshit crazy old coot who had probably escaped from an Alzheimer's ward and somehow wandered into Savior Land raving about a new bible and then desecrating a perfectly good one that made them tons of money.

"He's the Pope," Ravenel said calmly.

"Who's the Pope?"

"The old coot. He's the Pope."

"Angus, what in the hell are you talking about?"

"The man who was arrested on Friday at Savior Land was Pope Thomas. You know, the honcho from Vatican City. Also known as the Vicar of Christ, a.k.a. The Pope of Rome, a.k.a. the spiritual leader of a billion misguided Catholic folks. *That* Pope."

Ravenel now had Roland Jasper's full attention.

"Let me see if I have this right, Angus. You are telling me that the Roman goddamn Pope somehow snuck out of Rome, or Vatican City, or wherever the fuck he lives, flew to the U.S., rented a car or took a Greyhound bus or something, and paid a $15.95 admission fee to enter Savior Land and start a riot..."

"$14.95," Morris Greenberg corrected him.

"Goddamnit, Morris, I thought we talked about raising the admission price."

"We talked about it but decided to table it after the Jesus Loves You dating unpleasantness."

"Whatever... You are telling me that for $14.95, THE Pope hisfuckingself entered Savior Land, where he was responsible for all hell breaking loose, and he is currently residing in a cell next to Bubba Bodine at the Rhea County Detention Center? That's what you are telling me?"

"Well, I'm not sure about the Bubba Bodine part, but essentially, you have it right."

"Holy Christ on a pogo stick. What's he doing *here*? And how did we charge him?"

"I imagine he paid cash unless he had a Groupon deal," Morris offered.

"God damnit Morris! I meant, what did we charge him *with*? What laws did he break?"

"As for what he's doing here, your guess is as good as mine. Our crack Sheriff's Deputy, Emit Potterfield, a member of my congregation, threw the book at him. Disorderly conduct, trespassing, littering, and blasphemy."

"If he paid his admission fee," interjected Morris. "How can he have been guilty of trespassing?"

"Who gives a flying fart?" Jaspers waved his accountant off and gave him the *one more word out of you, and I will kill you* look. Then he thought about the blasphemy charge. "Blasphemy? We have a God damn anti-blasphemy law?"

"Indeed we do," Ravenel responded proudly. § 16-17-520. Disturbance of religious worship says...," He pulled a copy of the statute from his inside suit coat pocket.

"Any person who shall (a) willfully and maliciously shall disturb or interrupt any meeting, society, assembly or congregation convened for the purpose of religious worship, (b) or use blasphemous, profane or obscene language, utters language casting contumelious reproach or profane ridicule upon God, Jesus Christ, the Holy Ghost, the Holy Scriptures or the Christian or any other religion, at or near a place of worship shall be guilty of a misdemeanor and shall, on conviction, be sentenced to pay a fine of not less than twenty nor more than one hundred dollars, or be imprisoned for a term not exceeding one year or less than thirty days, either or both, at the discretion of the court."

"You're shitting me. Is that thing constitutional?"

"Yes and no."

"What do you mean, yes and no? I understand "maybe" or "possibly," but yes and no... Was Mary a virgin? Well, yes and no. Horseshit. She either was or she wasn't."

"Well, sir, it's like this. The Supreme Court..."

Jaspers looked at him suspiciously. "Of the United States or the great State of Tennessee?"

"United States. You know. The other one. Well, those boys declared most blasphemy statutes incredibly unconstitutional—freedom of speech and the establishment of religion by the state and all that crap. But the disorderly conduct parts have nothing to do with religion *per se*. It's like going into a PTA meeting and disrupting it with any kind of obnoxious or profane conduct. You don't have a constitutional right to act like an insufferable horse's ass in a public place. You can't get on a tabletop at Chez Francois (he pronounced "chez" with a hard Z) and start cursing the food... But none of that constitutional crap is going to matter in this case."

"How is it that a statute like this is still on the books," asked Morris.

"Well, statutes in half the states in the country make all types of sodomy, including fellatio and cunnilingus a felony, regardless of the participants' genders. These statutes have been on the books for 200 years, and members of the state legislature are reluctant to step forward and vote to repeal them for fear of being branded as "pro-blow" by the Evangelicals in the next election. So even though prosecutions never happen, they are theoretically possible."

"Start locking up people for blowjobs, and January 6th will look like a polite Mothers Against Drunk Driving protest," said Roland. "...But you said none of the constitutional crap was going to matter in this case... Why not?"

"Because the Pope and his fancy mick lawyer don't give a rat's ass about our constitution and any rights he may have under it. Pope Thomas, it seems, wants a trial on the merits."

Jaspers took a deep breath. "Let me see if I have this right. The Pope... The real Pope is here in Dayton, which I will assume is not a coincidence..."

"You assume right. As you may recall, there was a somewhat famous trial here in 1925."

"I recall that one... and he wants to be tried here in the Scopes courthouse on the charge of... *blasphemy* and an assortment of other piddling crap? He wants a trial on the merits of the charge based on a statute that probably hasn't been used since we burned witches at the stake?"

"Correct. According to his attorney, Pope Thomas thinks we have been reading the wrong version of the Bible. He thinks that *our* Bible and all the people who preach it have it all wrong. He called us spiritual terrorists. He has apparently written, found, or put together a new one. He wants to put his new one up against ours."

Jaspers folded his hands across his ample midsection and squirmed again in his seat. He looked over at his accountant, whose brain was operating on a level he could almost smell. Morris smiled. Jaspers smiled back and then turned his attention to the State's Attorney, whose smile had evolved into more of a smirk. Roland Jaspers laughed. It looked like a gathering of feral cats about to enjoy lunch at a Wels catfish carcass.

"Hmm. A battle of the Bibles... Son of Scopes... Well now. All I can say is hallelujah and honeysuckle. If this trial can be dragged out for a good while..."

Morris smiled. "Savior Land and the good city of Dayton will experience a resurrection that will rival the original."

"Indeed. Who says the power of prayer is a myth? I tell you, boys, it's a gift from God."

10

The Albino Option

[handwritten: *1) FICTIONAL DAN BROWN BOOK ALBINO MONKS SENT TO SLAY ENEMIES]

∞

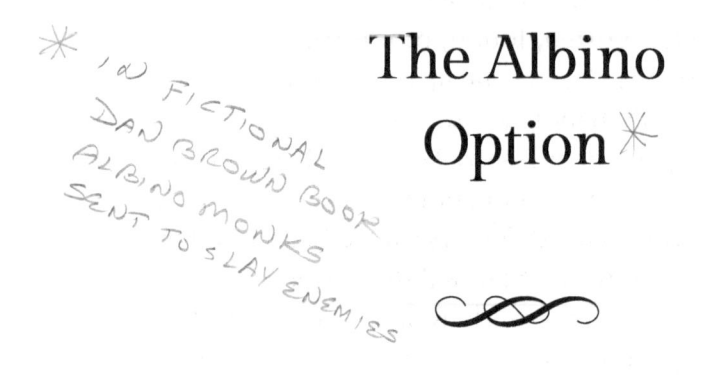

Maybe we should have him killed and blame it on the Protestants. [handwritten: PAGE 50 ANTI-DEFAMATION]

Warren Donovan tried to expel the thought from his brain as soon as it clawed its way into his consciousness. Once you start thinking about the unthinkable, it necessarily becomes thought of. Then you can't stop thinking about it. He knew it was only a matter of time before a variation of the idea infested everyone's mind. *Whatever you do, Cardinal, do not think of the pink protestant elephant. I understand. No problema. How about a pink elephant sitting on the Vicar of Christ?*

Alitalia Flight AZ4000, also known as "Shepherd One," carried an emergency Vatican strike force that included Cardinal Battista, Cardinal Calcagno, Chief Vatican Counsel Rodolfo Graziani, and five of his most trusted lawyers. A Mercedes van met them at Lovell Field airport and took them to the best hotel available for a large party on short notice – none other than the famous (by Tennesse standards) Chattanooga Choo Choo Hotel and Train Museum, where Warren Donovan was waiting to meet them. The hotel has a railroad museum; guests can choose a romantic stay in one of the train's sleeping cars or rooms inside the hotel. Warren Donovan was concerned that the accommodations would be substandard for the pontifical gathering, a group who were accustomed to the incomparable opulence of the Vatican. Still, he put the thought out of his mind for more pressing matters.

Like murdering the Pope.

The entourage was able to reserve the entire top floor of the Choo Choo Hotel after searching in vain for an accommodating, secure estate in the area. The absence of local Tennessee Catholic aristocracy left them little choice.

The initial meeting between the lawyers was thought best without the Cardinals present.

"Okay, Rodolfo," said Donovan. "Did you find a precedent that can get us out of this God-awful mess?"

Rodolfo sighed, and the look on his face told Donovan that nothing good was coming. "We have spent some time researching canon law and historical precedents for intervention in a situation like this. Unfortunately, there is very little guidance. In 1296, Pietro del Morrone – Pope Celestine V – was elected after a deadlock in a conclave that had lasted for two years. He was chosen because of his hermit-like monk lifestyle away from the politics of Rome. He was completely non-political and thought to be a spiritual compromise. At the time, he was eighty-five years old, and it is quite possible that his reported extended periods of silence had as much to do with the beginnings of dementia as with his spirituality. The new Pope had no experience in the day-to-day management of the Vatican. It quickly became evident that he was not remotely qualified for the office. He was – let us say – *encouraged* to resign. But technically, he was not removed. All of his official acts were annulled by his successor, Boniface VIII, who had him arrested and imprisoned to prevent him from being reinstalled as some kind of an antipope."

"I know all about the antichrist, but what in God's name is an antipope?" asked Donovan.

"An antipope is a person who attempts to usurp the position of leader of the Church of Rome in opposition to the legitimately elected Pope. Between the 3rd and 15th centuries, there were times when antipopes were supported by important factions within the Church and occasionally by secular rulers. Remember Warren, there has never been a Church procedure for *removing* a Pope. The only path available was to claim that the papal election was – as your President Trump claimed – improperly rigged."

"So there is no 25th Amendment for Popes, like if he goes nuts, or becomes incapacitated, or let's say he sexually assaulted a nun?" asked Donovan.

"I don't recall that particular remedy doing much good when your moronic president Trump went completely *matto* after your 2020 election."

"Matto?" [ITALIAN FOR CRAZY]

"Our expression for a sudden onset of insane stupidity."

"Rodolfo, I'm a Republican, but believe me, With Trump, there was nothing sudden about it."

"Warren, my dear friend, I'm afraid there is simply no

formal mechanism for getting rid of a Pope. I suppose we could come up with something. These men have reinterpreted scripture for two thousand years in almost every conceivable circumstance. The absence of a remedy in canon law by itself could be... well... a godsend, so to speak."

"So to speak..." agreed Donovan. "The problem, I surmise, is with that completely unnecessary 19th-century declaration of papal infallibility. What in the hell were those people thinking?"

"Actually, they were thinking that it was a good way to *prevent* this exact kind of thing from happening. The idea was that every Pope would be handcuffed by the declarations and interpretations of the Popes who preceded him. *Stare decisis*, as your Supreme Court has declared, and proceeded to ignore whenever they decided the occasion called for it. The idea was that a Pope could not go back on the pronouncements of his predecessors, who were also infallible. Therefore, papal infallibility was envisioned as the exact opposite of papal sovereignty since it bound the Pope to the canon proclamations of his predecessors."

"Wait a minute. You're saying that no one ever *considered* the possibility that this kind of absolute power could be used the opposite way?"

"Correct."

"But Rodolfo, If a Pope is infallible – correct me if I am wrong – that means he can never make a mistake. That would automatically trump, so to speak, the notion of ecclesiastical estoppel and *stare decisis*. A Pope could – God forbid – declare that everyone had to become a vegan because Genesis says that God gave Adam and Eve nothing to eat except seeds and fruit... You've got to be shitting me."

Rodolfo shrugged his shoulders. "I believe the saying in your country is 'I shit not on you.'"

"Well, I'm curious. How did they retrospectively fit the pesky matter of the Inquisition into this brilliant canonical reasoning framework?"

"They didn't. They pretended that it never happened. They still do. They changed the subject and said the numbers were misstated and exaggerated. Only a few people were tortured, and so on. Protestant Reformation fake news, so to speak. Remember, Warren, Papal infallibility was not formally adopted until the 19th century."

"Ah, so the Popes who had non-believers, blasphemers, and ordinary enemies tortured to death pre-infallibility were fallible and behaving mysteriously?"

"No. They were infallible, too." He shrugged his shoulders. "It's all very confusing, I grant you that. There are many invisible footnotes to consider."

Donovan shook his head in disbelief. "So I guess you are saying –correct me if I am wrong –you are saying..."

"I am saying, to use another popular American idiom, that we appear to be fucked."

Donovan shook his head in disbelief. "Once this gets out, parish priests will be scrambling to explain the church's actual position on these insane events. What do we tell them to say? Since birth, they have been told that the Pope speaks for Jesus Christ and that he must be obeyed without doubt or question. He is much more than infallible. He is a messenger of God. And suddenly, he is attacking a theme park, tearing out parts of the Bible, and ranting about a new one? Do we tell them he is still the Pope or that he has gone batshit crazy? Death or boofa,"

"I am familiar with death, but boofa is a new one. Enlighten me."

"Well, three Buffalo hunters trespassing on sacred Sioux Indian hunting grounds are captured by a war party, tied up, and brought back to the village. The tribal chief looks them over and says to the first hunter, "Death or boofa?" The man, having no idea what boofa is figures out that it has to be better than death so he chooses boofa. He is immediately tied to a log and stripped naked and the biggest brave in the village appears and has his way with him. The hunter struggles to his feet and limps out of the village. The second hunter is offered the same choice and undergoes the same terrible punishment. The chief asks the third hunter, "Death or boofa?" The third hunter is a proud man. He insults the chief, calling him a despicable savage, and bravely chooses death. The chief smiles at him and says, "Fine, asshole. Death by boofa!"

The Italian lawyer burst out laughing, took a deep breath, and said, "We are boofaed."

"Any ideas come to mind, Rodolpho?"

"I am at a dead end. We need to meet with him. This Kerrigan *stranzo* would love to bring down the church. He almost did twelve years ago. He seems to be the only one Pope Thomas is communicating with. Perhaps we can bring *him* to his senses."

"Kerrigan? Forget it. He equates the entire church with Father O'Grady and the legions of child molesters. He hates the Church."

"Then we must get to Pope Thomas. I suppose it is up to us. Battista and Calcagno are paralyzed with fear. They are worried that the Holy Father really might be speaking for

God and that, somehow, God may have changed his mind. They believe he really may be infallible."

"Well, that's exactly what you guys trained them to believe since birth. It seems to me that the Vatican will essentially crawl into the fetal position," said Donovan.

"*Hai voluto la bicicletta? E adesso pedala!*"

"Which means?"

They asked for this bike. They better start peddling."

"Where are *Opus Dei* guys and their albino problem-solver when we really need them?" said Donovan, catching himself immediately and then explaining unnecessarily, "I was just kidding."

"I didn't read *The Davinci Code*, but I did see the movie. It was quite good. The albino would not seem to be a viable option. Yet. Warren, why can't your government simply dismiss these ridiculous charges and let us take him back to the Vatican where we could try and get control of him and get him the medical and psychiatric treatment he needs?"

"Because we would have to get around the fact that *he* has decided to waive his diplomatic status and immunity protection. That is *his* right, not the Vatican's. And the local contingent of backwoods Baptist politicos can't wait to bring him to trial. Dayton is going to become the media center of the universe. This is going to make the O.J. Simpson trial look like a drunk-driving plea bargain. As long as he is competent to make his own decisions, there isn't much we can... Wait a minute. That raises an interesting question. I have an idea. Let's think out loud."

"I thought we already did that when you raised the idea of an albino hitman."

"Forget the albino. It was a stupid idea in the movie, anyway. *What did the killer look like, Ma'am? Well, I can't really describe him in detail. Oh, I almost forgot. He was an albino. But there was nothing really distinctive about him.* I have an idea. Okay, here is what we know. 1. The Pope sustained a head injury of undetermined severity. 2. He went nuts at the Savior Land Theme Park, a place that is owned by an idiot named Roland Jaspers, a wealthy former asbestos mogul who is probably not fond of Catholics. 3. It cannot be a coincidence that the Pope pulled this stunt off in a place within the legal jurisdiction of the same courthouse where the famous Scopes trial took place. 4. The Pope undoubtedly wants a trial with the entire world watching. 5. Once this gets out, the entire world *will* be watching.

"You've just bullet-pointed the phases of Armageddon. *That's* your idea? Sit back and watch the Apocalypse?"

Donovan ignored him. "What if the judge ruled that there was probable cause to believe the Pope was not competent to stand trial? That he needed to be extensively evaluated. It would solve so many problems."

"Hmm. We would still have the infallibility problem," said Rodolfo.

"It will go away, sort of like the Inquisition. The Holy Father suffered an unfortunate debilitating injury. The best physicians in the world are treating him for post-traumatic something or another. We are confident he will make a full recovery. Blah, blah, blah. We somehow sedate him and take him back to the Vatican."

Rodolpho took the handoff and began to run with it. "When he comes to his senses, he will thank the doctors and usher in a new era of bringing mental health issues to the attention of the world!"

"Yes. The Church will allocate a portion of its substantial resources to research and treatment of brain injuries. We will open our arms and treatment centers to American football players and other victims of head trauma. I see where you are going, Warren. I like it, and it just might work."

"If not, we can start compiling a list of unemployed albino hitmen."

"We would still have to do an end around that prick, Kerrigan," said Donovan. "But I have an idea about how to do that."

They refined Donovan's brainstorm for an hour. It was a long shot, but when a long shot is the only shot available, you take it and hope you hit your target rather than innocent bystanders.

11

Reality TV

Reality TV bears very little resemblance to reality. What it should be called is "pretend reality TV." Because that's exactly what it is—fake realness.

The first reality show was a 1950s radio broadcast called *Nightwatch*, which recorded Culver City, California, Police on patrol arresting people. This was the grandfather of FOX's *Cops*, a brilliantly conceived half-hour slice of Americana that consisted of weekly TV ride-a-longs with the Broward County, Florida Police who seemed to be on round-the-clock patrol of every trailer park in Florida on the dangerous missions of searching out and arresting drunk, unemployed, trailer-park residents who had or might in the future, beat up their wives, husbands, girlfriends, or neighbors. When there were no drunk and disorderly calls, there were unlimited numbers of traffic stops of motorists who were either guilty of DWI or DWB (driving while black) or DWS (driving while stupid.)

The producer of *Cops* once suggested, only half in jest, that the show be called *Drunks*. Police on the show were told to show a preference for arresting disorderly white drunks over black and Hispanic drunks because the network did not want to be accused of being racially insensitive. The Cops' arrest ratio was kept at five to two – five moronic drunken, stoned, or otherwise drug-using white people for every two moronic substance-impaired black or Hispanic people. The same quota ratio did not apply to male and female subjects. Drunken 200-pound plus out-of-control women covered in tattoos with a shortage of brains and teeth received the highest ratings and arrest preference. This formula seemed to keep everyone happy and the American Civil Liberties Union and the NAACP at bay.

No one bothered getting written consent or even oral permission from the weekly arrestees. The broadcast of their adventures with the Broward Police Department was the highlight of their otherwise anonymous lives. They often begged to be filmed by the FOX hand-held camera crew and insisted that they be notified as soon as the show was going to be aired. They were amazingly cooperative and would often ask for stage directions. "*Ya, want me to take a poke at you or spit when you are about to put the cuffs on? Can I say, Go fuck yourself, pigface?*" Friends and relatives would gather for pizza and beer to watch their debuts as TV stars. *Right here is where I called him a little limpdick cocksucker. Watch and see. They'll bleep it, but that's what I called him. This here is the good part!*

Americans are not sure they officially exist until they see themselves on TV. What other explanation could there have been for the legions of hapless idiots who lined up in the streets of Manhattan every weekday in front of 30

Rockefeller Plaza for *The Today Show*, behaving like they were recovering from brain injuries, waving their hands, shouting "Woo, woo," and holding up signs plugging NBC or Al Roker after telling everyone in Toledo to watch and listen for them shouting *woo woo. That was me, shouting woo woo. Could you tell it was me?* Or the even more exciting prospect that they will see *themselves* on the giant overhead TV screen, wave, and go into total narcissistic ecstasy at realizing they actually exist in the very spot they were standing. And there is always the possibility that they just might be *discovered*. It is the same phenomenon as wanting to be filmed on *Cops* with a slightly more educated and higher socio-economic idiot.

The reality TV storm, ironically, got its start from the people with the most to lose from the phenomena: The Hollywood Writers Guild. The same clever wordsmiths who would pen the highbrow social commentary of *The Dukes of Hazzard* and The *Beverly Hillbillies* would someday pitch *Swamp People* and *Honey Boo Boo*. This started the inexorable slide toward cultural Armageddon. The creator of *My 600 Pound Sister*, a prominent guild member, pitched a pilot for *The Defecators, a* show where a panel of celebrity judges would award cash prizes and trips to contestants whose excreta would be judged in the categories of volume and olfactory originality. The pilot episode showed what could be done, but the concept was rejected for technical reasons.

The originator of *The Defecators* had been inspired by a legendary episode of *Fear Factor*, a 2001 game show hosted by none other than Joe Rogan. Contestants were pitted against each other to face their worst fears. Among the terrors bravely faced by the show's guests were leeches, having one's head shaved, tear gas, and the immortal *He*

Haw! He Haw! episode. Two sets of beautiful twins were put up against each other to see who would drink the urine and semen from a donkey. Brynne and Claire Odioso of Tampa Bay, Florida, made their friends envious by fearlessly gulping the liquid without throwing up while wearing skimpy bikinis (it seemed like the appropriate attire for such an occasion.) As one earlier auditioner who was rejected as a donkey semen slurper because she weighed 215 pounds remarked, "It all tastes the same to me." The Odioso twins are remembered to this day for their unflinching bravery under challenging conditions. Joe Rogan went on to become a serious podcast journalist who tried in vain to save America from COVID-19 vaccines. He should be remembered, however, for hosting the Donkey Semen episode. And for being an asshole. When *Fear Factor* tried to make a comeback in 2006 with the short-lived *Celebrity Fear Factor*, it was hosted by none other than the rapper Ludacris. It made perfect sense.

And then there was *Trial TV*. It was the first reality TV show ever to broadcast actual reality.

Trial TV was one of the two live court format cable networks that exploded on the scene in 1982, shortly after cable TV began to expand. For the first ten years, there was a small but loyal following of viewers/voyeurs who loved to watch the courtroom drama. There was a limitless supply of murders, rapes, product liability, medical malpractice suits, defamation, and discrimination actions all waiting to be televised. The litigation explosion kept spewing forth countless live spontaneous screenplays.

Public trials were a constitutional mandate, and every hack litigator in the country mugged shamelessly as soon as the cameras were turned on. Just *how public* trials should be was open to debate after O.J., but once the door was opened to the media, it became all but impossible to bolt it again. Pre-O.J., things were going just fine for *Trial TV* and its executive producer, Angela Olsen, with a modest but stable cable market share, decent advertising revenues, a few stories in *Time* and *Newsweek* about real-life courtroom drama, and some genuinely exciting moments.

Angela Olsen thought it would be hard to top the trial of Mohammed "Shah-Boom" Ali Fouzgar, a failed Iranian oriental rug merchant and part-time Islamic fundamentalist, who managed to sneak a small amount of sub-cutaneous C-4 plastique explosives and a crude detonating device into his arraignment concealed in his hollow prosthetic leg during the days before sophisticated metal detectors were part of the security in courthouses.

Shah-Boom had lost his right leg below the hip during a reconnaissance foray into the Brooklyn sewer system while investigating possible positions from which to launch an attack on the dreaded symbol of Zionist oppression and expansionism, The Brooklyn Bagel Barn. He and his roommate, Muhammad Hamza, had entered the tunnels through a manhole cover. After discovering that neither of them had bothered to install fresh batteries in their flashlight when it began to lose power a minute after they began exploring the tunnel, they decided to exit the sewer and try again another day. As they turned around to climb back out, Shah-Boom slipped in raw sewage and landed on a rat he would later describe to friends as the size of a small goat. The rat bit him on his right leg. He did not seek medical attention for the bite until a week later. It was too late by then, and the infection had progressed to gangrene. His leg had to be amputated just below the hip. Still, as fate would have it, he was accepted as a candidate for an experimental prosthetic leg being tested, ironically, by the Brooklyn Jewish Medical Center.

The metal leg worked reasonably well and was hollow, providing the perfect place to conceal explosives. His plan to blow up The Bagel Barn using a powerful bomb hidden in a backpack was thwarted when the FBI received a tip from the Boise, Idaho publisher, *Military Press*, that a customer with an Islamic name had ordered copies of *Twenty Tips for Terrorists* and *The Anarchist Cookbook*. A search of the Muhammed and Sha-Boom's apartment found books detailing how to use explosives. They were arrested on unprovable conspiracy charges and, of course, released on bond and scheduled for arraignment the following week. That gave the would-be terrorists time to come up with the brilliant idea of concealing explosives and a crude detonating device in Shah-Boom's hollow prosthetic leg. They would blow up themselves and the assembled crowd in Manhattan Courthouse courtroom #12 to teach everyone a lesson in true Jihad. The virgins were waiting anxiously in paradise.

Fortunately for the assembled, which included the camera crew of Trial TV, the crudely made detonating device, which had been taped to the inside of Sha Boom's right upper thigh, malfunctioned and did not successfully detonate the plastique. It did, however, quite successfully, blow his bang-stick/virgin deflowerer cleanly off and across the courtroom, where it landed directly in front of the Trial TV camera. This appalling spectacle was replayed in slow motion (with appropriate warnings that the material might be unsuitable for younger viewing audiences) approximately four thousand times by every network in the country over the next ten days. Stock in

Media Broadcasting Corporation, the parent company of Trial TV, went up eleven points.

The Jihadist community ridiculed the two men for their failed plots and said they would not have been able to blow up a balloon with a bicycle pump. But their status was restored when Al Jazeera ran a story claiming that the innocent men were the victims of a dastardly Zionist castration plot.

Then came O.J. All of the networks had to get their feeds through Trial TV, which had secured the broadcast rights to L.A. County Court. The O.J. trial became a separate media industry. Lawyers nobody had ever heard of, and those everybody had heard far too much of lined up as expert commentators. America – and, for that matter – the rest of Western civilization could not get enough. But the unbelievable part, as Angela Olsen would modestly point out to her staff at least twenty times a day, was that it was all *free* for the taking. No high-paid prima donna actors, no screenwriter's union, no enormous production costs. All you needed was a camera crew and a couple of camera-ready lawyers, who were about as hard to find as aggressive rodents in the New York subway tunnels. The trial lawyers in the local markets would bribe producers at the affiliates to be commentators so they could put out brochures that showed them doing expert commentary on the O.J. case in a TV studio. Blowhards like Jerry Spence, who always wore his trademark fringed leather cowboy jacket and a cowpoke string tie, became instant celebrities. Legal "experts" sprouted everywhere like dandelions on an ugly lawn.

O.J., it should be remembered, gave birth to the Kim Kardashian phenomenon. How the daughter of the unknown third-rate O.J. lawyer Robert Kardashian became one of the most recognized and followed celebrities in the history of the planet – a woman who never did anything noteworthy in her short and brainless life aside from marrying Kanye West – is a mystery that dwarfs the question of who built the pyramids.

It was wonderful while it lasted. O.J. was all anybody wanted to hear or talk about. *Trial TV* had created what seemed like a permanent low-cost, high-revenue niche in the center of the American television industry. Or so everyone thought.

It came to be known as the O.J. effect. When the Juice was turned off, so were the fortunes of *Trial TV*. How were they going to top O.J.? Who cared about the high school home economics teacher sex scandal? Or the plea bargain of the Vermont Vampire killer. The banality of evil was a fact, not a theory. And banality didn't do a whole lot for ratings. When people tuned in to see Jeffrey Dahmer, they wanted to witness him baying at the moon or drooling, shouting obscenities, and praising Beelzebub. They wanted a Hannibal Lechter from *Silence of the Lambs*. They got a doofus who looked like he should be ringing up Slurpee sales behind the counter at a 7-11. The truth was that after O.J., the public got bored with ordinary trials. And when a media-friendly trial did come along, judges were becoming increasingly reluctant to offer themselves up as Monday morning quarterback fodder for Jerry Spence and Alan Dershowitz. Public trials did not require courts to allow them to be televised, and it did not take long for the collective patience of judges to wear thin.

Good civil cases are few and far between and almost always settled, and the gory criminal ones usually result in pleas. Sure, there was the occasional suit against a dildo manufacturer when the product "failed to perform" as warranted, but on the whole, those were rare. Ratings went in the toilet, and sponsors began to follow suit. It wasn't anybody's fault.

Angela Olsen was paid $256,000.00 a year to keep the ratings up. She did not relish the thought of going back to practicing personal injury law for a living. Myron Mulligan, the CEO of Mutual Broadcasting Company (MBC), had put her in charge of the dogs – *Trial TV, Cuckolded, Great Big Fatties,* and *Flat Earthers.* She only needed to save one of them to save her job. *Trial TV* had the least potential. How in the hell could anyone make an interesting trial *happen?* How could tedious trials compete with the fake judges – Judge Judy, Chrissy's Court, and Judge Joe Brown?

Angela was on her second snow toot on a Sunday afternoon trying to decide between pitching a transgender mixed martial arts league or a reality hunting show called *Real Survivor and We Ain't Kidding,* where the hunters hunted each other on the Indonesian island of Gili Montang while dodging hungry Komodo dragons. They both seemed like couldn't-miss concepts.

She would put together a proposal for the pitch in the morning. Or she could kill herself. It seemed like a jump ball. She lowered her nose to the glass cocktail table to do a third toot when she got the call.

12

Holy Shit Times Infinity

⸎

"Angela, it's Ricky."

Ricky was Ricky McLaughlin, her drug dealer.

"I know who it is, numbnuts. Caller ID. It's only been around for fucking ever."

"Whatever. Look, Angela, I just got an unbelievable tip you're going to want to hear about."

"When, Ricky?"

"When what?"

"When am I going to want to hear about it?"

"Huh? ... ah... now, Angie. Right-the-fuck now."

She sighed, put the phone on speaker, and went down to snow-land on the coffee table.

"Angie, did you just do a line? Jesus, girl. Clear your head and listen up. The Roman Fucking Pope just got himself arrested in Hairy Butt, Tennessee... Angie? Are you listening to me?"

"No, I don't think I am, Ricky. I thought I heard you say the Pope got arrested. What is in this shit you sold me?"

"I *did* say the Pope. You know. The little guy from Rome who wears a dress and a beanie always crosses himself. *That* fucking Pope."

"Ricky, what the fuck are you blathering about?"

"Well, I have a cousin who is a jail guard at some backwater town in Tennessee. Deals meth part-time to trailer parks. Anyway, he tells me that yesterday some crazy fucking little old man wound up in jail for causing a major scene at someplace called Savior Land. It's a jump-around-for-Jesus theme park and mall or something."

While he continued to blather, Angela pulled up the article from the Chattanooga Times Free Press on her laptop.

"Okay, Ricky, I'm reading about it. It's a very amusing story. But what makes you think the old guy is the Pope?"

"My cousin listened in on the conversation between the old guy and his lawyer. A hotshot from South Carolina. A guy named Connor Kerrigan. Flew into Chattanooga on a private jet. He showed up at the jail in a big-ass limo to represent the old guy on some piddling-ass charges. I'm telling you, Angela. It's the motherfucking Pope. And nobody knows yet. They are planning on having a trial in this little town. I think it's called Drayton."

That's when the light came on and it was blinding. Dayton, not Drayton. As in Dayton, Tennessee. *Dayton.* As in the Scopes Monkey trial, Clarence Darrow, William Jennings Bryan, Inherit the Wind, Spencer Tracy, and Frederich March. Holy shit.

No, holy shit times infinity.

"Ricky, stay right there. Don't answer any calls except mine. Give me ten minutes. I'll call you right back."

That's all she needed—ten minutes with Google. Connor Kerrigan *was* a heavyweight. He made a ton of money suing the shit out of the Catholic Church. That didn't make a lot of sense for a guy who would be representing the Pope, but she put it off to be made sense of later. The Vatican website said that the Pope was suffering from a case of the flu and had not made a public appearance in almost a week. He was said to be resting comfortably, and y*eah, thought Angela. He's resting in the Dayton, Tennessee Monkey Courthouse. Holy shit.* She dialed Ricky back.

"Ricky, it's Angela."

"Yeah, I know. Caller Id."

"Tou-fucking-che motherfucker. Ok, I had that one coming. What's your cousin's name?"

"Bobby Clanton."

"Okay, as soon as we hang up, get him on the phone and tell him to call me. Tell him to drop whatever he is doing and call me. Right-the-fuck now. Tell him there's a big payday in it if this thing pans out. The same goes for you."

She spent the next half hour on the phone with Bobby Clanton. When she hung up, she dialed Myron Mulligan. The transgender mixed martial arts league pitch would wait.

"Myron, It's Angela."

"I know. Caller Id."

She sighed and thought, *Karma really is a vengeful bitch.*

"To what do I owe the pleasure?" Myron Mulligan always regretted his occasional dalliances with attractive employees. But he was a hound. There was nothing he could do about that. Angela was a redhead, and Myron Mulligan had a thing for redheads. He called her The Great Red Snapper.

"Myron, I'll get right to the point. I am sitting on what may be the biggest story... " She hesitated for a few seconds before she launched the superlatives. "...the biggest story in the history of the planet. Maybe the universe. I need a plane, a strike force, and a pisspot full of money to throw around. And I need it all by tomorrow morning."

"I'm disappointed. When I saw it was you, I thought it might be something important. Okay, tell me about it."

13

Let's make a deal

―――― ∞ ――――

Angela flew into Chattanooga the next afternoon with Brad Whittington, III, the MBC head of legal, five top network account executives, and a technical crew who would be assessing Dayton logistics, assuming all went well at the meeting. She also had a virtually bottomless expense account, courtesy of CEO Myron Mulligan, that she could access from her iPhone, which pretty much assured that all would go well.

As fortune would have it, Mulligan knew Roland Jaspers by virtue of having been seated next to him at two Rudy Giuliani, legal fees rubber chicken fundraisers where they shared their mutual attraction to money and redheads. The call had gone well.

Jaspers had reserved a private room at Dayton's finest eatery, Bob Bodine's Restaurant on the River, which a

Yelp tourist had favorably reviewed. "Their french fries are pretty good, and their side salad wasn't bad either." A "Private Party" sign had been posted, and those at the meeting would, of course, be sworn to secrecy. Besides himself and the MBC entourage were the Mayor, Pastor Eugene Ingersall, Rhea County Council Chairmen Roy Blackstone, Chamber of Commerce President Ellwood Suggins, and Rhea County State's Attorney Angus Ravenel.

Dayton is a town of 5,217, and the two events that could be considered tourist draws are the annual Tennessee Walking Horse Festival and the Monthly reenactment of the Scopes Monkey Trial at the Rhea County courthouse. One hundred years later, monkeys are still the main downtown attraction. Wooden monkeys that will balance on the edge of a table and a jewelry box engraved with "Monkey Town U.S.A." are modest but reliable sellers. Books, pamphlets, and buttons are in every store. Tickets to the "trial" go for ten dollars. You can buy a painted model of the courthouse for $49.95.

If you do not count the town's tourist reenactments every summer, Dayton's Rhea County courthouse – the site of the most famous trial in the history of American jurisprudence – had gone without a memorable trial for a century.

That courthouse was the theater where Clarence Darrow and Williams Jennings Bryan staged their epic battle over the right to teach evolution in the Rhea County, Tennessee public schools. And "staged" is the appropriate description. The truth is that the whole Scopes evolution "monkey trial" was as artificial an event as was ever orchestrated in an American courtroom. It has been well documented, and conveniently ignored by almost everyone, that the trial was a theatrical spectacle performed for the world to attract attention, publicity, and big piles of cash to the small, impoverished town of Dayton.

The architect of the most memorable trial in American history was a civil engineer named George Rappleyea, who happened to believe in science and evolution. In 1924, he attended a Baptist funeral for a young man who died in an accident. During the service, he listened to a deranged preacher give a eulogy in which he told the parents of the young man that their son would burn in hell because they had failed to have him baptized in the preacher's church. George Rappleyea was furious.

Not long after the funeral, Rappleyea read about the Butler anti-evolution law and organized a group of community leaders at Robinson's Drug Store, where he pitched the idea of challenging the fanatically inspired legislation in a show trial that would make Dayton the center of attention of the country and perhaps the world.

The conspirators decided that John Scopes, the high school football coach and substitute science teacher, would make a splendid defendant and sent a young boy to fetch him from his favorite fishing spot. Scopes could not, for his life, recall whether he had ever even taught the legislatively banned subject of evolution. Nevertheless, he voluntarily incriminated himself to play the part of the defendant so the show could open. He even went so far as to coach some of his students on how to testify against him when they were called before the grand jury.

The most ironic part of the whole sham charge was that the mandatory Tennessee state science textbook already had a chapter on evolution and had been taught all over the state for quite some time. Science teachers would have violated official state policy by *not* teaching Darwin's theory.

It isn't clear whether George Rappelyea was the one who contacted the ACLU shortly before they publicly offered to defend anyone who was prosecuted under the Butler Act. The inane legislation was named after John Butler, a Tennessee farmer, state legislator, and head of the World Christian Fundamentals Association. Butler was part of a conservative anti-science movement that would argue forcefully that the theory of gravity was unnecessary and could be replaced with the straightforward pre-existing theory of "down," as in "things fall down."

A hundred years post-Scopes, a New York Times columnist writing about the Republican war on science and climate change observed that their concerted new effort to earn the title of "The Party of Stupid" revived the memory of Mark Twain's pithy observation that "One should never argue with an idiot. They will drag you down to their level and beat you with experience."

As fortune would have it, the ACLU was itching for a good fight at the same time the Mayor and City Council of Dayton were looking for an influx of cash. An unlikely and hasty wedding date was set. Feverish preparations took place between the indictment, May 25, 1925, and the trial date of July 10, 1925. There was a national avalanche of pre-trial publicity. Dayton's city center went through a makeover, and a pedestrian area was constructed almost overnight. The Dayton County courtroom was transformed with modern communication wiring, movie newsreel camera platforms, and radio microphones. WGN Radio arranged to have live broadcasts from the courtroom and spent the unheard-of sum of $1,000 a day for telephone lines so the trial could be broadcast to the world. Local businessmen, who had been instrumental in conspiring to get the trial going, went so far as to choreograph barroom brawls between soldiers of God and the secular forces of Darwin and Satan. Interest in the forthcoming spectacle was kept at a fever pitch. The press loved everything about the clash, gleefully aided and abetted it, reporting every event and interviewing anyone who had an opinion and would stand still. The scale of the media circus was breathtaking. History recorded that it all worked out marvelously.

No one would have paid the slightest bit of attention to the Butler Act any more than they do today regarding the thirteen states that have laws on the books banning oral sex as an "unnatural and perverted sex act" and a "crime against nature." Oral sex is still illegal in some places. As recently as June of 2013, Attorney General Ken Cuccinelli of Virginia, also the Republican nominee for governor, said he wanted to pass a new law banning fellatio. This resulted in a predictable grassroots campaign by a gay pride organization that used the attention-getting slogan on billboards around Richmond that said, *Let's lick Cuccinelli before he licks us! Oral is Moral*, and the equally sophomoric bumper sticker, *We blow, Cuccinelli sucks!*

Prosecutors, it would seem, sometimes get ideas to use the criminal courts to advance ludicrous causes.

Not much had changed in Dayton since the 1925 trial, which was reported to the world contemporaneously by my benefactor, H.L. Mencken, and later smashingly brought to the screen by Spencer Tracy, as Clarence Darrow and Fredrich March as William Jennings Bryant. As an accurate historical screenplay, *Inherit the Wind* was mostly Hollywood bunk, but it remains a classic.

Tennessee is still a Christian fundamentalist stronghold

and the big born-again buckle on the Bible belt. Jimmy Swaggart (pre and post-masturbation episode in the Days Inn with a fifty-dollar hooker), Pat Robertson, Kenneth Copeland, and Jerry Falwell, Jr. played well in this part of the country. In the 2020 presidential election, 11,000 Rhea County citizens voted for Donald Trump, 2000 for Joe Biden, and five votes were cast for Roque "Rocky" De La Fuente. Locals demanded an investigation into election irregularities, claiming there had been a nefarious conspiracy to rig the election, that there could not have possibly been 2000 votes cast for Joe Biden, and that the reputation of the county had been irredeemably tarnished.

Mayor Ingersall welcomed the New York delegation with his warmest good ol' boy southern charm routine. After lunch and the usual token exchange of views about the wonderful simplicity of small-town living versus the New York rat race, the Mayor asked the assembled if they minded if he partook of the pleasure of a good cigar. He offered everyone the same from a "Monkey Town" humidor. The New Yorkers demurred, and Angela surmised that the laws prohibiting smoking in restaurants must not apply in third-world states.

Mayor Ingersoll got the meeting going. "I gather from my preliminary discussions with Mr. Jaspers, here, that you people have in mind something more financially significant than a PBS-style documentary?"

"Yes. You gather correctly, Mr. Mayor," said Angela.

"No need to be so formal, my dear. We are simple people here in Dayton. Just call me Mayor."

He waited just a moment and then gave everyone the signal to guffaw, which they, of course, all did.

"Just funnin' with you, Ms. Olsen. Call me Eugene."

Angela considered reciprocating by telling the Mayor

he could call her Ms. Olsen, provided he did so from a distance after gargling with Listerine, but discretion held her back. She was used to dealing with assholes.

"What we have in mind... *Eugene* is securing the exclusive rights to broadcast the upcoming legal proceedings."

"Exclusive?" said County Council Chairmen Roy Blackstone. "Is that legal? I expect the boys from FOX, NBC, CBS, and ABC are gonna' be none too happy about such an arrangement."

"First come, first serve, I always say," said Roland Jaspers. Assuming, of course, that the price is right. The thing about MBC is that we can trust that the coverage will be honest and fair." Jaspers had years of experience spewing out bullshit with a straight face and lying under oath. Myron Mulligan had also suggested that a major documentary on the wonders of Savior Land would be part of the deal.

"Perhaps I can be helpful here," interjected Brad Whittington, III. A precedent for such an arrangement was established in 1994 when we secured the rights to broadcast the O.J. Simpson murder trial with the Los Angeles County Council. Perfectly legal."

"And I assume that every other network in the universe will want to cover this trial and be willing to pay for the right to have a camera in the courtroom," said Roy Blackstone.

"Yes," said Angela. "That is the way these matters are typically consummated."

Roland Jaspers felt the stirring of a pre-chubby when he heard the redhead say "consummated" and wondered if he could work some consummating of his own into the deal as part of a honeypot sweetener.

"Let me pose this to ya'll," said Rhea County Council Chairmen Roy Blackstone. Why wouldn't it be in our best interest to open the bidding to all the networks? The highest bidder is the winner. That would seem to be the fairest and most profitable thing to do."

"Because," Angela leaned forward, exposing her freckled and ample cleavage to the assembled, "such a bidding arrangement would preclude direct consulting fee payments being made to the people at this table."

They let the not-so-subtle bribery offer sink in for a minute. "Well, now," said Angus Ravenel. "Just what kind of consulting do ya'll have in mind?"

"The kind that pays very lucratively," said Angela.

The Dayton contingent looked at each other for another minute. A smile with the contagiousness of a group yawn went around the table.

"Well, now," said Roland Jaspers. "What say we roll up our sleeves, put this porker in the pot and get down to some serious cooking."

Angela and her lawyer's next stop was Bobby Clanton's trailer.

14

The Tom in My Cell, Part I

I was not in the best shape when they dumped me in the cell already occupied by an elderly white man wearing neatly pressed khakis and a white button-down collar shirt. Such is to be expected when an alcoholic spends the night in a liquor store after breaking into said establishment. How I survived after drinking the better part of an entire 5th of Uncle Nearest 1856 Sipping Whiskey probably qualifies as a medical miracle. I'm not sure if I was trying to drink myself to death or simply had arrived at a state where I did not care what happened next. In any event, I blacked out, and when I regained consciousness, there he was sitting on his cot reading a leather-bound book. He looked up at me as I struggled over to our shared commode.

"Good morning, sir," said the old man.

My back was to him as I struggled to hit the center of the target. I found it tough going. I waved to him with my free hand and wondered what he was doing in my bathroom and whether my wife knew he was there. I recall putting the seat back down in the event my wife might be next to use the commode. I then realized where I was and remembered that my wife died two years ago.

"Hello, there. When did you get here?"

"Actually," the old man said, "I have been here for three days. You arrived a few hours ago. You were not conscious when they deposited you in your bed."

"... Oh, yes. I remember now. I guess I was pretty shitfaced."

The Pope had never heard the term before but quickly figured out it was one of the many colorful American idioms for drunk. He then noticed that his new roommate had multiple bruises on his face, a swollen lip, and dried blood coming out of his nose."

"What happened to you, friend?"

"I believe my arrest involved more than an acceptable amount of required force. They beat the shit out of me."

"The police?"

"Yes." It happens for some inexplicable reason whenever they find me inside a store."

"I don't understand. You aren't allowed to go inside a store?"

"Not at 2:00 am. This incident happened to be the inside of the Drip Drop Liquor Store. It was closed at the time. I entered the spirits establishment to get something to drink and to sleep. There was an alarm, but that was part of the plan."

"The plan?"

"Yes. The plan was... it wasn't much of a plan...the plan

was to get arrested and thrown in jail; I was tired of sleeping on benches."

"But why did they beat you?

"Well, my good man, I vaguely recall telling Constable Slaven to kiss my black ass. He was one of the officers who showed up to arrest me. We have met before."

"Oh my. I see. Are you a homosexual?"

"No, it's a saying when you don't like somebody, you say, 'You can kiss my ass.' Crude but effective... I detect an accent. Where are you from, kind sir?"

"Originally? From Brazil. I've been living in Rome for the past eight years."

"Georgia or Italy?"

"Italy."

"How in God's name did you get from Rome to this Rhea County jail cell?"

"That, my friend, is a very long story. God's name actually has more to do with it than you can imagine."

The fog had cleared enough for me to recall the article I had read in the Dayton Herald two days before. This had to be the old man who had been arrested at Savior Land. "Ahh. You are the gentleman who was arrested for causing a commotion at Savior Land. It's a pleasure... nay, an honor to meet you. I look forward to hearing all about it."

"Well, that is quite a long story. But first, I would like to hear your story."

The jailer, one Bobby Clanton, whom I had met in a previous stay, came in with our breakfast while we were chatting. "Good morning, gentlemen. Getting acquainted, I see. I brought you boys an old radio we had in the broom closet in case you'd like to keep up on the news."

"That was very kind of you, Mr. Clanton," said the old man.

I learned later that when they booked Pope Thomas, he would only say that his name was Tom and offered no other details from which they could identify him. He had no identification, and his pockets were empty aside from some cash when they searched him for weapons and narcotics.

My story was not one I particularly wanted to share. But something about this old man made me want to talk to him. He radiated kindness, intelligence, and a genuine interest in who I was. He made me want to talk about my life for the first time in two years. He made me want to... well... confess.

"I came to Dayton about six years ago to research the town's history and write a book. I was a history professor at Vanderbilt and wanted to write a book about Dayton and the Scopes trial. But then... "

"Please, Go on. I would like to hear about what happened to you."

I hesitated.

"Confession, we like to say, is good for the soul."

"What are you, a Catholic priest or something?"

"... or something."

So I began. "I taught a course titled *Thomas Paine and the Founding of the American Republic* at Vanderbilt. I have a PhD in American history. My wife, Lucille, and I were unable to have children of our own, so we raised eight foster children. Every one of the children who came through our home graduated from college and went on to lead exemplary lives. Three became physicians, two social workers who investigated neglected children, and three worked as civil rights lawyers. Six years ago, I took a one-year sabbatical from Vanderbilt and rented a house in Dayton to research and write a definitive history of the 1925 Scopes evolution trial. Most of what people know about the trial – Clarence Darrow and William Jennings Bryan – is from the movie *Inherit the Wind*. It was a fine movie, but it wasn't history."

"I imagine that movies rarely are. They do, however, make people who do not have the time or inclination to devote to history books think about things they might not otherwise bother themselves with."

"I suppose that is correct. Movies need heroes and villains to sell tickets. Movies about history are rarely accurate. In the real world, heroes are often flawed, and villains are sometimes unfairly caricatured and vilified. Clarence Darrow, for example, was not always a knight in shining armor fighting for truth and justice. He started out as a labor lawyer. In 1911, he was hired by the American Federation of Labor to defend two brothers accused of bombing the Los Angeles Times building. He was later indicted for attempting to bribe a juror. He went through two trials as a criminal defendant."

"Was he found guilty?"

"He was acquitted in the first trial, and there was a hung jury in the second. The State was going to try him again, but at the last minute, a deal was reached. The prosecutors agreed not to retry him if he gave up his right to practice law ever again in California. His actual guilt is a matter of historical debate, but my research leads me to believe he was more likely than not, guilty. He was a champion for civil rights and the American working man, but he was not a saint."

"And William Jennings Bryan? Was he the

fundamentalist buffoon that was portrayed so unforgettably by... I believe it was Fredric March?"

"He was misunderstood, and his story is even more interesting. The man had concerns that went far beyond evolution's threat to biblical literalism. He worried about the rise of a Hitler before anyone had ever heard of Hitler."

"This is fascinating. Please go on."

"Bryan's concern was not so much the idea of evolution as blasphemy as it was a fear that the idea of survival of the fittest – a phrase, incidentally, that Darwin never actually used – that was Herbert Spencer – would become a rallying cry for men like Adolph Hitler, used to justify doing away with or denying rights to people they considered unfit. Might made right, they argued. So it was in nature, and so it should be in the affairs of man. The strongest race of the human species would always survive, rule, and weed out the weakest. The Nazis would argue that they had a moral obligation to make it so. Bryan may have been among the first to see the warning signs. Let me see if I can remember how he put it. 'Science is a magnificent force, but it is not a teacher of morals. It can perfect machinery, but it adds no moral restraints to protect society from the misuse of the machine. It can also build gigantic intellectual ships, but it constructs no moral rudders for the control of the storm-tossed human vessel.'"

"I had no idea," said the Pope." This seems to me to be a part of history worth retelling. What kind of storm took your ship off course?"

"Five months into the project, Lucille was diagnosed with pancreatic cancer. She died seven weeks after the diagnosis. Some men deal with the painful loss of a spouse and go on with their lives. I was not made to be one of them. I would guess that Spencer would have found me to be among the unfit."

I remember starting to well up. I fought back tears as I recounted what happened. They came anyway. The Pope placed his hand on my knee, his fingertips an inch or so from mine. And then I saw something I will never forget, and if you ask me if it was from the residual alcohol in my system or brain damage I had sustained from living the life of a derelict – I will tell you it is quite possible. I just don't know.

I saw a blue light extending from his five fingers to my five fingers. It looked like tiny bolts of electricity. Then he covered my hand with his. The lights went away and I felt something that I do not know how to describe. Again, it was probably my mind playing those tricks you hear about or a trick of the light or something else. It doesn't really matter what it was. All that matters is that it was. I slowly regained my composure.

"Your turn, my good man. What was the inspiration for your occupation of Savior Land?"

"Well, for starters, the place is an abomination. Did you know they have a ride they call the Holy Roller Coaster?"

I burst out laughing. "I hadn't heard that. It does strike me as an edifice that makes the episode with golden calf a rather minor transgression."

"Indeed," agreed the old man. He took a deep breath and then decided to tell me who he was. Or perhaps it would be more accurate to say who he had been. I was, of course, stunned. He told me that he came to realize the House that Peter built had been built on seriously shifting sands. But he didn't tell me how he had come to this earth-shattering realization. I decided to ask him.

"What happened, Your Holiness?

"If we are to speak more of these things, I would very much like you to call me Tom."

"All right. What happened, Tom?"

He hesitated. And then he looked at me and said, "Well, for one thing, I watched Jurassic Park."

"The dinosaur movie?"

"Yes. The dinosaur movie."

"*You* watched Jurassic Park?"

"I did. And I enjoyed it. I watch a movie almost every week. It is my way of keeping up with popular culture. There are more things in heaven and earth than exist in the Vatican."

"Who knew?"

"But back to your question, I did not seem to be able to make use of my apologetic skills to even approach reconciling the conundrum of the dinosaurs."

I would like to think that I am a fairly insightful man. I trust my intuition and can usually figure out the answer to a well-constructed Poirot story before the detective announces the culprit. I did not have a clue where he was going. The only word that popped into my brain was, "Huh?"

"There is a rather pithy soliloquy delivered by Jeff Goldblum, the mathematician character. He is contemplating the enormity of what has been created on the island where they cloned and made the dinosaurs, and he says, 'God created dinosaurs. God destroys dinosaurs. God creates man. Man destroys God. Man creates dinosaurs.' I spent the next few days reading about the history of life on this planet. It was the first time I ever really appreciated the enormity of time that has passed since the creation of Earth."

"I imagine the whole 6000-year New Earth concept went out the window...?"

"Actually, it went out the window, as you put it, many years ago. We have accepted the fact of evolution for over fifty years. Did you know that in the four billion years that Earth has been orbiting around the sun, the life form that has been the most successful and outlived every other life form in the planet's history was the dinosaurs?"

"I don't believe I knew that," I said, thinking that was interesting, but I still didn't have a clue.

"Yes. 165 million years. They were the most successful living things that ever inhabited the planet."

The proverbial light bulb came on. I now knew where he was going because I had been there myself.

"Well," the Pope continued, "... there is every reason to believe that if that asteroid made a 2-degree course deviation, they would still be here today, and mammals would not have inherited the earth."

"So it occurred to you that man may have resulted from an accident rather than a well-thought-out plan?"

"Something like that. If it was a plan, it seemed to me to be one that was very hard to accept. It would have been a plan that could only mean that the planner – God, the Creator – would seem to have made after realizing a design mistake. It would mean that one day, God looked down at what he had made – the evolution of enormous living creatures – and thought something like *this really was not going in a direction that pleases me,* and decided to start over. So he threw an enormous rock at them or knew it was coming and declined to do anything about it. Either way, it would seem that he rid his house of every last dinosaur. I could not find another way of looking at it, and I could no longer comfort myself with the sidestep of 'mysterious ways.' We would seem to be here by chance, not because the dinosaurs did anything *wrong*. Brontosaurus could not have committed any kind of original sin."

"And then there is pancreatic cancer."

"Yes, and then there is cancer. Your wife. Innocent children. Ironically, I had no problem dealing with the so-called problem of suffering up until that point. Another movie comes to mind. The one with Mr. Miyagi."

"The Karate Kid? Did you watch The Karate Kid?

The Pope lifted his eyebrows and shrugged his shoulders as if to say, what are you going to do? "It was a slow Sunday night. I did. Wax on, wax off. It was our answer to everything. You may not understand what the great Mr. Miyagi was up to when he made young Daniel wax all those cars, but his plan became apparent in the end. He was wiser than Daniel could have imagined and Daniel should have had faith."

God as Mr. Miyagi. That is how our marathon college dorm-style bull session went. The college professor who lost his way and the Pope who was trying to find his. After dinner on the second day of our encounter, Pope Thomas looked up at me and said, "Mr. Jefferson, it occurs to me that you should get back to doing meaningful work. I have a proposition for you."

And here I sit, writing this book. Oh, I almost forgot. I have not touched a drop of alcohol since that day in jail. And there was no withdrawal. It was as if I had never touched a drop. I can't help but think about those strange fingertip blue lights when I think about that.

15

The Tom in My Cell, Part 2 (The Tale of the Toms)

And that is how I came to write this recounting that you are reading.

I was still trying to grapple with the idea that *Jurassic Park* was the *casus belli* of this papal cataclysm, and I said so.

"There must be more to this story than the destruction of the Jurassic world."

"Yes, you are correct. There is more."

"Well, if I am to be your chronicler, I need to hear about it."

And so he recounted the tale of the Toms—the other ones.

"Henry, have you read the Gospels?"

"I think it would be more accurate to say that I have read *about* the gospels."

"That is the way most people come to know them. Reading the original texts is difficult, and gaining the necessary insight is best understood by reading them in Greek. They have been rewritten and translated innumerable times, and many of the translations are, at best, woefully inadequate and, at worst, completely wrong in important details. As an example, almost every Christian translation of the Hebrew Bible translates the 6th Commandment as *Thou Shall Not Kill*. That creates all sorts of problems as it would seem to forbid taking a life in self-defense or even taking the life of an animal for food. As I'm sure you are aware, there are no footnotes, only learned and not-so-learned commentaries. The original text is accurately translated as *Thou Shall Not Murder*."

I thought about it. "Yes, that would seem to provide a defense of sorts for Canaanite genocide when God ordered Moses to kill everything that breathes, including women and children. God sanctioned the killing, and therefore, by definition, they were not murders."

"Precisely. And as hard as that story is to accept, the distinction between divinely sanctioned killing and murder is an important one. The Canaanite massacre described in Numbers 31 raises an interesting and disturbing apologetics problem that I will explore with you later."

"That is one I look forward to."

"When I was elected as Pope, I chose the name Thomas

after the apostle Thomas and his namesake, Saint Thomas Aquinas."

"The apostle Thomas of Doubting Thomas fame?"

"The same. My choice was not met with universal approval at the Vatican. And I did not choose the name because of the *doubting* part of the story. The recounting of Thomas saying, *"Unless I see the nail marks in his hands and put my finger where the nails were, and put my hand into his side, I will not believe"* is from *John* 20:25. It appears in none of the other Gospels. *John* was the last Gospel written between sixty and seventy years after the crucifixion. It appears nowhere else, and it is, therefore, difficult to determine its accuracy. One of the methods used by historians to assess the credibility of events described in historical documents is how often those events appear in different historical accounts."

"You mentioned Thomas Aquinas."

"Yes, the philosophical father of physicotheology."

"I am not familiar with that term."

"Natural theology. It was an attempt to synthesize Aristotelian philosophy and natural science with the fundamentals of Christianity. I found his thinking to be both compelling and inspirational. I credit his influence with the Church's acceptance of the theory of evolution some fifty years ago."

"Intriguing. I will put him on my sober days reading list."

"Let us hope there will be many of them. It would be a sin to waste such a fine mind. Aquinas is well worth your time. But, interestingly, it was the first Thomas who caused me to begin to think about my faith in different ways. Did you know, Henry, that we have found fifty-three gospels to date?"

"I did not. I knew other gospels existed that were not incorporated into the New Testament – I have read about the Gospel of Philip and the Gospel of Mary – but I had no idea there were so many."

"Yes. One was discovered very recently – in 1949 at Nag Hamadi in Egypt. The Gospel of Thomas. In case you are wondering, it is not titled "The Gospel of Doubting Thomas." It is titled *The Gospel of Didymus Judas Thomas.*"

"Didymus?"

"Yes. Didymus means twin."

"Jesus had a twin?"

"We will never know for certain, but interestingly, the same reference to Thomas appears in John 11:16."

"But if Jesus had a twin...?"

"Yes, it raises all kinds of thorny questions and problems."

I thought about it. "It occurs to me... forgive me, Tom... it occurs to me that a twin would imply a kind of divinity for Thomas, as well as Jesus. They would both have to have been virgin births."

"That is certainly one conclusion." He looked away. It was clear to me that he did not want to go there. After a few uncomfortable moments, he continued. "There are other interesting issues raised by *The Gospel of Didymus Judas Thomas*. There is no mention of miracles or the resurrection. Not one. It recounts only the words spoken by Jesus. It begins with the statement, '*These are the secret sayings that the living Jesus spoke and Didymo's Judas Thomas recorded.*'"

"Jesus..."

"Perhaps."

We both chuckled.

"One would think that mention of the miracles and the resurrection would be in every Gospel."

"Yes," the Pope went on. "Miracles certainly figure prominently in *Matthew, Mark, Luke,* and *John.* The original *The Gospel of Thomas* is kept at the Coptic Museum in Cairo. I was permitted to examine it when I went to Egypt last year. Many of the sayings are identical or similar to those recorded in Mathew, Mark, Luke, and John. But there is one that was not. It caught my attention and stunned me. I might have even thought about *Jesus* the same way you did a moment ago."

"What was it?"

"Verse 29. *If the flesh came into being because of spirit, it is a wonder. But if spirit came into being because of the body, it is a wonder of wonders. Indeed, I am amazed at how this great wealth has made its home in this poverty.*"

"I don't understand."

"Well, Thomas is saying that Jesus was musing and perhaps had doubts about whether God created the universe or the universe created God. He is saying that it would be wonderous indeed if God did create the universe, but if the universe – the body – created the spirit... God... that would have been even more wonderous."

He began a sentence with "*Jesus*"... just as I said *Jesus!* We both said "Jesus!" at the same time. We laughed.

"Jesus's teachings were everlasting and miraculous. I have always believed they were much more important to Christianity than the miracles. That may be the message of Thomas's Gospel. And then there is yet another Thomas who thought the same thing."

"Who was he?"

"He was your third president, Thomas Jefferson."

"Of course. Our Diest in Chief is a man who either believed in all the gods or none of them. It is difficult to pin down one way or the other. I have read everything he wrote on the subject and remain unsure about his ultimate conclusions about God and Jesus. He did, however, say that he loved the teachings of Jesus. He called them the most sublime and benevolent code of morals which has ever been offered to man... I assume you are referring to his famous cut-and-paste job of the New Testament."

"Yes. As I'm sure you know, it is kept at the Smithsonian. President Jefferson used a knife to cut and then paste Jesus's words from the King James Bible into his own version. I was allowed to examine it carefully on my trip to Washington. It is often referred to as *The Jefferson Bible*, but that is misleading. He titled it *The Life and Morals of Jesus of Nazareth*. Like his namesake, the Apostle Thomas, he declined to include any narration or mention of miracles.

"... or a description of the resurrection," I added. "I also remember that he completely rejected *Revelation*. I wrote an article on his exchange of letters with his friend, Brigadier General Alexander Smyth, who asked Jefferson for his thoughts about a commentary he had written about Revelation. Jefferson said, *I then considered it as merely the ravings of a maniac, no more worthy, nor capable of explanation than the incoherences of our own nightly dreams.* And your thoughts on *Revelation?*"

"I suppose this is as an appropriate time as any," said the Pope. I have come to believe that Revelation was the stick of carrot and stick fame. It was included as the official version of the New Testament in the 4th Century to frighten the masses into believing. Referring to it as the believe-or-else Gospel would have been more appropriate.

That brings us to one of the final nails in the coffin where my old beliefs are buried."

"Revelation?"

"Yes, Revelation. Specifically the idea of the Lake of Fire. The final destination of those who do not believe in Christ. I could not reconcile dooming a child belonging to a tribe in the Amazon rainforest who never had the opportunity to know Jesus or reject him, to burn in the fires of hell for eternity, with the idea of the Jesus Christ I knew and loved. And there was not enough apologetic sophistry in the history of the Church to convince me that President Jefferson was in error when he called it the ravings of a maniac. That is the part they saw me tear out before I was arrested."

I was stunned. The implications and the enormity of what he was saying were hard to grasp. *Earthshaking* was a superlative that I took great pains to avoid in my discourse and writings. I could think of no other word to capture what was about to happen once *this* revelation became known.

"It seems to me – please allow me to address you this one time as 'your Holiness' – it seems to me, your Holiness, that the Toms may all be of one mind."

His Holiness smiled.

16

Lightning Hath Struck the Shithouse

～∞～

Bradley Simpson, the anchor of MBC's *New Day Today* – *a duplicative name for a morning show that* sounded fresh – actually shot his Starbucks almond milk latte out of his nose. "Are you fucking kidding me? Wait a second. Are we sure? This is a prank, right? It has to be. How many sources do we have on this bullshit story? You do realize, Steve, that if we are being pranked, this network will be the laughingstock of the galaxy."

Steve Danson, executive producer of *New Day Today* nodded. "We're sure. It's true, Brad. I got a call from M&M. Myron actually picked up the phone. He said he fully expected our jaws to drop. More sources have verified this than we had for the Stormy Daniels story. The local State's attorney, the Mayor of Dayton, the jail guard serving him meals, and his attorney, a guy named Connor Kerrigan; aside from those people, I suppose you could conclude it's just a rumor."

"What the fuck, Steve? Is it a sex scandal? Did he get caught with a boy scout?"

"No. Wishful thinking. But the more I think about it, this is even better. Pope Thomas I, the Vicar of Christ, is in a county jail cell in Dayton, Tennessee, after causing a minor riot at some theme park called Savior Land in the shadow of the Holy Roller Coaster, where he was arrested for disorderly conduct, trespassing, blasphemy, and littering."

"Littering? Did you say littering?"

"... and blasphemy."

"Blasphemy?? Jesusfuckingchrist..."

"Exactly. And it would seem that we are the only news network on the planet that knows. The Red Snapper, of all people, got the story."

"Angela? Angela Fucking Olsen? You're telling me that the producer of *Great Big Fatties* got the biggest scoop in the history of the planet?"

"The same." Steve thought of the wild coke-filled nights he, and probably half of the executives at MBC, had spent with the Red Snapper and then noted to himself that *Fucking* would have unquestionably been an appropriate middle name.

BREAKING NEWS!!

The introductory news banner was the largest ever used by the morning show. There were discussions about using the phrase "Unimaginable Breaking News" but cooler heads went with the more dignified approach and added a seldom-used double exclamation mark.

Bradley Simpson put on his most all-time severe announcer face. The one he had been saving for an occasion like a surprise Russian nuclear strike on London. "Good morning, America and the world. In an exclusive to MBC News – we are the only network with this story – (*Steve put his hand over his face and remembered that two days prior he had explained to Bradly that "general consensus" was redundant*), we have just learned that Pope Thomas, the spiritual and religious leader of over a billion and a half people worldwide, has been arrested and jailed in Dayton, Tennessee after allegedly causing a disturbance at Savior Land, a religious theme park on the outskirts of Chattanooga. This story is exclusive to MBC News. We have these details so far in this exclusive breaking story..."

"Exclusive" would be mentioned fifty-seven times in the next two hours. In the three minutes after the story broke, every news network around the globe carried the MBC scoop with the caveat (CNN, NBC, ABC TASS, FOX, Xinhau, Agenzia Nazionale Stampa Associata,) *We have not yet independently verified the story, but we expect to have details shortly.*

MBC News Operations Chief Roger Farnsworth claimed to have personally fielded more than 200 *What the Fuck* and *What the Actual Fuck* queries from news organizations around the world. His responses covered the bases from *You can take it to the bank* to *Well, verify it yourself, motherfucker.*

Within two hours, more corporate jets were scrambled than SAC bombers and fighters during the Cuban Missile Crisis, and every hotel room, VRBO, and Air B&B room within 100 miles of Dayton was booked at profiteer rates that would make oil companies blush.

When the story broke, Roland Jaspers was watching MBC with his CFO and remarked, "Well, now. It appears that lightning hath struck the shithouse."

17

The Deacon of Doubt

❦

The media had crowned Sean Patterson as The Deacon of Doubt. He was a spokesman for science, critical thinking, and America's atheist-in-chief. His detractors revived the phrase made popular by Richard Nixon's disgraced criminal Vice President, Spiro Agnew, when he referred to the press as those "nattering nabobs of negativism." Agnew was much too ignorant to have any idea what a nabob was. Pithy alliteration was what mattered. The success of the nabob zinger inspired him to follow it up almost immediately by referring to critics of Nixon's Vietnam War policy as "hopeless, hysterical hypochondriacs of history." When he pled no contest to a felony charge stemming from a storied career soliciting bribes from contractors while governor of Maryland, one journalist tagged him as "a cantankerous, conscienceless, corrupt criminal whose career ended in calamity when he copped a plea."

Sean Patterson held PhDs in philosophy and psychology. He published 17 books on the philosophy of science, critical thinking, the psychology of fanaticism, the history of religious thought, and a New York Times bestseller titled *Homo-non-sapien (The Evolution of the Irrational Belief Machine)*. But as the editor and publisher of *Freethinker*, he received fame and became known in the media as the Deacon of Doubt. Sean Patterson had a rapier-sharp mind and a George Carlin-style take-no-prisoners approach in dealing with ideologues and religious fundamentalists.

He was the child of a Catholic father and a Jewish mother. His father was a part-time Catholic, and his mother was not at all religious but insisted that he be mindful of his heritage. The only religious tradition she insisted he observe was Yom Kippur, the Jewish day of fasting, atonement, and repentance. She told him those same guilt skills would also be useful if he ever decided to become a Catholic.

He grew up in Lawrenceville, a working-class section of Pittsburg, which, along with Boston and New York, has the highest percentage of Catholics in any city in the United States. His choices for school were public schools ranked among the worst in the nation or the local Catholic school, Saint John The Evangelist. It wasn't a difficult choice for Mr. and Mrs Patterson. He attended Saint John, where he learned about Catholicism and the peculiar form of celibacy practiced by some priests. He also learned that a priest could abuse a young boy without fearing repercussions from the school, the Church, or possibly even from God. Punishment and the school spanking paddle were reserved for children.

In high school, Sean Patterson had studied the religious philosophy of the great writer C.S. Lewis, whom most people remember for The Chronicles of Narnia, but who was also an ardent atheist who converted to Christianity at the midpoint of his life and became a universally respected and accomplished modern apologist. An Anglican, he was an admired and loved theologian by all denominations. In his 1952 book Mere Christianity, he wrote of Jesus, *"Either this man was, and is, the son of God, or else a madman or something worse. You can shut him up for a fool, you can spit at him and kill him as a demon, or you can fall at his feet and call him Lord and God, but let us not come with any patronizing nonsense about his being a great human teacher."* The argument had been distilled to *liar, lord, or lunatic*. It was a laconic, frightening, and logically unassailable trilemma. Father O'Malley, his religion teacher, told his class those were the only choices. Choose wisely or at your eternal peril.

Except for the fact, Sean thought, that they might not be the only choices. Sean could not get the question out of his mind. He saw a flaw in C.S. Lewis's seemingly impenetrable logical fortress.

"Father O'Malley," Sean asked one day. "What if he never said it?"

"What, Mr. Patterson, are you talking about? We have Mr. Lewis's words in his book. You have the book in front of you."

"Not Mr. Lewis. Mr. Lewis's argument seems to be based on the assumption that Jesus *said* he was Lord. He claimed he was the son of God. But Jesus is only recorded as having said that in the Gospel of John, which you told us was the last Gospel written sixty-five years after Jesus was crucified. I cannot understand why Matthew, Mark, and Luke would not have written about Jesus saying something that important. So my question is, what if John... well... got it wrong? Or what if he made it up? I'm not saying that John invented the story, but what if Jesus never said it? The whole liar, lord, or lunatic argument would collapse, wouldn't it? There would be a fourth alternative. The one where he never said it."

Father O'Malley was aghast at the boy's sense of intellectual self-importance. Children his age should not be asking such questions. God inspired the Gospels. To question the integrity of an apostle and Gospel author was to question God. The boy was sent to the principal's office, where The Diocesan Superintendent of Catholic Schools happened to be paying a visit. The two men asked Sean to recount why he had been sent from class. He explained and said that he felt that he had done nothing wrong. He had simply asked a question.

He was told to ask God for forgiveness and given the choice of suspension from school or the paddle. He chose the paddle and told the Diocesan Superintendent that he thought it best to follow the example given by Jesus. He would endure the pain and suffering rather than abandon his principles. This last act of impertinence earned him an extra ten paddles.

Sean Patterson had already decided to take the fork in the road that led away from Damascus after having been abused as a seven-year-old by his 4th-grade teacher, Father Francis Gallagher. During the class action suit eight years later against Father Gallagher and Our Lady of the Immaculate Conception Parrish, the defendant apologized and said he was at a loss to understand why "God had made him that way." That was what they all asked when exposed. That was their defense. It was God's doing.

The positive aspect of the outcome of Sean Patterson's encounter with Father Gallagher was that his higher education would be taken care of as far as he wanted to go. And Sean Patterson went far. But the financial settlement did nothing to ameliorate his hatred for the Catholic Church, which he called The Fear Factory.

His experience left him with a binary choice about the character of God. If God had made Father Gallagher that way, then God was the demiurge of the Gnostics – a first-century largely forgotten Christian sect whose followers believed that the creator god made the world where lions ate lambs, children died in natural disasters, divine intervention had no discernible rhyme or reason, and priests were made as predators. He let that be the nature of things because the demiurge was an intrinsically flawed god. That was one deduction that seemed unavoidable. The other way out was to accept that the entire god thing was nonsense. Shit happens. There never has been a plan or reason. Man became a belief machine to cope with inevitable suffering. Evolution sculpted lions to kill and eat meat and humans to believe in nonsense to deal with random suffering.

The Deacon of Doubt was born long before he was named.

Connor and Sean, college roommates, called themselves The Irish Twins. It was a disparaging 19th-century term used against Irish immigrants who were stereotyped as having large Catholic families with siblings that were as close as a year apart.

Religion, philosophy, and history were the subjects of late-night bull sessions during their years at Georgetown

University in Washington, D.C. They often went at it well into the early morning hours.

2000 was their sophomore year, and they both registered for a course titled *Theodicy and the Philosophy of Evil* taught by the world-famous author of *The Exorcist*, William Blatty. On the first day of class, Blatty had asked them to think about an all-powerful and perfectly benevolent God, which everyone seemed to agree were two qualities that the Almighty would necessarily have to come equipped with. So how, Blatty asked, had this perfect supreme being allowed evil to enter the world? And why? Why, Blatty asked, hadn't God simply kicked the crap out of Satan after his mischief in the Garden of Eden? Either He was not perfectly good, or He was not all-powerful. Where else was there to go? Blatty had assigned his novel, *Legion*, and told them to write an essay by the end of the first week.

"Blatty seems pretty cool," said Sean.

"For sure. I read an article about him. He not only wrote *The Exorcist* and *Legion*. The guy wrote the screenplay for the second *Pink Panther* movie. I think it was called *A Shot in the Dark*."

"No shit? I saw it. Laughed my ass off."

"His first lecture was pretty provocative," said Connor. I think a lot about evil. What kind of a schmuck god would create a world like this and then become an absentee landlord?"

"It's a fair question. *Schmuck*, by the way, was one of my mother's favorite expressions. Did I ever mention she was Jewish? Which makes me technically Jewish. Maternal bloodlines determine Jewishness. If a Jewish girl ever brings me home, I get a pass on the Irish part. Under Jewish law, it doesn't count. Keep the Jewish blood thing between us if the Nazis make a comeback. Anyway, I read *The Exorcist* when I was about seventeen. It scared the shit out of me. I was already probably an agnostic on the way to becoming an atheist, but I finished it and couldn't help asking myself, *what if I'm wrong...?* As a kid who was raised as a part-time Jew, I used to wonder what would happen if I broke the fast early on Yom Kippur when God was opening his big books. There were two of them. *The Book of Life* and *The Book of Death*. Both were sort of a Yahweh's *Farmer's Almanac* for the coming year. And as the Santa Clause song tells, *He knows when you are sleeping. He knows when you're awake. He knows if you've been jerking off so don't do it for goodness' sake!* He's watching. He knows if you've been bashing your bishop – spanking your monkey – for Christ's sake."

"Why would you bash your bishop for *Christ's sake?*" said Connor.

Sean laughed, choked, and started coughing on his hit of Maui Wowi. "Why would he watch? That's the real question. We were supposed to fast from sunset to sunset, and there was a tradition among reformed Jews – I was never quite sure what it was that we had reformed from doing or whether we were supposed to attend some kind of reform school – of breaking the fast by going to a Chinese restaurant. Anyway, I was not a good faster. I cheated. I don't recall being a particularly good anything as a kid, but I somehow made it into the right book year after year. So, after I read *The Exorcist*, I decided I was going to try and find out... well... if there really was a god. That got me paddled more than once in Catholic school. I wonder how Blatty will get us out of the conundrum. I hear he's a devout Catholic."

"I heard that too," said Connor. "Should be interesting."

"But here's the thing," Sean went on. "Science staunchly maintains that it has nothing to say about the nature of evil and why it exists. None of it can be quantified or empirically verified so these human concerns are better left to the religious folks and the philosophers. From what I have read, science says. *It's not in our job description. It's above our pay grade.* I decided they were just ducking the issue. I think it's up to us to sort it all out. You and me."

"You sort it all out, my Irish-Jewish friend. Me? I think I'll try and do something about it."

Sean Patterson spent the next twenty years trying to sort it out and Connor Kerrigan went to law school and did something about it."

18

The Straitjacket Plan

◦◦◦

The meeting between the Irish/Italian legal axis and State's Attorney Angus Ravenel had reached an impasse regarding conflicting interpretations of applicable principles of jurisprudence.

"Are you fucking kidding me, Mr. Donovan? Let me get this right. You boys – you and Rodolfo Linguini over there – want me to help you have the Popesecola declared crazier than a shithouse rat so that there *won't be a trial?* Let me explain something to you, boys. Follow closely here. He stood up. That's the motherfucking Mick defense lawyer's job, not mine."

Donovan took a deep breath. His temper was mercurial, but he knew it would be counterproductive on this day with this man. "Mr. Ravenel, with all due respect... (which was the universal go-to expression used by a lawyer when

[handwritten margin note: GRAZIANI VATICAN COUNSEL]

addressing opposing counsel who was an idiot or a judge about to rule against him. The accurate translation of the patronizing phrase was, "*Could you be any fucking dumber and avoid being picked up for continuing legal education class in a short yellow bus?*") ...you do not really want to try this case. This will be the second time in one hundred years that Dayton, Tennessee, becomes the laughingstock of the country. This time, it will be the world. Are you going to try the Vicar of Christ on a *blasphemy* charge? I'm giving you a dignified way out of this mess."

"Let's not forget the destruction of property, littering, and disturbing the peace charges," Ravenel pointed out, "No man is above the law."

Donovan sighed and tried to keep his composure. "I haven't forgotten. It's unlikely anyone will ever forget if you take these charges to trial."

"Exactly," said Ravenel with a smirk that seemed like it would jump off his face and smother Donovan. "I will repeat what I said when we started this conversation. You can tell it to Judge Sebastian Sunderbahl in..." he pulled his pocket watch from his vest pocket with a flair that could have only been duplicated with a monocle" – in about thirty-five minutes.

What kind of a stupid name was Sebastian Sunderbahl, Donovan wondered. Probably English hailing from the village of Pomposity. This was going to be a total shitshow. No way around it.

His plan had a chance. It also would launch the beginning of a cut-our-losses PR campaign for the Church. The Pope sustained a brain injury in his fall over the stupid presidential yapper. The man needed to be under observation. In Rome. In a basement. Wearing a fucking straitjacket. It was a perfectly reasonable solution based on his insane behavior at Savior Land and his insistence on remaining in jail pending trial. Any prosecutor with half a brain would have been all over the idea. But it needn't have gotten that far. Any prosecutor with half a brain would have entered a *nolle prosequi* on the charges before the ink was dry and whisked him off in the night to a warmed-up and ready-to-fly Shepherd One.

But Angus Ravenel wasn't just any prosecutor. He was an ambitious Baptist fundamentalist asshole relishing the thought of pandering to the MAGA-Evangelical-what-we-need-is-a-Christian-Caliphate zombie hordes. Hell, this might even propel him to run for the Senate.

And then there was the problem of Kerrigan, thought Donovan. Why, in God's name, had he chosen Kerrigan? Was it precisely *because* he was an arch-enemy of the Church? Kerrigan was a glorified ambulance chaser who hit the big-time with multimillion-dollar hits against O'Grady and the Boston parish. He had done more damage to the image of the Church in a half hour on *Sixty Minutes* than the Spanish Inquisition had accomplished in 350 years. The man was a showman. Donovan would give him that. Kerrigan was the Pope's lawyer, and there was a legal presumption that he spoke and would continue to speak for the man in court. Every man had the right to choose his lawyer, and this lawyer wanted a trial.

But what if, Donovan thought, the lawyer had a conflict of interest and was objectively not acting in his client's best interest? What if it could be shown that he was simply a glory hound looking for a publicity explosion to benefit himself? Donovan felt confident he could convince the judge that the court should assume the role of *parens patriae* and appoint the Church leaders as *guardian ad litem* to act in the pontiff's best interest. At the very least, the court should appoint an independent temporary *guardian ad litem* to make an objective recommendation. And while all that horseshit was taking place, the court could, on its own, grant bail, and the Church could drug the old man or something and get him back to the Vatican, where he could be put under observation.

Forever.

It seemed like a good plan.

19

All Rithe

The Dayton courthouse had not exactly been a hotbed of precedent-setting legal conflicts in the days since *Scopes*. Judge Sunderbahls had, however, presided over the case of *Marbury vs. Madison*. Not the case of the same name that established the principle that courts have the power to strike down legislation that violates the Constitution. This was *Estelle* Marbury vs. *Junior* Madison, a landmark (some would say a pockmark) case dealing with land rights and personal property. The litigation ensued after a severe thunderstorm with sudden high winds microburst uprooted six pink flamingo lawn ornaments, blowing the hideous plastic sculptures from Estelle Marbury's double-wide lawn in the Pleasant Times Trailer Park, nearly three hundred yards onto the pig farm of Junior Madison. Mrs. Marbury discovered the landing zone of her plastic birds and demanded they be returned. Junior Madison refused and referred Mrs. Marbury to the time-honored legal principle of "finders keepers" and told her to go sit on a sharp stick. The case landed in the Rhea County Legal Aid Office, where it was assigned to two hapless local attorneys who were required to fulfill their yearly *pro bono* duties by taking one case a year. It then wound its way from Judge Sunderbahl's courtroom (verdict for Junior Madison upholding the principle of finders-keepers) to the Court of Appeals, where the appellate court reaffirmed the finders-keepers-losers- weepers principle, citing precedent that went back to the Code of Hammurabi.

The only other newsworthy trial was *McCoy vs. Nails by Nadine*. Judy McCoy had purchased a deluxe pedicure with miniature confederate flags guaranteed to last for ten normal baths or three hot tub encounters. The artistry went for $11.95. In a landmark ruling, Judge Sunderbahls held that Mrs. McCoy had the right to bring a pedicure malpractice suit when she suddenly developed a mysterious case of toenail fungus with accompanying ecchymosis after having visited Nadine's shop on four successive occasions. Ms. McCoy was able to lay blame for the incurable condition at Nadine's feet after showing that her cleaning procedures did not include sterilization of nail brushes and related equipment in a dental quality autoclave as required by the National Association of Pedicurists Good Practices Manual. The case was on appeal but most legal observers felt that the cause of action would be upheld.

When a judge enters the courtroom, tradition demands that the judge's courtroom clerk announce his entrance by saying Oyez, Oyez. (Not to be confused with Oy, Oy, a Jewish expression used when Nanna forgets to put horseradish on the table with the gefilte fish.) Oyez is followed by "All rise," announcing that the Court is now in session and the name of the Judge presiding over the proceedings. Judge Sunderbahl's new courtroom clerk was Donna Mae Dorfman. Her responsibilities included the Oyez announcement and keeping track of and numbering exhibits entered into evidence. This required her to be proficient in both letters and numbers. P is for the plaintiff, D is for the defendant, and S is for the state. Exhibit tracking was the most challenging part of her duties. The rumor was that she beat out the other applicants for the coveted county position because of her legendary ability to suck a bowling ball through a fountain straw. The rumor around the courthouse was that Judge Sunderbahls spent a good portion of his downtime surfing the waters of flaminghotpussy.com

Donna Mae had trouble managing her money. Her county salary barely paid for rent, gas, and food. It certainly didn't help matters that she was addicted to the California Psychic Hotline. California psychics were in fashion as the real deal. The Golden State was so far ahead of the rest of the country when it came to non-dairy lattes, sprouts, and new-age trends. That explained the mercurial success of the Hotline and the absence of any Iowa or North Dakota psychic hotlines.

Donna Mae was convinced that she would not have achieved her present career success were it not for the daily advice of the "Astounding Methuselah" (California Psychic Hotline consultant 1047) at $1.95 a minute. Methuselah was a woman named Beth Bowers who loved the sound of the biblical name but never bothered to find out that the original Methuselah was a man. The psychic knew everything about Donna Mae. A cynic might point to an explanation that took into account the fact that Donna Mae spent $120 an hour telling Methuselah everything the psychic with the tortured Eastern European accent needed to know to repackage the same information and demonstrate her amazing psychic insight by feeding that information back to her. Nevertheless, it was Methuselah who had correctly predicted that she would be hired as Judge Sunderbahl's courtroom clerk the very evening after her chambers interview, after which Donna Mae had confided that the amorous jurist was "hung like a Budweiser Clydesdale" and "came like a B & O freight train." Donna Mae just knew Mathusela's prediction that she would get the job could not have been a lucky guess. There were, after all, four other well-qualified applicants for the position.

Donna Mae's courtroom clerk position paid a paltry county salary of $27,500 plus limited medical benefits. Dental insurance was not part of the benefits package and shortly after she was hired, while she was still in training she had been bowling at the Dayton Bowl-A-Rama. Her Thursday night ladies league team, *Dolls with Balls*, was in a heated match with *Les Miserabowls*. Donna was not paying attention when Ellie Johnson was practicing her takeaway extension and hit her square in the mouth with a Brunswick TZone Indigo Swirl Bowling Ball, knocking out four front teeth.

The following day, the local dentist, Dr. Harvey Woland, learned that Donna Mae had no money to pay the considerable cost of an expensive set of implants or even dentures. However, purely in the interest of dental science, he discovered that the errant backswing had enhanced her legendary talents in the art of oral pleasure. Therefore, he agreed to do the work on a barter-for-service basis, including twice-weekly "follow-up" visits. Dr. Woland had taken pride in the specially designed dentures that could be removed effortlessly in appropriate circumstances. The result was a set of teeth that looked borderline passable, but Donna Mae had great newfound difficulty adjusting insofar as her ability to deal with the letter "s."

Methuselah had been right on the money, somehow knowing that Donna Mae was struggling financially. It was positively uncanny. And who else could have foreseen that Donna Mae would be able to earn additional money by using the same abilities that had won her favor with Judge Sunderbahls? Her "special talent from God," Methuselah had called it. Methuselah was never wrong. A girl had to make use of what God had given. And if the good Lord had seen fit to place her in harm's way on the Brunswick backswing, then this is what He must have had in mind. The extra money she earned three nights a week servicing long-haul truckers at The Truck Stops Here went to pay Methuselah. The Lord did, indeed, work in mysterious ways.

As fate would have it, the first time she was called upon to begin a court proceeding post-bowling trauma was the Pope Thomas hearing. It did not go well.

"Oyeth, Oyeth, Oyyeth. All Rithe. The Thircuit Court for Reah County Tennethee ith now in thethion. The honorable Thebastian Thunderbahls presiding."

The New York Times correspondent turned to the Reuters reporter and said, "Did she just say *Thunder Balls?*" It took five painful smashes of Judge Thunderball's gavel before order was restored. His first thought after the laughter subsided was that carpel tunnel syndrome was a bitch. His second thought was he was doomed to be known as "Judge Thunderballs" for the rest of his life. That was followed immediately by the question of what other job he could find for Donna Mae that would keep her under his desk. It seemed like an insurmountable set of problems.

"Your honor," began Donovan, "We are here on a motion to intervene as *parens patriae* on behalf of His Holiness, Pope Thomas I. As you may recall, Pope Thomas sustained a quite serious head injury just four months ago while visiting the White House. We are prepared to present testimony from an internationally recognized expert in the field of traumatic brain injuries who will testify that His Holiness sustained a serious insult to his brain, which resulted in frontal and temporal lobe syndrome. This injury is well known to cause moderate to severe personality changes, impulsivity, mood dysregulation, impaired social judgment, and the inability to appreciate the effects of one's behavior or remarks on others."

Judge Sunderbahls turned to Connor Kerrigan for a response. "Mr. Kerrigan, what is your position on Mr. Donovan's Motion to Intervene?"

"Your honor, with all due respect, neither Mr. Donovan nor his client are parties to this proceeding. He is the proverbial jilted ex-boyfriend and uninvited wedding guest who stands and objects when the officiant asks if anyone objects to this union."

There was laughter from the gallery. Judge Sunderbahls smashed his gavel down and winced. Until this point in his career, he had only used the ceremonial gavel to crack walnuts and end the day's proceedings.

"Mr. Kerrigan, The Court will take your response as an opposition to the motion to intervene."

"That would be a reasonable interpretation, Your Honor."

"Mr. Ravenel, what is the State's position on this matter?"

"Yah Honah," Ravenel began, slipping into his I'm one of us, good old boy, Tennessee accent. "If we had competency hearings for every person who committed a crime on the sayso of some so-called expert, the criminal justice system would come to a complete halt. The defendant is not raising an insanity defense. We should leave the matter of guilt or innocence up to a jury of the good citizens of Tennessee. The state opposes the intervener's motion. We cannot allow foreign strangers to a proceeding to put a halt to any legal proceeding and intervene because they don't like the nature of that proceeding. What we have here are some folks that aren't even Americans who would like to interfere in our great State's administration of justice for their own purposes, and we all know what those purposes are." He winked.

At this moment, it occurred to Connor Kerrigan to call an audible at the line of scrimmage.

"Your honor, may I have the court's indulgence for a moment to confer with my client?"

Judge Sunderbahls nodded and thought that anything that delayed the circus of a jury trial he was about to preside over would be welcome. He wondered how long it would be before the New York Post ran a headline with "Judge Thunderballs" in the copy.

Kerrigan turned to Pope Thomas and whispered, "Tom, do you trust me?"

"I have... how to best put this... I have complete faith in you, counselor."

Connor smiled. " I should warn you that I sometimes work in mysterious ways."

Pope Thomas nodded and smiled.

"Your Honor, we have reconsidered. We do not wish there to be any doubt in the minds of the Court or the world, for that matter, as to Pope Thomas's competence. Mr. Donovan has raised an issue that will now be a matter of public speculation. The media will run with it, and I am quite certain that that is exactly what his friends at the Vatican want. Therefore, we would be delighted to have a full and fair hearing on the competency issue."

It was at this moment that Warren Donovan's sphincter began to tighten reflexively and he caught himself wondering if he had just stepped in a very sticky shitpile of his own making. At about the exact moment, Angus Ravenel saw his highly anticipated glory train leaving the station and realized he might not have a seat.

"Mr. Kerrigan," the judge asked while rubbing his wrist. "How much time do you need to prepare for this hearing?"

"Fifteen minutes, your honor... on second thought, twenty just to be cautious and completely prepared. I assume Mr. Donnovan's expert witnesses are prepared to enlighten the Court."

"And your side, Mr. Donovan?"

"Your honor," Donovan was unprepared on multiple levels. "We will need time. This is a complicated matter and we will need to contact and prepare expert witnesses."

"If I may, your Honor," Kerrigan stood again. "Mr. Donovan filed this motion. My client would have been happy to have a trial on the merits as soon as the State was prepared to go forward. Where I come from, he who asks the court for relief had better be prepared to back it up. As I understand it, Mr. Donovan already has a qualified medical expert witness who gave him the medical opinion he summarized for the Court a few minutes ago. If so,

I believe the expression used in Tennessee is *Lock and Load*."

"You honor," Donovan pleaded, "Our witness must be flown in from Rome."

"How soon can you have him here, counselor?"

Before he could answer, Judge Sunderbahls ruled. "I'll give you two weeks. This hearing will commence at 10:00 a.m. on July 10th." He adjourned court, bringing the gavel down with considerably less enthusiasm."

"All rithe," said Donna Mae. And the first hearing came to a close.

20

The Wisdom of Mike Tyson

"Warren," said Rodolpho. "What was that quaint expression you used in describing our collective predicament after I explained the lack of exceptions to the Church's vexing infallibility conundrum?"

Warren Donovan stared out of his hotel window, weighing the options of suicide versus albino recruitment. "We are fucked."

"Yes, that was it. And we certainly appear to be. It occurs to me that Mr. Kerrigan plans to use this hearing to hoist us on our own petard. Warren, do you know what a petard is?"

Donovan sighed. "No, and I don't really give a shit."

Rodolpho ignored his co-conspirator's despondency. "Well, we have the same expression in Italian, about petards. Come to think of it, we also have one for not giving a shit. *Issato dal suo stresso petardo.* Most people assume that a petard is some kind of uncomfortable 15th-century undergarment. Actually, it is a crude type of small bomb."

"That is fascinating, Rodolpho. When it goes off, I assume it is followed immediately by *We're fucked?*"

"That would be appropriate."

Donovan thought about his plan and the hearing. He recalled the wisdom of Mike Tyson when he said *When you get in the ring, everyone has a plan until they get punched in the mouth.* When Connor Kerrigan did his impromptu 180 and told Judge Sunderbahls that they would be delighted to have a competency hearing, Donovan remembered a story about the man who went to a house of pleasure where one of the options was for the patron to choose a prostitute who would be positioned on the other side of a wall. The patron would then insert his erection through a hole in the wall where his chosen pleasure giver would be waiting to engage it. It was said to allow the patron to let his imagination lead him to an incomparable conclusion. The story was that his golf buddies then had substituted a transvestite bodybuilder for his chosen courtesan. Ergo, you never know what is waiting on the other side of the wall.

Donovan now realized that his plan had been ill-conceived. He had assumed that this country bumpkin Judge would be thrilled to get rid of this can of worms and, therefore receptive to a finding that the Pope required mental health and medical attention that would best be administered in Vatican City. The Vatican's expert witness had impeccable credentials that would give the judge the ammunition to issue an unappealable initial ruling that would order the Pope to be confined for evaluation for seventy-two hours. Plenty of time to get in, drug him just before his release, and get him over the Atlantic. But Kerrigan had a mid-hearing epiphany. He would counter the expert testimony by putting the Pope on the stand, thereby giving him an excellent platform to not only convince the court that he was perfectly rational but to spew his poisonous secular humanist blasphemy to the entire world. *My actions at Savior Land may, indeed, have been inappropriate, but I will explain why I felt compelled to say something about this disgrace to Christianity.* Everyone knew this Pope to be the most articulate extemporaneous the Vatican had ever known. And it now appeared that this entire goat rodeo would be televised to the far corners of the known world by MBC. Everyone would be able to see exactly what the Vatican was up to. *Holy shit.*

"It would appear that we have a rather immediate need of a plan B."

"I agree," said Rodopho. "One that takes the unforeseeable variables out of the equation."

The problem, of course, with unforeseen variables is that they are unforeseeable. Kerrigan had just proven that principle... well ... brilliantly.

"We still need to get him out of here, somehow," Rodolpho thought aloud. "Out of this stupid local jail and onto a plane. What we need is a good action film-type kidnapping."

"Great idea. We could see if Tom Cruise is between films. Breaking into jails and snatching a Pope should be a piece of cake for the Impossible Mission Force. We have to be sure and tell him the part where the Vatican will disavow any knowledge of his mission. Why don't you have your people get started on it?"

At the same time, if the albino option wasn't feasible,

perhaps a pope-napping was. There had to be a way. After all, the Pope wasn't an American citizen. The U.S. Government wasn't going to demand that he be returned to Tennessee to stand trial for the horrific crimes against humanity of littering and blasphemy. But to accomplish that outlandish idea, they first had to get him out of this backwoods jail. Tom Cruise and his boys were not a viable option. The Pope had first to leave the jail of his own free will. How do you get someone out of jail who does not want to leave?

"You were right about this, Connor Kerrigan *bastardo*. I must confess I did admire his guile in strategically reversing his position to gain the upper hand. And to do so during a hearing where the whole world was watching, knowing that a wrong move could have a disastrous outcome. Quite a move. And so simple."

"Yes, it was so simple."

"If only we could get him to post that ridiculous $100 bond, said Rodolpho."

"We can't force the man to...Wait a second. Hold the phone. Maybe we don't have to force him..."

Rodolpho looked confused. "What phone?"

"It's an expression. When someone is in the middle of a call, and you want to interrupt them. You say, *Hold the phone*."

"Ahh, In Italian, we say..."

"I don't give a shit what you say in Italian. Let me make a couple of calls."

Fifteen minutes later, Donovan was all smiles. "It will work. Nothing Kerrigan can do this time. And there isn't any risk. It's perfectly legal." He explained what he was thinking.

"Well, the first part would seem to be. But the second

part is highly illegal and that is where the problems come in. It will require the cooperation of the Cardinals. They could be an obstacle. Breaking the law is frowned upon in the Vatican."

"Oh, really? It didn't seem to bother them too much when they were aiding and abetting O'Grady, moving the pervert around the country to keep him one step ahead of the pedophile hunters."

Rodolpho cleared his throat. "Yes... Well, I believe we could appeal to their duty to the Church. We are talking about the possible destruction of Catholicism as we know it."

"Not to mention their cushy jobs."

"There is that..."

Donovan felt guardedly upbeat for the first time since Kerrigan seemed to have run around behind him in court and pulled his pants down. He thought again about Mike Tyson and assured himself that he would be looking for the punch this time.

21

Plan B

Cardinal Battista, crossed himself four times during the meeting. Not a good sign. Cardinal Calcagno seemed deeply contemplative. He had never been in such a position. He wondered if anyone in the history of the Vatican had been in such a position. Then he remembered the O'Grady mess.

Rodolfo knew that these were not men who could be easily manipulated. On the other hand, this was a crisis that was impossible to blow out of proportion. Whatever hyperbole he could come up with would not do this disaster justice. He decided to dispense with his advocate's instinct to argue a case. There had never been anything like this. The dangers of an irreversible *stare decisis* rewrite of Catholicism by a possibly deranged and brain-damaged pontiff was cataclysmic, and they all knew it.

Cardinal Calcagno let out a deep breath. "It seems to me that the first part of your plan is well thought out, and there is nothing morally or legally wrong with it. It is what you – *we* if we decide to assist – what we are planning to do afterward."

"Desperate times, desperate measures," said Rodolpho, aware of the emptiness yet undeniable appropriateness of the cliché.

"I see no alternative," said Calgano, surprising everyone. "If there is to be no divine intervention… if the Pope doesn't come to his senses…"

"Neither would seem to be a realistic possibility," said Donovan.

"Then I agree it is up to us to do something."

"Well, this certainly does qualify as something," agreed Calcagno. "But I don't know about involving these men from the ranks of the integralists. We have come very close to designating several of their groups as terrorist organizations."

"What about Defenders of Catholic Faith International?" offered Donovan.

"They are a possibility," said Rodolpho. I recall there are several former Mafioso in the Italian branch who came back into the fold while serving their sentences. Our Lord seems to do some of his finest work within our prison systems."

"Well, that would take care of our Tom Cruise part of the plan," said Donovan.

The Cardinals looked confused.

"Never mind," said Donovan. "The less you two know about this aspect, the better."

Catholic integralists are to Catholicism what ISIS and Hamas are to Islam. They espouse a Sharia law-type view of the world that predates Mohammed by hundreds of years. Integralism argues that the tenets of the Catholic faith should form the basis of all public law and policy. They believe Catholicism should be declared the official religion of every country and that the separation of church and state is heresy. They argued that Jesus never said a word about the separation of church and state. Separation of church and state originated with the deists and Thomas Jefferson. Their theology is anti-pluralistic in the extreme, clinging to the quaint belief that practitioners of all other beliefs (including any form of progressive Catholicism) deserve to burn slowly in hell. Called "the new Catholic radical right" by the Southern Poverty Law Center, they are thought to make up the largest organized antisemitic group in America. Their core belief is that Jews then and now are to blame for the crucifixion of Christ. The Romans who convicted Jesus and drove the nails in his extremities got a pass because they were only guilty of the misdemeanor of DWIJ (driving under the influence of Jews.) Plus, they came around and saw the error of their ways. All Jews are deemed to be part of the collectively responsible gene pool. Marjorie Taylor Greene, who is definitely not Catholic and would therefore also be thrown in the Lake of Fire on Judgment Day like the Romans, may also get a reprieve because she identified the cause of California wildfires as Jewish space lasers.

Donovan had attended meetings with two such groups, The Slaves of the Immaculate Heart of Mary and the Boston chapter of Catholic Traditions in Action, as part of his fundraising duties supporting Catholic conservatism. He believed them to be barking mad lunatics. Still, he accepted courting favor with such groups as not much different from Donald Trump entertaining white nationalist neo-Nazi Nick Fuentes at Mar-a-Lago. Trump wasn't a Nazi. He was much too stupid to have a worldview that included an organized ideology. He was simply a modern-day Nero who lived for the attention that came with being the most powerful man in the world. This was how politics worked, requiring one to make allowances for the crazies who supported your team. And on occasions like this and January 6th, they come in handy.

After the Cardinals left the room, preserving the fiction they were not part of the plan B pope-napping, Donovan and Rodolpho continued to kick the idea around. They justified the plan as no different from any cult deprogramming intervention.

"Look, I like your idea of using Italians. Those Mafia guys know how to do a good kidnapping. But we need to move on this thing. Let me call my people in L.A.

"Do you think you can get them to do it?"

Rodolpho, these people are hardcore integralists who believe this liberal Pope is the Antichrist."

"Point taken." He thought about it for a moment. "But what if they were to take it upon themselves to take care of our mutual problem with, as they say, *extreme prejudice*? We agreed that the albino option is off the table."

"And so it shall remain. The last thing we want is a martyr. They would have to be convinced that *they* would be responsible for the acceptance of his radically liberal views and the end of the true Church of Jesus Christ if they were to kill him. It shouldn't be difficult to get them to follow orders. These people are fanatics."

"The hearing is in nine days. Can you get this thing moving? If the hearing goes forward and the world gets to hear him articulate his views in detail..."

"Well then, we *are* fucked," said Donovan.

22

Jesus!

◈

Angela was losing track of the number *holy shit!* responses she either heard or was directly responsible for uttering. Myron Mulligan's *holy shit* was particularly enthusiastic.

She and Brad Wittington III were on speaker.

"How in the hell did you get this recording?"

Angela told him about the Yakumano miniature spy voice-activated transmitter their audio technician had put inside the old portable radio Bobby Clanton had so thoughtfully left in the Pope's cell.

"Bradley, is that legal?"

"It's in the iffy category, Mr. Mulligan."

"What the fuck is the iffy category?"

"It's not that simple, Mr. Mulligan."

"Well pretend it is. Make it fucking simple, Bradley."

"Okay. In Tennessee, like most states, recording phone calls without the consent of a party to the conversation is illegal. But this conversation did not take place on the phone."

"What's the law in cowtown jail cells?"

"If the party being recorded has a reasonable expectation of privacy – such as when a prisoner is having a conversation with his attorney – recording the conversation is unarguably illegal."

"Get to the fucking point, Bradley. This guy he was talking to... what was his name? *[PROLOGUE XV WROTE THIS "BOOK"]*

"Henry Jefferson," said Angela. He's the town drunk."

"He told all this stuff to the town drunk? Are you shitting me?"

"I would never shit you, Myron. But this wasn't just any town drunk. This guy happens to hold a Ph.D. in American history, and he was a tenured professor at Vanderbilt. He had been on sabbatical and was going to write a book about the Scopes Monkey trial. His wife died suddenly, and he lost it. Oh, I almost forgot. He's also black."

"This gets better by the minute. Okay, the Pope wasn't with his lawyer, who you guys had already eavesdropped on, as I recall."

"We are in the clear on that one," said Bradley. "The jailer did the eavesdropping on his own. He was the one who told Angela about the Pope being in jail in Dayton. Mr. Clanton is the one who may have legal issues with his..."

"Who gives a shit about Mr. Clanton."

"Right. So, to get back to your original question..."

"Let's. Today would be wonderful."

"I don't think we have much to worry about. There is a conceivable civil cause of action for invasion of privacy, but the Pope intends to make this story incredibly public at trial, so it would seem to be a no-harm-no-foul situation."

"Good. Next time just tell me the answer and dispense with the goddamn law school lecture on civil rights in jail cells."

"Yes, sir."

"Angela, I'm turning this puppy over to Network News. We're going to run with this. It's 4:30. We'll do a bulletin in half an hour and a full story at 6:30. Right on the heels of the blockbuster we let fly this morning. My God, this is unbelievable. Do we have a broadcast studio in – where are you again – Buttfuck Tennessee?"

"Dayton. No, but Chattanooga is only half an hour away."

"OK, as of this moment, you have been promoted to Very Important Network Current Affairs Correspondent or whatever the fuck we call them these days. Start writing your story and get your ass to Chattanooga."

"Myron, sweetheart. Does this mean I am officially finished with *Great Big Fatties?*"

At about the same time that Myron Mulligan and Angela Olsen were doing long-distance fist-bumps, Connor Kerrigan's cell phone rang in his hotel room. Caller I.D. showed the call originated at the Rhea Country Detention Center.

"Hello, Connor. This is Tom."

"Tom, is everything all right? Are you Okay?"

"Yes, I'm fine. I'm in the Sheriff's office. I'm calling to tell you that I am being... well... I guess I'm being evicted."

"Evicted? They are evicting you from jail?"

"Yes. They are releasing me. It would seem that I am suddenly a *persona non grata.*"

"What happened? Did they drop the charges?"

"Not that I am aware of. They tell me that someone posted my bond."

"Did you ask anyone to do that?"

"No. I was perfectly comfortable here."

Connor thought about it. Could someone post a bond and get a person out of jail without their consent? He had never heard of anything like that. Then again, it was probable that in the history of criminal arrests, no one had ever *wanted* to stay in jail after a bond had been posted. The fact that the bond was only $100 meant that anyone could have posted it and taken responsibility for the accused. It wasn't like there was any risk associated with posting a $100 bond that the Pope would flee the jurisdiction or that if he did, anyone would possibly care.

"If it wouldn't be too much of an inconvenience, I was wondering if I could impose on you to give me a ride someplace."

"Of course. I'll be there as soon as I can."

"There is a bench in front of the bus stop in front of the detention center. It is quite a lovely day. I will wait there for you."

As he got into his rental car, he thought he had a good idea who had posted the Pope's bond. It had to be Donovan at the behest of the Vatican. It made sense. They wanted him out of jail so they could talk sense to him and convince him to give up this decidedly unholy crusade. The last thing they wanted was a show trial in Dayton, Tennessee, with a wildcard pontiff. They were probably on their way to pick him up. He shrugged his shoulders. The Pope was still the Pope, and he could do whatever he wanted including listening to the pleading from the Vatican delegation. But for some reason, he couldn't quite put his finger on; he felt that the whole thing didn't feel right.

He made the turn from Main Street onto Rhea Highway and pulled up at the Detention Center bus stop fifteen minutes later behind a black Mercedes. A man was getting out of the back door. It was Warren Donovan. Connor got out of his rental car.

"Warren, what a coincidence. You meet the nicest people at the Detention Center bus stop."

"What are you doing here, Kerrigan?"

"His Holiness asked me for a ride. I'm assuming that you and your friends posted the bond."

"It was high time to end this shit show. Enough is enough."

"That would seem to be his decision, not yours. Of course, it's easy enough to find out what he wants to do. Why don't we ask him?" Connor walked around between his car and the Mercedes. Donovan followed.

There was no one on the bench.

"Let's check inside. Maybe he decided to wait in the Sheriff's office."

"We just checked," said Donovan. "They were the ones who told us to check the bus stop."

He was gone.

"It's a nice day. Maybe he walked to town," said Donovan.

"That doesn't make sense. He called fifteen minutes ago and asked me to pick him up."

"I'm sure he'll turn up."

"I'm not," said Connor. "I'm going back inside."

The Sheriff took the same position as Donovan. There was no reason to think anything had happened to the old man. He would turn up. Connor went back outside. He saw two teenage boys across the street playing whiffle ball.

"Hey, guys. Did you happen to see an old man sitting at the bus stop a little while ago?"

"Yeah," said the taller kid. "Short guy. Khakis and a white shirt."

"That's him. Where did he go?"

"Two men pulled up in a white SUV. No more than a minute ago. They got out of the car and started talking to him. Then they sort of led him over to the car and put him in the back seat."

"What do you mean, *sort of* led him?"

"They each took an arm. You know, like you would with an old guy who had trouble walking."

"Do you know what kind of car it was?"

"Yeah, my uncle has one. A Ford SUV. I think it's an Explorer. Like the one the cops use."

"Which way did they go?"

"That way," said the shorter kid, pointing. "Toward the Hardees. And mister, you ain't allowed to park at a bus stop."

Connor ran back to his car. "Donovan, he's been kidnapped! Follow me."

He pulled around the Mercedes, took off in the direction the kid had pointed, and dialed 911. "This is Connor Kerrigan. I'm the Pope's lawyer. He's been kidnapped. Two men in a white Ford Explorer. They are headed north on Rhea County Highway past the Detention Center toward... " And then he saw the sign. Mark Anton Airport – 13 miles. "they are headed for the airport."

"Chattanooga or the Mark Anton?" said the dispatcher.

"Mark Anton! Get the state police on the line. I'm not kidding. The Pope has been kidnapped."

While Connor was on the phone with the 911 dispatcher, Donovan, his driver, and the two Cardinals were in full panic mode. "Oh my God," said Cardinal Battista. Cardinal Calgano crossed himself and started to hyperventilate.

They had planned to show up at the jail and ask to see the Pope, be told he was released, and then "be unable to find him." They would then ask where he went so they would not be suspected of being part of the pope-napping. They had not counted on the Pope calling Connor Kerrigan to pick him up. The good news was that their alibi was now rock solid. The bad news was that they were now following Kerrigan to the airport, the police were on their way, and a G5 that could be traced through a Cayman shell corporation back to nefarious Italian interests that were connected to the Vatican was *en route* and probably about to land. To make matters infinitely worse, the two pope-nappers were looking at life without parole if they were caught and would cut a deal and turn on them faster than green grass through a goose.

Rodolpho dialed his Mafia connection in Rome. "Abort. Abort the flight. Tell them to land somewhere else... I don't care where! Into the side of a mountain would be terrific." Donovan thought that this entire operation would someday be taught in police classrooms as the model for the term "clusterfuck." They had been so close to getting him out of the country. No witnesses, no harm, no concern by anyone. And now...

Trooper Emit Sewall happened to be sitting in his Ford Interceptor Police Special on the side of the road on Walter Squire Road a mile north of the Mark Anton

Municipal Airport, about to chomp down on his 1150-calorie Double Frisco Burger when he got the dispatcher's call. A kidnapping in progress was about the most potentially exciting thing that had ever happened to him. And she said this was no ordinary kidnapping. This was the Holy Pope of Rome! First things first. He carefully placed his Double Frisco Burger in its cardboard container and fastened the lid. Then he pulled his cruiser across the two-lane road, activated the emergency lights, grabbed his Mossberg 870 pump action shotgun, and stationed himself behind the hood facing south. *Kidnappers! Fuck me, this is gonna be great!* He imagined the headline. **The Trooper who Saved the Pope of Rome.**

Larry Salter and Gerald Heeney, the two zealots who had been recruited by the White Knights of the Immaculate Heart of Mary, Pensacola, Florida Chapter, were doing 80 when they came around the bend and saw the Trooper's cruiser. *Oh, fuck me!* was the last thing Larry Salter, Warrior for Christ, ever said.

They are called Live Oaks because they keep their leaves through the winter when every other leafy tree looks dead. The occupants of a car that collides with one do not generally take any consolation from the fact that they are about to experience one of the South's most stately and sturdy trees up close and personally. Larry swerved doing 80 to avoid the Trooper's car and Mossberg combination. The big Explorer is not known for its cat-like agility, and when the speeding SUV's front right side clipped the giant oak, it went airborne, rolled twice, and exploded on impact. The whole spectacular crash was captured on Trooper Sewall's body camera. His first thought was there goes my hero's commendation for bravery in the line of duty and interview on *The Today Show*. His second thought was that nobody could survive a crash like that and that the occupants were going to be crispy critters. He called for backup, described the accident and explosion, and said there were fatalities.

Connor and the Vatican Mercedes pulled up just after the explosion.

All of them ran to the scene at the same time. And then they looked to the right of the flaming vehicle about twenty yards from the wreck. The old man was standing next to a live oak, wearing khakis and a white shirt without a hair out of place. The only word that came to their minds was *Jesus!*

23

The Resurrection

～

Seven people were standing at the accident scene, shielding themselves from the flames. Trooper Seawall, Connor, The Vatican's limo driver, Rodolpho, Donovan, and the two Cardinals. When they saw the Pope there were four simultaneous *Holy!* exclamations. Two *holy mother of Gods!* by the cardinals and two *Holy shits!* by Trooper Seawall and Donovan.

"Holy Father, Holy Father," said Cardinal Battista. "Are you...?"

"Yes, thank you. I seem to be fine."

"Sit down, please," said Trooper Seawall. "The EMTs are on the way."

"No. Thank you, officer. I feel fine. Just a little... disoriented."

The ambulance pulled up less than five minutes later,

and they convinced the Pope to let them transport him to the Rhea Medical Center to be checked for any non-obvious internal injuries. While he was being escorted to the ambulance, the seven witnesses stood there stunned.

Rodolpho's mind was racing. He texted his Mafia connection in Palermo and told him to abort immediately. He got a "?" back. He responded, "Get that fucking plane out of here now!"

"It's impossible," said the Trooper. "I've come to the scene of a hundred fatal accidents. I've been trained in accident investigation and reconstruction. No one could have survived a crash like that. Look at that wreck. The doors are all still closed. How could he have been thrown clear and unscratched? I've never seen anything like it. The man should be dead."

Cardinal Calcagno was the first to say it. "Praise our Lord and Savior, Jesus Christ. It is a miracle. We are witnesses to a miracle."

Donovan's mind was running at warp speed. His first thought was, *well, that takes care of our problem with the kidnappers ratting us out as the ones who put them up to it.* That was immediately followed by the thought that the Cardinals would now officially be off the *ad hoc* intervention team, having been convinced that they had been witness to a miracle and that the hand of God had intervened on behalf of their beloved Pope. Third came the realization that Catholicism, as the world knew it, was, in all probability, doomed. No one was going to get in the way of a Pope whom seven witnesses saw walk away from a certain death when there was no rational explanation. It was as close to a resurrection as anyone had gotten in more than two thousand years. Fourth was, *We are fucked.*

I'm not exactly sure how it is going to happen, but we are surely fucked.

The ER doctor, an African-American woman who looked young enough to still be in undergraduate school, came out to the waiting area.

"Gentlemen, we cannot find a thing wrong with him. Not a scratch. All of the neurological tests are negative."

Rodolpho spoke first. "Thank you very much, nurse, but is the doctor available?"

"You are?"

"I am an adviser to His Holiness, The Pope."

"Well, yes, sir. The doctor is available. You are talking to her."

Connor looked at the Italian and shook his head. "Doctor, Are you going to release him?"

"Not today. I want to keep him under observation for twenty-four hours. I've ordered a CT Scan of the brain to rule out the possibility of a cerebral hemorrhage. And you are..?

"Connor Kerrigan. I'm his attorney."

"Oh, yes, Mr. Kerrigan. He asked to see you. Follow me."

"May I see him?" asked Donovan.

"I'm afraid not. He said he only wanted to see Mr. Kerrigan at this time."

Donovan was growing weary of all the *fuck me(s)* that seemed to have taken over his thought processes. He feared he would never again be able to keep them at bay. He wondered if they had exorcism rites for such things.

Connor entered the room to see his friend sitting up in a chair wearing a hospital gown. "I'm glad you are okay, Tom. It's a new look for a pontifical robe. Should I begin addressing you more formally now that you have returned from the dead?"

"Tom it was, and Tom it shall be."

"Okay, tell me what happened?"

"Starting at the bus stop, I assume..."

"Yes, please. Starting at the bus stop."

"Well, after I called you, I chatted with Sheriff about my release for a few minutes and he explained to me – he's a lovely man – he explained to me that as much as they enjoyed having me as an honored guest, his jail was not a hotel and once bond had been posted he could no longer let me reside at his facility. He asked if I had a place to go and I asked him if I could use his phone. I called you, I thanked him for his kindness and professionalism, and I walked across the parking lot to the street where the bus stop was located."

"Did you or anyone else call Mr. Donovan and tell him you were being released?"

"I did not. No one called him while I was there."

"What happened at the bus stop?"

"A white vehicle pulled up. It was large. Two men got out. They apparently knew who I was because they addressed me as 'Your Holiness.' They told me that you had sent them and asked me to get in the car. I was somewhat suspicious but they said they were taking me to where you were staying. I got in the car and here I am in the hospital being told I am lucky to be alive."

"Well, I did not send them. You were kidnapped. My guess is that they had a plane waiting to take you somewhere out of the country."

"Oh, my goodness. They did seem to be driving quite fast. I was in the back seat with one of them. He was asking me about the conditions at the jail. Just chatting. Then... then my memory goes blank. That is the last thing I remember. I do not remember the crash or anything else before the crash. The next thing I recall is standing where you found me by the burning car and you, the police officer, and my people from the Vatican were standing there looking like they had seen a ghost."

"Did these men say anything else while they were driving?"

"Not that I recall."

The TV in the Pope's room was on the FOX cable news show. Bret Baire was reporting. *I've just been handed a bulletin that MBC News is reporting that Pope Thomas, who was arrested four days ago and is being held at the Rhea County Detention Center, told his cellmate that the movie Jurassic Park contributed to his reevaluation of the Gospels and his crisis of faith... wait just a second. I'm now being told that there was a kidnapping attempt. Apparently, the Pope was released from jail this afternoon, and two men forced him into a vehicle. The state police set up a roadblock, and the vehicle swerved and crashed into a tree at high speed. We are awaiting confirmation and word on the Pope's condition... wait... I'm being told that the two kidnappers were killed in the crash and the Pope is in an undetermined condition at the Rhea County Tennessee Regional Hospital. We will bring you more information as soon as it is available.*

"That was quick but not unexpected," said Connor. "What is this stuff about *Jurassic Park* and your crisis of faith?"

"That is a story I need to discuss with you. But..." A nurse came into the room.

Gentlemen, there is a man out here named Henry Jefferson who said he needs to speak with both of you. He says it's urgent.

Before Connor could ask about the visitor, the Pope said, "He's my friend. Please, send him in."

The Pope stood up and hugged me. "Henry, this is my lawyer and friend, Mr. Connor Kerrigan. Connor, this is my new and good friend, cellmate, and future biographer, Mr. Henry Jefferson."

Connor looked confused. We shook hands. "Cellmate? How did you get out?"

"Someone posted my bond. My guess is it was one of the news organizations looking for a story. A dozen correspondents and reporters were waiting when they released me. I refused to talk to them and came straight here when I heard about the accident. I was listening to the news on that old radio the jailer left in our cell. When I heard the reference to *Jurassic Park*, I was confused about how that could have possibly gotten out because it wasn't me. Then it hit me. They were listening. I'm not sure who *they* were, but I opened the back of the radio and found this." He handed Connor the transmitter."

"Son of a bitch. Sorry. They had your cell wired. Someone paid off your guard," said Connor.

At that moment, the aforementioned guard, Bobby Clanton, was in panic mode. He hadn't thought this thing through. Of course, they were going to be able to figure out who put the recording device in their cell. He was going to lose his job. Fuck it. He still had most of the ten grand that tasty redhead had given him. He would expand his meth sales operation. There were a hundred trailer parks within a four-hour driving distance. He would be his own boss. All things work out for the best. He comforted himself with these thoughts as he drove to Walmart to get plastic baggies for his product. He had taken his third hit just before he left. His last thought was that pine trees don't usually jump out in front of cars. He was *not* standing beside his car unscathed when the police found him.

24

The Making of a Sow's Ear

~~~

Transcript (unedited) of interview by MBC correspondent Angela Olson with Trooper Emit Seawall.

AO: We are here at the scene of yesterday's crash involving Pope Thomas and his kidnappers just south of the Dayton Municipal Airport. I am going to play the footage from Trooper Seawall's body cam of the horrific crash that happened here a few miles from Dayton a short while ago. Trooper Seawall, tell us what happened.

TS: Well, Ma'am...

AO: Let's Start over. I need you to try and keep your eyes on the camera behind me rather than my tits.)

(TS: Okay, I didn't mean to stare.)

(AO: It's ok. Winking. That's what they're there for. It's just that for this interview, I need you to look at the camera.)

(TS: Yes, Ma'am.)

(AO: You can stare all you want after we are finished. Give me a good interview, and I'll let you give them a squeeze.)

(TS: *Eyes wide.* Yes, Ma'am. Now?")

(AO: Yes... No. Your statement, not the tit squeezing. Okay, let's try it again.)

AO: We are here at the scene of yesterday's crash involving Pope Thomas and his kidnappers just south of the Dayton Municipal Airport. I am going to play the footage from Trooper Seawall's body cam of the horrific crash that happened here a few miles from Dayton a short while ago. Trooper Seawall, tell us what happened.

TS: Well, I was patrolling along Walter Squire Road – we get a lot of kids drag racing out by the airport – and I got the dispatcher's call about a kidnapping in progress. She said to be on the lookout for a white Ford Explorer headed toward the airport. I pulled my vehicle across the road, blocking it, and no more than three minutes later, here comes that Explorer that I could tell was traveling at a high rate of speed. We are trained to recognize speeders regardless of the angle – whether they be heading toward us or away from us – and...

AO: Yes, I'm sure your training is top-notch. What happened then?

TS: Well, sir... I mean, well, Ma'am... Sorry, I'm kind of nervous... The Explorer kept coming at me. It was apparent that the gentlemen were not gonna slow down, and I was behind the hood of my cruiser with my Mossberg 870 – that is a very powerful shotgun... would you like to see it? I can get it and hold it up for the camera if you want.

AO: Maybe after the interview, (*If he doesn't get on with it, this is going to be a fucking disaster.*)

TS: Okay. Well, at the last possible second, these fellers... I assumed they were fellers. You couldn't tell after they'd been burned up... Anyway, these individuals (AO: *kill me*) swerved to try and get around my cruiser, lost control, and hit that live oak over there. (Would you like me to say something about those trees? They are pretty big and old and all, and if you hit one, it's like hittin' a building. They don't move much.)

AO: (*No, on second thought, I deserve to live. Let's kill this dumb sonofabitch*) No, that won't be necessary. Please continue with your story.

TS: Well, like I said, these individuals hit that live oak doing about sixty. There was a tremendous crash, and then the vehicle exploded. There was nothing we could do. Just then two other vehicles pulled up. The people got out to see if they could help, I guess. We all looked over about fifty feet from the wreck, and this older gentleman was just standing there. He didn't have a scratch on him. At first, I thought he came on the scene from someplace else. Then I realized who it was. It was Pope Thomas, the man the dispatcher told me had been kidnapped. I had seen his picture on the news. The dispatcher said he had been in the Explorer. The one that crashed and was on fire. I called for the EMT people, and we checked to see if he was okay.

AO: You confirmed that he had been in the vehicle?

TS: Yes, Ma'am.

AO: Trooper, do you have any explanation for how Pope Thomas could have possibly survived that crash and exited that vehicle?

TS: Offhand, I'd say it was impossible. All of the doors

were closed. I know that vehicle. It's built like a tank. He was just standing there. Like he'd been standing there when the crash happened, I'd say there were only two possibilities. Either the good Lord got him out of that car, or he came back from the dead like Jesus.

AO: This is Angela Olsen reporting from the Dayton Country Tennessee Municipal Airport.

The cameraman lowered his camera and said, "I'm assuming you will want them to cut out the part about letting him squeeze your tits."

Roland Jaspers was meeting with the Mayor, Pastor Ingersall, and State's attorney Angus Ravenel when he got the call from Angela Olsen to turn MBC at 6:00 to watch her exclusive (under-the-table-paid-for) interview with Trooper Emit Seawall.

Jaspers spoke first. "Unbelievable. This is fantastic. Every news organization on the planet is covering the whole Pope in the pokey thing, and now... now we have the guy walking away from a car crash inferno, and nobody can explain it. This story is going to make nine years of 24/7 Trump coverage pale by comparison. Dayton, Tennessee, is ground zero and the center of the universe!"

"I don't know," said Ravenel, stroking his chin. "You know what they are going to say. You know what's gonna be next?"

Mayor Ingersall knew, and he wasn't happy about it.

Ravenel went on. "They are going to say it's a motherfucking honest-to-God miracle. The Catholics are going to do a 180 and say he's the second coming. They are going to start to say he came back from the dead. They will say he is Jesus Christ or something."

"Get real, Angus," said Jaspers. "There has to be a

rational explanation. People don't come back from the dead."

Pastor Ingersall took a deep breath and didn't respond, hoping that the short, fat bastard would realize what he had just said. He didn't. Ingersall knew exactly what road Angus was going down, and he was sure that it wasn't the road to Damascus. "He's right, Roland. This could be bad. The more I think about it, the more I am concerned that it's worse than bad."

"What are you two talking about? Money is pouring into Dayton. I have the only theme park/shopping mall within a hundred miles. Why, just yesterday, we took in..."

"It's more than that," said Angus. "We were going to have a trial. (*I was going to be famous and a champion for Jesus*) I was planning on dragging it out. We had the guy in jail, and that would have continued to make us the center of media attention well into the future."

"So what? The charges are still there. He still did all that shit. All hands on deck and full speed ahead."

"Roland, it isn't that simple. You expect me to march into the Dayton courthouse and try the man who the media is about to proclaim as the second coming of Jesus Christ for littering?"

"He's right, Roland," said Ingersall. "It's worse than you think. Christianity itself is on the chopping block. Remember, this guy was babbling about a new bible. If it looks like he came back from the dead, he's gonna sell more than a bunch of them. Our version could become as worthless as two-day-old bubblegum on a boot heel. Remember. it didn't take much to convince the Evangelicals that a bleach-blond whoremonger was sent by God to lead the United States on a path back to glory and a Christian nation."

"Yeah, well, let's not forget that we all voted for him," said Ravenel.

Jaspers and Ingersall ignored him, and the Pastor continued. "Imagine how they will react if they think this guy came back from the dead. Need I remind you that he believes in evolution? You know that exhibit ya'll have where the cave boy is playing polo riding a dinosaur? I'd be thinking about scrapping that puppy."

"Wait a minute, boys," said Jaspers. "1. He did NOT come back from the dead. There's an explanation. 2. He's the Roman Pope. Seventy percent of American Christians are different flavors than Catholics. I read somewhere that Catholics only make up 11% of the Christians in this great country. Who do you think comes to spend their hard-earned money at Savior Land? It sure as hell ain't the Catholics. Most of the people on our team think the Pope is the fucking Antichrist."

There was a moment of silence while Pastor Ingersall and Ravenel thought about that. Then the Pastor said, "Wait just a minute here... Roland, maybe you're on to something. Maybe we can turn their silk purse back into the sow's ear."

25

It's A Good Book

~~~

Connor arrived at the hospital at 8:00 a.m. the following day. The Pope was sitting up in a chair with the hospital bedside tray pulled over as a makeshift desk. He was reading something on a laptop. I was sitting in a chair beside him.

"Good morning, Gentlemen. Where did you get the laptop from?"

"Good morning, counselor," I said. "A very kind nurse lent it to us."

"Catching up on the headlines?"

"No, actually, Henry and I have just finished making some final edits on the Introduction to... well... let's call it the revised edition of the New Testament."

"Is that what you are really going to call it?"

"No. I have decided to call it, *A Good Book*."

"Not *The* Good Book."

"No, that would be presumptuous of me, don't you

think? It was Henry's idea. Anyway, I believe the timing is right to release it."

Connor smiled. He hadn't read it, but I'm pretty sure he knew exactly what was coming. "I assume you are going to launch it out there into cyberspace."

"Yes, I still have access to the Vatican servers if they have not changed my passwords. If they have, Cardinal Battista will help me. He tells me a growing number of people have come around. Cardinal Battista believes in the resurrection."

"The original one or yours?"

The Pope smiled. Henry laughed. "Both, I think."

"About the new one... I wanted to ask you..."

"Plenty of time to chat about that. Have you an idea where I should go after they release me this morning?"

"Actually, that was what I wanted to talk to you about. Every rental property and hotel room within 100 miles is taken, and there is only one place I could find that is both secure and private. A place where you can be protected."

"And where might that be?"

"Your recent residence. The jail."

The Pope laughed. I was confused

"Your kindly jail guard – a fellow named Bobby Clanton – was found deceased inside his truck that had crashed into a tree yesterday. Turns out he was in the drug business. He sold methamphetamine, a synthetic drug—the poor man's heroin. My guess is that he was bribed by the good folks at MBC to put the transmitter in your cell. They are doing a toxicology test, and I think it is safe to assume that he had sampled his product shortly before the crash. The Sheriff tells me they had figured out that the folks at MBC had compromised him. They were going to fire him. Anyway, the Sheriff is a good man.

He strikes me as honest and sincere. He has offered to let you stay at the jail. They have a kind of VIP cell that they use for prisoners that they want to keep isolated from the general population. You can have a computer, internet access, a TV, and cell phones. All the comforts of home. He says he can make it into a protective custody retreat."

"Excellent," said the Pope. "Will Henry be allowed to visit me?"

"Yes. I told him I had hired Henry as my paralegal. He can come and go with me or by himself anytime."

"It sounds perfect."

"Henry, do you have a place to sleep?"

"Not really. Which, I guess, means no."

"Okay, you can stay with me. I have rented a three-bedroom Air B&B house that has an office. Plenty of room for a co-conspirator."

"Thank you."

Angela Olsen's *Resurrection at the Live Oak?* story started a journalistic wildfire. Reporters jammed onto planes from every country with a news organization that could afford to send a contingent. The Governor of Tennessee called up the Tennessee National Guard to erect an emergency tent city for pilgrims. Every hotel room, rental home, rental car, and RV Park within 100 miles was booked at rates that would make the oil companies blush.

Roland Jaspers was sitting in his office reviewing the day's receipts with his CFO and watching the news. He went back and forth between FOX, MBC, MSNBC, CNN, and El Jazzera. "Jesus, Morris. How could this possibly get any better?" He happened to have flipped to CNN (*The Commie News Network*) when Wolf Blitzer broke the story.

We just received a digital copy of Pope Thomas's promised

new version of the Bible that he mentioned when he was arrested nine days ago at Savior Land, a religious theme park and shopping mall located near Dayton, Tennessee, the site of the famous legal battle between Clarence Darrow and William Jennings Bryan – the Scopes evolution trial that took place almost 100 years ago. Our experts are going through it as I am bringing you this report. So far, I can tell you that it has an introduction written by Pope Thomas, and the entire book is only 143 pages long. As a point of comparison, the King James Version of the Bible — the most popular version in the world – contains 1360 pages. We expect to have an analysis by Professor Bart Erhmann, a noted scholar and expert on religious studies who has published 14 books on the history and theology of Christianity. We have also submitted the work to three different Artificial Intelligence programs, and it should be interesting to compare and contrast the analysis of Professor Erhmann and Chat Gbt 6. We are told that while much of the text consists of quotes attributed to Jesus, there are also passages from the Sutras and Vinaya Pitaka. As You know, Pope Thomas was kidnapped by two men after being released on bond from the Rhea County Detention Center. Police have not yet been able to determine the identity of the kidnappers. The vehicle swerved to avoid a roadblock that the state police had set up, struck a tree, and exploded into flames. Miraculously, Pope Thomas was uninjured and found standing not far from the crash when witnesses arrived. The police have been unable to determine how he survived the violent crash and fire without so much as a scratch. The State Trooper at the scene has gone on record saying it was impossible for anyone to have survived and that he had never seen anything like it. All four vehicle doors were still closed when the fire department extinguished the flames. The windows were damaged but had not been broken in a manner that would have allowed for a passenger to have been ejected. CNN asked

James Butterfield, the leading accident reconstruction expert in the country, to speculate how the Pope could have survived the crash. Mr. Butterfield. Tell us what conclusions you have been able to come to.

Good to be with you, Wolf. I flew into Dayton this morning and was permitted to examine the vehicle and the accident crash site. I also interviewed State Trooper Emit Seawall, the officer who was at the scene and whose body camera filmed the crash. We, therefore, had video evidence of the entire occurrence as well as statements from the seven eyewitnesses who arrived within moments after the accident. Wolf, I have been investigating fatal wrecks for twenty-four years. I have never seen anything remotely like this. If Pope Thomas was in that car – and everyone seems to agree that he was – there is simply no way he could have survived, let alone been standing there unscathed. His clothes were not even soiled. The doors of the vehicle were locked, and even if the windows were broken before the explosion, the Pope could not have been ejected through one of them. An adult cannot be ejected through a vehicle window unless it is the windshield. The front of this vehicle was crushed against a tree, and an occupant would have hit that same tree. Wolf, I am at a complete loss to explain this. That does not mean that there isn't an explanation. It's just that I have not been able to find one yet.

Thank you, Mr. Butterfield. Please stay in touch with us if anything else develops. Well, there you have it. No one can explain how Pope Thomas survived... Wait just a moment. My producer has a late-breaking story. It is coming through to me now. I'll read it to you." Jose F. Cardinal Advincula, archbishop of the Philippines, has just declared Pope Thomas to be a living miracle and has called for an immediate global meeting of Bishops and Cardinals to sanctify Pope Thomas's new gospel. Cardinal Advincula, in a released statement, said, "Pope Thomas is the Vicar of Jesus Christ, and He stands in the place

INFALLIBLE 179

of our Lord and is the guardian of His authority in the Church. Pope Thomas's authority in matters of faith and scripture is infallible, and I will follow the teachings and wisdom of His Holiness as he leads us into a new era."

This extraordinary development will undoubtedly send shockwaves throughout the world among conservative Catholics. We will continue coverage of these astonishing events after this break.

Jaspers clicked over to Fox

... our correspondent in São, Brazil. Steve, I just interviewed these people in front of Catedral da se De São. I asked what they thought of the events involving the Pope in America. This woman is typical of the reactions I received. (Crossing herself) "He is the incarnation of Jesus. He returned from the dead. Only one man could accomplish such a thing. Our Lord has risen."

Click to MSNBC: *Mika, these events are reverberating around the world. People are calling it the resurrection and asking...*

Click to MBC: *... and so the speculation continues. Miracle or an earthly explanation? And now we are getting word about the release of Pope Thomas's new version of the Bible. It is called simply "A Good Book."*

"I would say we are pretty much dominating the news cycle. Trump must be beside himself," said Morris. "I'd be surprised if he didn't post something on Truth Social that started with Pope-a-Dope. This is all great. But where in the hell are our people?"

"Our people? Morris, do I have to remind you again that you are Jewish?"

As it turned out, "our people" were about to unleash the hounds of hell.

26

2 Thessalonians Walked Into a Bar

Pastor Ingersall felt a chill go up his spine and the hairs on the back of his neck came to attention. "What if this Pope surviving an unsurvivable accident and explosion *really was* a miracle? What if it was a *black* miracle and this man was... " He paused because he didn't think he could bring himself to say it out loud. Ravenel and Jaspers were waiting for him to say it.

So he said it.

"The real Antichrist. Not just one of the legions of nonbelievers who deny the true divinity of the Father and Son. But the actual Antichrist foretold in the Gospel of John and Revelation. Think about it. It makes perfect sense. The Antichrist is the man prophesied to oppose Jesus Christ and substitute *himself* in Christ's place before the Second Coming."

Jaspers rolled his eyes. "I thought we agreed that Obama was the Antichrist. Remember him? It was all over YouTube. Barrack *Hussein* Obama. The Muslim terrorist former president of these United States?" He squirmed in his seat. His ass was killing him, and he had forgotten to load the afflicted area with sandpaper. He reached behind and gave his asscrack a violent scratch.

"This is serious," the pastor went on. "Think about it. This man who claims to be the infallible Vicar of Christ comes to our town, goes to your holy theme park and mall, starts tearing up the Bible, and claims there is a new one. What does the Bible tell us about the Antichrist?"

"I forget," said Jaspers, clearly bored.

"I used to know it, said Ravenel. Haven't read that part in a while."

Pastor Ingersall graduated from Jerry Falwell's Liberty University in Lynchburg Virginia, class of '83, knowing his Bible. "Daniel 7:25 *He will speak against the Most High and oppress his holy people and try to change the set times and the laws. The holy people will be delivered into his hands for a time, times, and half a time.* And then in 2 Thessalonians, it says, *The coming of the lawless one, the antichrist, is through the activity and working of Satan and will be attended by great power and...* he paused for dramatic effect... *with all sorts of miracles and signs and delusive marvels.* Gentlemen, tell me that ain't a perfect fit. It explains everything. We could be... no, we are... in the middle of the final war."

The Roman Pope as the Antichrist, thought Jaspers. *I know it's bullshit, Ravenel knows it's bullshit, but who gives a flying fart. It will sell. Hell's bells, it will be a motherfuckin bestseller. And if it's 2 Thessalonians why did they roast Trump's nuts for saying 2 Corinthians? 2 Thessalonians walk into a bar and...*"My god, Angus. He could be right," he said, trying to sound as sincere as he could.

"Indeed he could be," said Ravenel. "But does it matter? We need to get out ahead in front of this thing before they declare him as the Second Coming. This could be the perfect way to do it. He certainly fits the bill. No arguing with that."

"Think of it, Angus," Jaspers said encouragingly. "Angus Ravenel, the fearless prosecutor who went up against the Antichrist."

Ravenel rubbed his chin. "It does have a nice ring to it."

"Jesus Christ," said Jaspers. "This thing gets better every hour. Boys, we could actually turn the chicken salad into chicken shit."

"Roland, I think it's the other way around."

"Huh? Whatever."

"We need help with this. We need to get the word out. We need credibility for this idea," Angus went on. "With all due respect, Pastor, you are the Mayor of a small town in Tennessee, and your church has what? A few hundred members? The New York Times will roast us."

"Yes, you are probably right. But what if we mobilized the leaders of the non-Catholic churches all over the country? What if we got the boys at Christian Broadcasting Network on our side? Those boys reach millions."

"Pastor," said Jaspers. "That is genius. CBN! Pure genius," he said while thinking *I wonder if we could get them to plug Savior Land while they are preaching about the End of Times and the Antichrist?* Boys, I need to make a call."

"Rick Hawkins Ministries. How may we help get closer to Jesus and prosper today?"

"This is Roland Jaspers. I need to speak to Rick, and I need to speak to him now."

"I'm sorry, sir, but Reverend Rick is in a meeting with..."

"Look here, sweetheart. I don't give a roasted pig turd if he's in a meeting with Jesus Christ and the Apostles. Tell him it's Roland Jaspers – the rich guy – or I can assure you you'll be greeting people at Walmart instead of at Reverend Rick Ministries."

"Please hold sir."

Thirty seconds later, Reverend Rick answered the call. "Roland. How are you?

"Fine as frog's hair cut four ways. Look, Rick, how'd you like to lead the next crusade?"

"A fundraiser? Roland, I'm committed to a lot of appearances all over..."

"No. Not that kind of crusade. The real crusade. Like the one the Catholics fucked up in olden days."

"What in the hell are you talking about?"

"The Antichrist. The real one. He's here in Dayton. And it's up to you to help us roast the sonofabitch."

27

ShalamaKoraba niRendoshalaZ abarenuTalame nde

~~~

Every show began with the Christian rock song *The King is Alive* and a spring-loaded platform under the stage, launching Reverend Rick jack-in-box style ten or so feet in the air. His left ACL [A LIGAMENT] was starting to go, and he was not sure how long he could continue his flawless landings. He wore an electric blue cowboy shirt with gold fringe and matching pants. The crowd went wild every time.

When the spirit of the Lord overcame Reverend Rick – when he had something important to impress upon his flock and felt possessed by the living Christ, he would speak in the language of the Lord. This was his first and most important public statement since Pope Thomas's blasphemy and desecration of Christianity at Savior Land.

ShalamaKorabaniRendoshalaZabarenuTalamendeYaramas hiBerendakaGaramondiJavarekaiShikantruMenorastiVaraken daAlmazuriQuilantroDoramakiPalindraniSoerashuTuramendi FendalariBragamisto.

Which, translated from the Pentecostal language called Tongues, means... absolutely nothing. Then again, that interpretation could apply to most of Reverend Rick's sermons. But in all fairness, it might have also meant, *Send me a large portion of your Social Security or disability check because I just bought a very expensive used G5 from the disbanded rock group Talking Heads.* That group, you may or may not recall, depending upon whether you have peculiar tastes in music or did excessive amounts of drugs in the late 70s, recorded an album titled *Speaking in Tongues*, which included their unforgettable songs, *Swamp, I Get Wild, Making Flippy Floppy, Psycho Killer,* and the classic *Pull Up the Roots* which coincidently was the theme song one heard when logging on to flaminghotpussy.com.

No one would ever bother to check, but Reverend Rick's gibberish was the identical tongues monologue he used when defending Trump's 2015 *grab em by the pussy* comment that had caused such a furor. And just in case his string of syllables was misinterpreted, he had quoted Corinthians 11:8-9 *"For the man is not of the woman; but the woman of the man: for neither was the man created for the woman; but the woman for the man."*

Glossolalia is the generic term describing the ability to speak in an unknown language, usually while engaging in religious worship. The idea that the language the speaker is blathering in is *unknown* may imply that it is actually a language. It is not. It is a series of noises that sound vaguely like syllables that a victim might speak after a severe head injury or a prefrontal lobotomy done by a stoned surgeon. However, neurological and psychological studies have concluded that a belief or attempt to speak in tongues is not necessarily a symptom or sign of a mental derangement. It can also be an indication that you are listening to the stage act of a prosperity preacher who is encouraging his followers who suffer from the mental derangement of stage five gullibility (something they share with attendees of Donald Trump rallies) to give him lots of money for reasons that are never fully explained. For some reason, Jesus always seems to be short of cash.

When Reverend Rick finished babbling in tongues – a skill he picked up by interning with the entertaining charlatan Jerry Copeland – he arrived at the point of tonight's important sermon.

"Pope Thomas, the so-called Vicar of Christ, had demonstrated in the clearest possible manner of deeds and speech that he was the true Antichrist. His supposed resurrection was either 1) the work of Satan or 2) a cheap parlor trick pulled off by clever papist coconspirators. Mathew 24:24 tells us *For false christs and false prophets will arise and perform great signs and wonders, so as to lead astray, if possible, even the elect.* Great signs and wonders, my people. Like pretending to have been in a terrible car crash and surviving or coming back from the dead! We live in an age of CGI where Hollywood's liberal dinosaurs can roam the earth and fake everything can spread across social media like the fires of hell... But 2 Thessalonians 2:3 also tells us Let no one deceive you in any way. *For that day will not come unless the rebellion comes first, and the man of lawlessness is revealed, the son of destruction.* Good people, the time has come. This is the first act foretold in Revelation. The Beast is among us."

Reverend Rick's call to arms was joined almost immediately by every TV evangelical or prosperity preacher who had ever demanded money to support their lavish lifestyle, which is to say every TV preacher. The 700 Club has a worldwide audience of 360 million. The first message one encounters on their website is GIVE NOW!; a message which is routinely followed up by the idea that GIVE NOW really means GIVE NOW OR ELSE!

It is safe to say that there had not been a more energetic outpouring of outrage directed at a competing sect of Christianity since Martin Luther nailed his *Disputation on the Power and Efficacy of Indulgences* to the Roman Catholic church door in 1517. The thread that ran through every vitriolic fundamentalist rant was The Antichrist!

Confusion surrounds the coming of The Beast because in different parts of the Bible the term "antichrist" is used to describe 1) the multitudes of nonbelievers all over the world who refuse to acknowledge Jesus as God, and 2) THE Antichrist, meaning the literal incarnation of Satan. Among the famous people who have been positively identified as *The Man are* Emperor Constantius (the father of Emperor Constantine), who persecuted orthodox Christians, Pope Leo X, who was positively identified by Martin Luther, Martin Luther himself, who in turn was positively identified by Pope Leo X, Napoleon Bonapart, called out by Leo Tolstoy in this novel *War and Peace*, John F. Kenedy who frighteningly received 666 votes at the Democratic convention, Henry Kissinger, the Antichrist of the Jewish persuasion who astute observers pointed out had a Hebrew name consisting of 111 letters and 666 divided by 6 equals 111. Along these same lines, Ronald

Reagan, aka Ronald Wilson Reagan had three names with six letters each. And most frighteningly, Barney the Dinosaur. An astute Suma Cum Laude graduate of Jerry Falwell's Liberty University found out that if you write "cute purple dinosaur" in Latin, it translates to "CVTE PVRPLE DINOSAVR." If you remove the Roman numbers and add all the numerals together [C+V+V+L+D+I+V], you get ... 666. This important revelation was published shortly after the Reverend Falwell sounded the alarm that the cartoon character Tinky Winky of *The Teletubbies* was part of a plot to expose Christian children to homosexuality. Falwell also proclaimed that the Antichrist was a then-living male Jew.

The immediate worldwide Catholic reaction was, predictably, mixed. The vast majority were stunned by the developments in Dayton. Conservative Catholics were horrified. For many, it was like waking up one morning to the news that the father, mother, daughter, son, husband, or wife you adored had just been charged with working for a Mexican drug cartel. They hoped that there could be a rational and consistent explanation for the news but feared the worst. Progressive Catholics were cautiously optimistic that a second Reformation was underway, was unstoppable, and would spread around the world. Surely, this would herald the end of birth control, male exclusivity in the priesthood, and celibacy.

The atheists, secular humanists, agnostics, and nones (people who simply did not take any position on religion and would answer surveys or questionnaires asking about religious affiliation by checking the box "none") watched from a comfortable distance with the same curiosity they would have had for any amusing religious upheaval.

Among the most interested observers was Sean

Patterson, the editor of *Freethinker*, the most popular skeptic publication in the world. He dropped everything he was working on and canceled a scheduled debate in San Francisco with a popular Australian religious fundamentalist. This was an intellectually earthshaking event the likes of which had never occurred in his lifetime. The more he thought about it, the more it was possibly an event that had never occurred in anyone's lifetime. And the lawyer for the Pontiff happened to be his college roommate, Connor Kerrigan.

28

Jihads and Crusades

◆

Shah-Boom and Muhammed were granted parole after serving twenty-five years of their life sentences. They had both convincingly owned up to the error of their ways and swore on the Quran that they would never again take up the cause of Jihad. Both men were offered jobs in Nashville by Muhammed's cousin, Fareed Ali Atwa, the leading Midwestern frozen falafel distributor who, as cruel fates would have it, had been sent to paradise in a hail of AR-15 bullets after filing his discrimination suit against Savior Land for refusing to allow him entrance to The Wrath of God Gun Exchange.

Sha-Boom knew that his Jihad calling had been renewed by this turn of events and consulted a local Imam about whether his manhood would be restored in paradise if he was killed in Jihad. The Imam explained that it was a certainty that the faithful who are the victims of earthly misfortune will have great rewards and high status with Allah if they bear their infirmities with honor and seek reward in the afterlife. Allah knew of his earthly travails, and he would be glorified and exalted in this world and the hereafter if he dedicated his life on earth to the glory of Allah. He also received an official null-and-void ruling regarding his pledge not to engage in Jihad.

After being assured that his *shishna* would be restored in all its former glory if things went wrong and that a plethora of vivacious virgins would indeed be on the menu, Shah-Boom and Muhammed agreed that Jihad was back on their agenda. They fist-bumped and decided to reorder a copy of *The Anarchist Cookbook*, the best seller on how to blow things up found in every terrorist's library. But this time, they ordered it under the name Shlomo Goldstein and had it delivered to a Nashville post office box. The question they needed to resolve was what to blow up and how to get the materials they would need to do it. Potential targets were limitless, although their former target, The Brooklyn Bagel Barn, had gone under and was now the site of a trendy Pilates-hot yoga studio. Still, there were so many infidels to choose from. They prayed to Allah for guidance.

While Sha-Boom and Muhammed were waiting for orders and inspiration from Allah, Aloyisis Comacho, the Grand Master of the Knights Templar of Catholic Apologetics International, was meeting with one of his most trusted knights about the disaster in Dayton. Integralism was an extremist religious ideology, and Camacho was on the most extreme edge. He had bragged to confidants of being able to put his hatred of the Jews up against Hamas, and he raised money from like-minded wealthy radicals who funneled millions to the Palestinian terrorist organization. Revelation was the most important part of the Bible, and it predicted that before Christ's return to Earth, the armies of an Antichrist would invade Israel, and the Antichrist would be defeated at the Battle of Armageddon. Hamas was in the best position to lead the charge and his fundraising could play an important role in lighting the fire that would begin the End of Days. The enemy of my enemy is my temporary friend and all that.

Two of Camocho's crusaders had been burned beyond recognition (thankfully) in the crash with The Pope, and he was in a foul mood. He would have been in a much fouler mood if he had known that his fundraising activities had been brought to the attention of Special Agent Nathan Abramowitz, an FBI agent who had been detailed to Homeland Security and was investigating homegrown terrorist and terrorist support organizations. Agent Abramowitz was trained as an accountant and was a follow-the-money specialist. He was very good at his job. Tracking the activities of groups like Catholic Apologetics International and Hamas was the next best thing to hunting Nazis, and the Jewish FBI Agent loved his work.

"It is hard to imagine a turn of events that could have gone any worse," said Camacho to his second in command.

"Yes," agreed Antonio Guzman, who had recently been awarded the rank of Noble Knight of the Knights Templar. The two crispy-fried knights held the rank of non-noble sergeants. "We lost two good men."

"I beg to differ. We lost two idiots. They had one job to do. Get the Pope into the plane and out of the United

States. And now..." he sighed, "...the man is seen as a revolutionary hero. I know this man. He taught biology at a high school I attended in São Paulo. I have followed his career with concern. I knew we were in for it after the incident with the little girl and the cat in Poland. And now, people worldwide are proclaiming that he is the Second Coming. Donovan called me a while ago screaming about our incompetence and babbling that he would have been better off calling on the Opus Dei albino to get the job done."

"I beg your indulgence, but who is the Opus Dei albino?"

"Dan Brown. *The Da Vinci Code*? Ever heard of it?"

"Oh yes. Now I remember. The blasphemous trash about Jesus being married and having children."

"Forget I mentioned the albino," said Camacho, losing patience. "We have a real problem now. The fate of our faith is up for grabs. Don't you understand? Our people have been drifting away from our true faith and toward the sin of secularism for the past three decades. 84% of American Catholics believe in birth control. 55% approve of same-sex marriage." 75% favor ending celibacy for priests and favor letting women into the priesthood. Less than a third think homosexuality is a sin. Men doing unspeakable things to each other. It's unimaginable." The thoughts made him gag involuntarily.

"We have never had a crisis like this. And now the Pope – a man who took the name of a man who refused to acknowledge Christ's divinity – a man who has rejected the words of God, has taken it upon himself to rewrite the Gospel."

"Yes. I agree. It's very serious."

"Very ser... Yes. Yes, that is how I would characterize it.

It's very serious. Like a leak in your kitchen faucet. Good to know you fully appreciate the potential apocalypse we are in the middle of."

"What should we do? What can we do?"

"Well, one thing is for sure. We can no longer count on Donovan and Cardinal Battista. If any of this comes out... and it usually does... the two of them will be spending their prayer time in a Tennessee prison chapel. We are at war, Antonio. There has not been a war like this since... since that bastard, Martin Luther started the Reformation. What we need is a good old-fashioned ex-communication. This Pope needs to be deposed."

"How do you depose the Pope?"

"I have no idea. Sylvester III was driven out of office in the 11th century. Some claim he wasn't really the Pope. He was called the Antipope. In any event, this Pope... I cannot even bring myself to utter his name... this Pope needs to be driven out of office."

"Tell me what I can do."

"I don't know... Start with a Google search for names and phone numbers of Catholic hit men."

"What we need," said Antonio, "is somebody to give us a tip about a juicy scandal. The problem is that the man is as clean as Mary Magdalene in a church pew."

"Wait for just a second, Antonio. That is brilliant."

"Mary Magdalene in a church pew? It's a cleaned-up version of *clean as a whore in church*."

"No, you imbecile. The juicy scandal part. What do you do if you don't have evidence of a scandal?"

"I don't know... make one up?"

"Exactly. Make one up."

29

Finding the Ether

〜∞〜

We got together shortly after Sean Patterson arrived in Dayton. We were an *ad hoc* investigative triumvirate – a lawyer, a professional skeptic, and an over-educated alcoholic scribe determined to stay sober.

"... and the reason," Sean asked Connor, "that the holy successor to the son of God wanted *you*, out of all the slick ambulance chasers there were to choose from – *you*, the guy who almost forced the entire organization into bankruptcy – to be his advocate is...?"

"He's an interesting guy," said Conner.

"He's certainly proving to be. I found it hard not to like the guy from the day he was elected. For me, liking anybody in that organization is saying something. The story about the cat and the little girl in Gdansk... if you're going to have a heaven, it's hard to argue with a man who says that good cats should be allowed through the gates. The Cardinals must have shit themselves."

I laughed. "I would say that for the past six days, a significant percentage of Cardinals, Bishops, and priests all over the world are mainlining Imodium."

"And then there's the Evangelicals and the prosperity church crowd," said Connor. "I'm guessing there had been an End of Days run on bottled water, freeze-dried meals, and AR-15s," said Sean.

I learned that Sean and Connor hadn't connected since the publicity surrounding Connor's verdict against O'Grady et al. in 2014. Sean had called to congratulate him, thank him for taking the church to the woodshed, and told him for the first time about his abuse at the hands of Father Francis Gallagher. Like many victims of sexual abuse, it was a source of irrational and uncontrollable shame. The victim has done nothing wrong, yet there was an undeniable stigma about having been violated *like that.* Were there people who would think he enjoyed it? People who would think he encouraged or provoked it somehow? It was a sad fact that people looked at a young man differently when they knew he had been sexually abused by another man. Sean Patterson held a PhD in psychology, but when it came to *his* childhood trauma, I learned he had as much difficulty dealing with it as anyone else.

What the three of us seemed to share was an inclination to mistrust and dig up the basis for assumptions. Sean had used the *liar, lord, or lunatic* lesson in articles, lectures, and TV appearances throughout his career to encourage people to step back and question the positions they took for granted. I had heard him use it once, and I asked him how it was that a 14-year-old boy had the balls to go there.

"I'm not sure about the *balls* part. The question seemed

innocent enough at the time. I just remember being curious. Years later, when I was at Georgetown, I was reading a book about Einstein in my first philosophy of science course. There was a chapter about how he came to figure out his theory of relativity. It turned out he had a *liar, lord, or lunatic* epiphany of his own. It was a lot more sophisticated than mine, but at its core, it was the same."

"I remember this one," said Connor. "You made a career out of it."

"Yeah, I guess you could say that." He turned back to me, and Connor went to get a cup of coffee.

"Okay. At the turn of the century, every physicist agreed that all the great problems of physics had been solved. There was nothing left to figure out. Except for one pesky little problem with light. They knew that light traveled in waves, and waves, as everyone knows, need something to travel in. They do not exist independently. Waves are not *things*. They are characteristics of things. Think of ocean waves. They cross the oceans in water. In the same way that birds need air to fly. Flap your wings in the vacuum of space, and you go nowhere. Space was the problem. There's nothing there. It's a void. So, what medium was light traveling in? They decided that there was something they called ether. An invisible and very difficult-to-detect substance that carried light all around the universe. The problem was nobody could find it. And believe me, they tried. But they didn't care. They figured the answer would turn up eventually."

"Einstein found it?" I asked.

"No. He struck out like everybody else. It seemed undetectable. Then, one day, it hit him. The reason no one could find it was that it didn't exist."

"But you said light waves have to travel in something."

"Ahh, you are paying attention. Good. That assumption – ether had to exist – was the one he began to question. He decided it was bullshit. Light was unique. Light waves didn't need *anything* to travel in. Light was its *own* transportation system. It made no sense. It seemed impossible, but it was true. There never had been any ether, and questioning that one assumption is what led him directly to the theory of relativity. It changed the world. Physics underwent the most radical revolution in the history of scientific thought."

"It is, indeed, very much like your *liar, lord, or lunatic* quandary."

"Pretty much."

Connor came back with his coffee. Sean's story brought me back to the problem posed by the Pope's crash.

"I know I am on *terra firma* in assuming that none of us believes that Pope Thomas was saved from that crash by the intervention of Jesus or that he came back from the dead. Let's apply Einstein-Patterson reasoning to the mystery. Everyone is at a loss to explain it, and the world is about to engage in a holy war between those who do believe he is the second coming and those who believe that he is the cleanup hitter batting for the other team and wearing a black uniform under his khakis."

"Perhaps a visit to the jail is in order," said Connor. "Sean, would you like to meet the Vicar of Christ?"

"Yes. I most certainly would. I once said being on the dais with Richard Dawkins and Sam Harris at Berkeley was the most exciting thing that had ever happened to me. This, believe it or not, is right up there."

When we arrived at Pope Thomas's special unlocked cell, I made the introduction to Connor's newest paralegal. Ironically, it was the ardent atheist who had the most difficulty with the idea of addressing Pope Thomas as Tom. When I introduced him, the author-celebrity simply said, "Sir, it's an honor."

"The honor is mine," said Pope Thomas. "I took the liberty of doing a bit of Googling... is that the correct term? Googling?"

"Yes, that's correct," I said.

"... I Googled you when Connor told me you were going to visit me. First, I would like to apologize for what happened to you as a boy. We always say that the Lord forgives all sins. I know that some are more difficult to forgive than others."

"There is no need. I am well-versed in the steps you have taken to make sure that the institutional aspect of these crimes will never happen again, and I appreciate what you have done. To err is human... but I am far short of divine, so forgiveness... I have never quite understood what forgiveness is. Does it mean that it is okay now that O'Grady did it? I'm afraid it will never be okay for me and the other boys. Does it mean that we should feel love and understanding for Francis Gallagher? I suspect that most people who say that they forgive such men cannot possibly mean it. But that is why I am who I am, and you are the Pope and a man of God. If I may ask, with respect, do *you* forgive O'Grady? Are there get-out-of-hell cards for monsters if they confess and ask for one?"

The Pope sighed. "I could quote scripture. Many verses might apply, but I sense they would not be of much comfort."

"Thank you anyway. And thank you for your restraint in that regard. I did not mean to put you on the other end of what happened to me. You are not my enemy."

"Tom," I said. "Let's go over the kidnapping again from

the beginning. From the time you found out you were to be released."

"All right. I was at the front of the jail in the Sheriff's office talking to the Sheriff about my release, and he asked me where I would be going. As I told you, I asked if I could borrow his phone, and I called you."

"If I may ask a question here," said Sean, "Was that the first time you learned you were going to be released and that someone had posted your bond?"

"Yes. But, now that I think about it... when Mr. Clanton brought us lunch..."

"That may have been the worst tuna salad in the history of the tuna fish sandwich," I said, remembering and thinking it must have been spoiled.

"I remember you reviewing the food and threatening to write a social media critical review, Henry... Mr. Clanton was the one who told me."

"What did he tell you?"

"He told me that my bond had been paid and that they were going to release me."

"And then?"

"After I walked to the bus stop, the two men came and said they were picking me up to take me to Connor's rental house."

"What do you remember about the ride?"

"As I told Connor, I remember chatting with the man who was in the back seat with me. He asked me about my stay at the jail. Just small talk. And then... I do not remember anything else until everyone came running up to me."

"And they found nothing wrong with you at the hospital? asked Sean. "The CT Scan was negative?"

"Yes, that is my understanding."

"One more thing, If you don't mind. Is your memory of the rest of the day clear, or are there gaps?"

"My memory of everything else is clear. I even remember the tuna sandwich Henry mentioned. He is right. It was terrible. I took a bite and left the rest."

"Thank you, said Sean. "I can't think of anything else."

"Connor, what will happen next?" I asked. Is there still going to be a trial about competency?"

"Henry, as of this moment, I don't have any idea. I have a meeting with Mr. Ravenel later this afternoon. I will let everyone know as soon as we finish."

Something was bothering Sean. His brow was furrowed, and he was drumming his fingers on his knee. "Sean," said Connor, "What are you thinking? I can see you thinking."

Sean turned to Henry. "Henry, what did you do after they released him and he left your cell?"

"Do? There isn't a lot to do in a jail cell. I... as I recall, I took a short nap. I was sleepy and I laid down and went out."

"Do you usually take naps after lunch?"

"Well, now that you mention it, no. If I am drunk, I black out quite regularly, but sober, I rarely nap. I have a great deal of trouble sleeping without alcohol."

Connor and Sean looked at each other. Connor was the first to say it. "The tuna fish. Do you think somebody drugged the tuna fish?"

"Yeah, I think so. But where does that get us?"

"I'm not sure it gets us anywhere."

30

Truck Stop Mary and the Twelve Opossums

The lure of extra undeclared cash brought Donna Mae Dorfman to The Truck Stops Here on Interstate 81. Three nights a week, she went from rig to rig (never on league bowling nights) like a hungry anteater in a field of termite mounds. This additional income was exactly what Donna Mae needed to keep her head bobbing above water and Methuselah on call as her infallible psychic spiritual adviser.

Horace Ledbetter was a regular visitor to The Truck Stops Here, having locked up a run between Knoxville and Amarillo, Texas, taking pork bellies east to Tennessee and toxic waste west to Texas where it could be disposed of illegally in abandoned Minute Man missile silos sold by the federal government for fourteen-hundred dollars an acre to a Mafia-run waste disposal company. On this fateful evening, Horace was carrying a shipment of decomposing trivalent chromium glutaraldehyde, a particularly harsh chemical used in the final stage of leather tanning. The foul liquid could do lethal and rather horrid, science-fiction-looking damage to almost anything it came in contact with, with cow and pig skin being the exception. As far as anyone could determine, this chemical had a toxic life span of about a billion years. Environmental scientists were unanimous in warning of the danger posed by TCG as the specially constructed barrels used to store it only had a life span of one hundred and twenty-five years. This meant that a major part of Texas was flat-out doomed to irreversible toxic devastation for the next generation of Dallas Cowboy fans. Still, on the other hand, the Tennessee leather tanning industry would be assured of meeting the demand for much-needed Bocca Roataan "soft as melted butter on freshly baked bread" leather used in the Cadillac Escalade Sport Platinum, the vehicle of choice with successful drug dealers everywhere.

Paid-for sex tends to bring out what would normally be considered embarrassing and peculiar peccadillos in some men. Horrace Ledbetter liked to articulate blow-by-blow descriptions of his state of arousal as he progressed toward the paradise stroke. A big rig operator for twenty-three years, Horace thought of his sexual adventures as a process of going through the gears. *"First gear... oh my ye'as, we are extending out the chute... second gear, can you feel the power...? keep stoking that shift knob...*" etc. On this evening, Horrace was cruising in 6th gear (his rig had eleven, but he rarely made it out of 7th) with Donna Mae firmly in control of his stick shifter when Horace yelled something about the hammer being down and his tachometer redlining and reflexively kicked out with his right foot knocking his gear shifter into neutral. This would not have amounted to much had it not been for the fact that he had forgotten to set the emergency brake and he had parked the big Kenworth on a three-degree incline. The ensuing minor collision between the rear ends of his Kenworth and Lonnie Bladsman's Freightliner hauling a large resupply shipment of two-ply Tissue Genie Toilet Paper for Dollar Stores in Tennessee and Kentucky did not cause much damage to either vehicle, although Lonnie's favorite souvenir license plate "IF YOU SEE THE DRIVER OF THIS VEHICLE DRIVING IN AN UNSAFE MANNER PLEASE CALL 800-FUCK-YOURSELF", was knocked off the rear of his truck and seemed irreparably bent. The collision damage was settled in a gentlemanly fashion without resorting to insurance company intervention or billboard lawyers. Donna Mae arbitrated the dispute by suggesting that Horace pay for a complimentary session for Lonnie. All parties to the settlement agreed that if more disputes could be resolved this way, the country could be cleansed of fucking personal injury lawyers. Unknown to the parties to this impromptu mediation was the fact that one of the barrels of TCG had become sandwiched between two others at just enough pressure to cause a small leak of the contents onto the trailer floor, where it ate through the floor panel and puddled on the asphalt parking lot of The Truck Stops Here.

Horace, Donna Mae, and Lonnie were long gone the following day when Rudy Boone, a deacon in the Baptist Congregation of Dayton who worked the morning short order cook shift at The Truck Stops Here, was walking across the parking lot and came upon the miracle.

Rudy was in a particularly foul mood that morning. Although he was thirty-two, he still suffered from recurring isolated large pimples on the end of his nose that had earned him the derisive nickname "Rudolph." Again, he wondered about his dalliance with that goat he had as a 12-year-old boy that had angered the Lord and cursed him with this affliction.

Among TCG's unique chemical characteristics is the kaleidoscopic effect it leaves behind when it comes in contact with asphalt. As it eats through the initial layer of basalt, it causes a veritable explosion of colored patterns that are well off the chart in terms of toxicity but are, nevertheless, as perversely compelling to the human observer as the incomprehensible painting style of Yayoi Kusama. Rudy stopped dead in his tracks when he saw the colors. Almost instantly, he was drawn to the shapes. It was undeniable.

"Sweet mother of Jesus..."

There, on the asphalt parking lot of the I 81 Truck Stops Here, it appeared to be as clear a message as God had ever sent. It was Mary – mother of baby Jesus. And she was magnificently adorned in technicolor robes that would have been the envy of any 80s heavy metal band.

Rudy dropped to his knees at the edge of the chemical apparition. Almost immediately, the TCG ate through his overalls, burning his kneecaps. He yelped and backed away, knowing instinctively that God's message was powerful and real. Hadn't Moses been told to look away from the burning bush? He began to pray but had difficulty deciding what he should pray for. His mind went blank. Instead, he began to yell at the top of his lungs,

"Hallelujah, praise the Lord Jesus! God has come to Dayton! Praise the Lord, Praise the Lord! Come and see his wondrous paintin'!"

Larry Mosely had been sound asleep on the front seat of his rig, having passed out well into his third six-pack of Coors, followed by a meth chaser the night before. He jumped up, smashing his head on the steering wheel, and after yelling "fuck a duck" several times, began to focus on where the noise was coming from. Finally, he came as close to his senses as his residual blood alcohol would allow and grabbed his Donald Trump Special Edition bump stock-equipped Armalite AR-15 from under his seat. This much commotion probably deserved to be shot, and he was just the fellow to do the shooting.

Rudy was still shouting, "Praise the Lord!" but with somewhat less exuberance than before as he was holding both kneecaps and wincing in pain as the TCG did its' nasty chemical dance on his knees.

"What's all this fuckin hollerin' about, you crazy asshole," Larry asked, holding his AR at the ready.

"Look there, brother," said Rudy, pointing at the image of Mary. He then immediately realized that this was an event of truly biblical proportions, so he said, "Behold... It is Mary, the Mother of God!"

"What the fuck are you..." and then Larry saw her. He recognized the image immediately from a come-to-church billboard he passed regularly on his way to the Skagsville Liquor Mart. Then, he saw something else he recognized from the same roadside religious sign. He gasped and took a step backward.

"Holy shit on a shingle. Lookie there, behind her." He pointed with his assault rifle and began to count out loud. He had noticed some images surrounding Mary. When he had exhausted the fingers on both hands and added two, he gestured in a circle and said to Rudy,

"Fuck me and the horse I rode in on if those ain't... *the Twelve Opossums!*"

Rudy had no intention of engaging in biblically proscribed sexual relations with this automatic-weapon-wielding maniac or his invisible horse. Still, when he looked again, he saw the additional features clearly as he had seen Mary. There were twelve distinct figures surrounding her, and they could only have been the opossums. Larry was standing in almost the exact spot where Rudy had sustained the kneecap burns, and before Rudy could warn him, Mary and the Opossums had burned clean through the bottom of his Shoe Carnival Road Runners, resulting in burns that were far more painful than anything he had ever experienced. He screamed and dropped the AR-15, which discharged half a magazine into the side of a Walmart delivery trailer, fatally wounding six 72-inch Samsung UHD 4k Smart TVs, which it turned out were not nearly smart enough to get out of the way.

It did not take long for the commotion from the religious revelation, singed lower extremities, and shotgun blasts to reach Fred Farner, owner of The Truck Stops Here. Fred, like everyone else in Dayton, had been completely caught up in the Pope Thomas events. He was every bit as religious as the next guy, and almost immediately after gazing at the asphalt mural and being told what he was looking at, he realized that 1. God was weighing in on the side of the good people of Dayton against the Antichrist, and 2. he was now in a position to cash in big time on the current events even though his place of business was located four miles out of town. He sent an employee for KEEP OUT – DANGER construction site tape and cordoned off the entire area of the parking lot with temporary five-foot-high highway barriers, which he was able to "borrow" from a nearby I 81 roadworks project.

Every carnival man and successful magician knows that the anticipation of seeing something makes the viewer all the more receptive to believing what he has been told about what he sees. Word of the miracle spread like wildfire, and just before Fred was able to cover the image with a huge tarp stretched over the barricades, a WKBC News Action helicopter got an aerial shot that went over the wire services to every news organization in the world. This turned out to be fortuitous for Larry Mosely and Rudy Boone, who sold their respective stories to the National Inquirer and the Globe. Rudy's deal with the Globe pulled in a thousand more because he was first on the scene, and he was claiming that the viewing had caused the unsightly blemish on the end of his nose to completely disappear the following day as if treated by the magical waters of Lourdes. Fred Farner said he was preserving the image as a holy place and awaiting instructions from local religious leaders as to the appropriateness of opening the sight up to public viewing. In the meantime, he tripled his wholesale food orders and began negotiations with two Chinese souvenir manufacturers and a New York public relations outfit that specialized in promoting theme parks and MAGA rallies.

31

Lepers and Lourdes

"There is a God! There is a God indeed," said Roland Jaspers to his CFO at breakfast in the Simia Inn dining room the following morning.

"This is fantastic, I just love it. Just look at this shot the helicopter took," Morris said as he passed a copy of the Dayton Inquirer with the AP photo that took up half of the front page along with the headline, IMAGE OF VIRGIN MARY APPEARS AT TENNESSEE TRUCK STOP.

"How can they tell she was a virgin in this image, anyway?" asked Morris.

Jaspers raised his eyes to heaven. "What the fuck are you talking about, Morris?"

"Well, I get that she was a virgin when she gave birth to

Jesus. But she had other kids. Was she a virgin until she died?"

Angus Ravenel sighed and patiently explained. "It's called the doctrine of perpetual virginity or some shit. Once a virgin, always a virgin if you give birth to one child as a virgin, you get to keep your virginity status forever."

"How does that work? The birth, I mean. How does it get out of there without..."

"Yes-indeedie," said Angus Ravenel, grabbing the newspaper and cutting Morris off, "It certainly sure does look like Mary to me."

"Or a huge dick covered with a diner napkin, depending on how you look at it," observed Jaspers. "I always wondered how anybody knew what Mary looked like in the first place. I mean, as far as anyone knows, she never sat for a photo session. If only we could convince that greedy fucker Fred Farner to keep the thing covered. We all know what's going to happen if the skeptics get hold of that mess and analyze it."

Morris and Angus Ravenel were examining the WKBC aerial photo to see if they could concur with Jasper's visual perspective.

"Yeah," said Angus. "I kind of see what you mean. Although I can't think of why anyone would cover a dick with a diner napkin."

"You would at a formal state diner," said Morris. "Let's say you got a Viagra hard-on and...

Roland Jaspers held his hand up, signaling that the conversation was getting out of hand. There was work to do. He snatched the paper away from Angus.

"OK, boys. I think we should get somebody to wrap up a deal with Mr. Farner. Tell him we don't want anything from his future ticket sales or whatever the fuck he has in mind. Convince him to keep the thing under wraps until we can have some Jesus-believing scientist conduct a detailed bullshit analysis. Then we can make him an offer and have the goddamn thing excavated and moved to Savior Land. We could promote it like the Catholics did with Lourdes. Maybe we could bring in some fake lepers in to be healed or something."

"Well, we have to be able to do better than the asshole with the disappearing pimple," said Angus. We need to have somebody research how faith healers run their scams. What was that guy's name with the funny nose that sounds like Gomer Pyle?"

"Earnest Angley?" said Jaspers.

"Right." Jaspers Looked excited. "That guy healed more delusional hypochondriacs than the American Psychiatric Association. All we need are a few unverifiable amazing stories. I mean, half the fucking world wants this to be a sign from God. They're going to believe it if we give them any excuse to."

"Can you imagine? I can see the headline," Angus said, holding his hands up as if he were writing across an imaginary newspaper in the air, "GOD TESTIFIES AGAINST POPE THOMAS IN DAYTON."

"Well, technically, The Truck Stops Here is outside the Dayton city limits," Morris corrected and immediately wished he hadn't.

"God Damnit, Morris, who gives a shit!? This is show business. Nobody cares about the fucking city limits."

An intern at Savior Land who was majoring in Religious Studies at Bryan University could not find any curable *faux* lepers on short notice, but she did turn up some interesting facts about Lourdes, the famous French center of faith healing. In 1858, a young peasant girl named

Bernadette Soubirous claimed she had a visitation from "The Lady" at a spring that flowed into the town. "The Lady" was later, of course, identified as the same lady who was making a special guest appearance on the asphalt of The Truck Stops Here.

No one knows exactly how it was that the Catholic Church decided to proclaim the site a holy place or when it was the first sickly person bathing in the springs claimed to have been healed by the magical waters. Bernadette herself visited the hot springs in another French town to treat her multiple ailments associated with chronic tuberculosis and asthma, and she died an excruciatingly slow and painful death at age thirty-five. What is known with certainty is that more than four hundred hotels, two hundred and thirteen restaurants, countless souvenir shops, curio carts, and gift stands account for more than seventy percent of the economic activity generated by the three million yearly visitors to the city. Virgin curios are sold in every size, shape, and color. There are somber virgins, baby virgins, virgins with flashing lights, virgin corkscrews, virgin silver serving sets, a virgin VegaMatic, and a doll that looks curiously like a virgin Barbie. The local chamber of commerce claims more than thirty thousand miraculous healings a year. The Catholic Church recognizes sixty officially miraculous episodes associated with the shrine, a statistic that is also applicable to the number of cancer patients who have experienced stage 4 testicular cancer remissions after dining regularly at The Waffle House. Very much unpublicized are the eighteen thousand or so yearly cases of dysentery and related ailments picked up by tourists who bathe in and surreptitiously drink the foul water from a spring that has turned into a bacteriological convention center for various water-borne diseases that exist because sick people bathe there.

Roland Jasper's attempt to recruit a faith-healing candidate turned out to be unnecessary. Mildred Sumpford was a disabled twenty-four-year-old woman who had not been able to walk a step in two years since her slip and fall in a pile of hog entrails at the Manville Tennessee Meat Processing Plant where she worked cleaning up the remnants of butchered hogs. In addition to her clean-up duties, she had been required to engage in sexual liaisons with the plant manager, who would imitate hog mating noises as he was finishing up.

There were, of course, those cynics who suspected she was unsatisfied with working conditions at the plant and that she faked the injury but her father, who took all of her money, testified at the workman's compensation hearing that she loved her work. Mr. Sumpford, who ran a one-man septic tank cleaning business, had been killed in an unfortunate accident when the suction pump on his Sterling 815 Crudsucker mysteriously reversed, causing the twelve-inch diameter hose to buckle suddenly, knocking him into Elmer McFarlan's septic tank where he drowned. His friends agreed that it was a shitty way to die.

Mildred begged her mother to take her to The Truck Stops Here after hearing of the appearance of The Virgin Mary and the Twelve Apostles. Mrs. Sumpford prevailed upon Fred Farner to let her daughter approach the holy site. Neither Farner nor Mrs. Sumpford was surprised when Mildred had stood for the first time in four years and praised Jesus, Mary, the Holy Ghost, and Fred Farner, proclaiming to all within earshot that she had been healed. Fred Farner wasted no time relaying the miraculous healing to Barry Carp at the Dayton Inquirer, who was able to track down Mildred's family physician in Pigeon Forge. The doctor was able to sober up just enough to look very persuasive on the *New Day Today Show*, where he verified that he had, indeed, conducted extensive neurological tests before and after the accident and was convinced beyond any doubt that the girl's paralysis could not have been faked.

During the ensuing forty-eight hours after the *New Day Today Show* report, there was a mass influx of people with assorted ailments to Dayton and Chattanooga. It didn't take very long for Roland Jaspers and his co-conspirators to realize that The Truck Stop Mary might be the final touch needed to do for Dayton what Wayne Newton did for Branson, Missouri.

32

The Day of the Mildly Injured

~~~

Shortly after the January 6th, 2021 insurrection at the Capitol, an anonymous White House source told a Rolling Stone reporter that the President had bragged about getting the best non-viagra-assisted stiffy he had experienced since Stormy Daniels. He said it happened when he saw protestors turn into an angry mob and storm the Capitol on his behalf screaming "Hang Mike Pence."

Angela Olsen, Roland Jaspers, and Angus Ravenel did not quite experience Trump's reported level of excitement, but they did clap and fist-bump when the Dayton riot got into full swing.

Two days after the Antichrist and *A Good Book* stories broke, thousands of people came from all over the country to gather in Dayton to protest or praise Pope Thomas. For some reason, most of them found their way to Savior

Land. It may have had something to do with the fact that Roland Jaspers put up signs every mile on every road into Dayton announcing that Savior Land would be hosting a huge protest (with a 1/3rd off discount on refreshments) against the Pope and in favor of God and Country. Additional admission discounts would be offered to all the best exhibits (*The Lake of Fire* and *Dinosaurs Living With People Exhibits are not included with this offer*). Jaspers had raised these prices by 20% the day he found out the old man's identity in the Dayton County Detention Center, so the discounts were a net wash.

There are more than 200 Christian denominations in the United States and on July 7th, 2025, it seemed like representatives from most of them had found their way to Savior Land. But it was far from one-sided. There were progressive Catholics, secular humanists, atheists, Buddhists, Hari Krishnas, Sikhs, Muslims, Wiccans, and even a contingent from the Milwaukee Parish of The Church of Satan.

A line of vehicles stretched for two miles, waiting to get into the parking lot of The Truck Stops Here, where Fred Farner was charging $20 for the chance to see and/or be healed by the chemical stain apparition of Mary and the Apostles. For an extra $5.00, Pastor Amos Seabrook stood at the entrance to the cordoned-off image and would sprinkle official baptismal holy water on those in need of healing. Admissions at Savior Land broke all previous records. Roland Jaspers ordered his staff to run the Lake of Fire exhibit continuously. A drone shot of Savior Land and the surrounding five-acre parking lot resembled the scene at Super Bowl LVII. Morris came up with the idea of ordering a new fire-proof mannequin they would call Pope Thomas the Apostate, whom visitors to the park could push into the flaming lake for $100 a push. He was told it would take a while to manufacture, but Jaspers agreed it would be worth the wait.

Stephen Galt, a billboard accident attorney (Are you injured? Do you want to be?) who represented seventeen of the riot's mildly injured plaintiffs, would argue that the clash between the Christian fundamentalists and the people they identified as apostates, and the servants of Satan was recklessly inspired and entirely foreseeable.

Cindy "Big Sin" Calhoon started the whole kerfuffle, but she hadn't meant to. Cindy worked as the foot exfoliation specialist at Nails by Nadine, having taken and passed a demanding three-day online course given by Barefoot Cosmetics Corp. (Motto: We put your feet first!) who made their mark in the industry selling Bertha's Miracle Foot Cream, which they claimed cured athletes' feet, toe fungus, unsightly bunions, and Donald Trump-type bone spurs. The fine print on the ads said that their claims "Have not yet been evaluated by the FDA" but were said to be backed by independent double-blind testing, which consisted of rubbing what was nothing more than ordinary generic hand lotion on the feet of two people wearing blindfolds who said, "it felt good."

Cindy tipped the scales at 222 having lost three and one-half pounds in only six months after paying $19.95 for the classic CD, *Jumping with Jesus* exercise video, co-produced by Richard Simmons and Karen LaFonta, the Pensacola, Florida prosperity church mogul who made her fortune bilking the elderly and disabled by threatening to put in a bad word in with Jesus to let him know who was holding back and paying their utility bills before paying her.

Big Sin was carrying a sign that said, ROMAIN POPE! REPENT, FOR THE END IS SURELY ABOUT TO BE

UPON YOU. The lettuce sign partially obscured her vision and when she slipped in a freshly spilled puddle of Diet Mountain Dew Baja Blast, she fell backward, and her prodigious rear-end landed surely upon WGNP Action 4 News Team reporter Karl (known in the industry as "Karl with a K") Sandman who, as he fell, knocked a very goth looking wiccan transvestite into a Pentecostal snake handler who had traveled to Dayton from Possum Crossing, West Virginia. Punches were thrown, but fortunately, the most serious injury was sustained by the reporter, who suffered three broken ribs, a bruised kidney, and the destruction of his prized and irreplaceable Oscar de la Renta salt and pepper hair piece which was soaked in the highly acidic Baja Blast. The news anchor's workers' compensation claim would subsequently be settled without a fight, but his claim for the full replacement cost of the hairpiece was denied.

The problem for the would-be rioters was that it was difficult to tell who was on which team, so no one knew who to hit. There was a lot of random pushing and shoving, yelling and cursing and even some chanting in tongues. The papists were severely outnumbered and wisely kept a much lower profile than those who had come to bury the man who had been identified by Reverend Rick Hawkins as a reincarnation of the 4th-century Roman emperor Julian the Apostate.

Morris thought he had never seen his boss happier. The Pope gets himself arrested at Savior Land and insists on staying in jail and having a trial. That blessed event is followed by the miracle of the Truck Stop Mary and the Twelve Opossums, a pope-napping, a fiery car crash, and supposed resurrection, and then, praise the Lord, the identification of Pope Thomas as the Antichrist by

Reverend Rick Hawkins and ten of the most influential TV preachers in the world. And now... praise Jesus... *now* a minor riot with the cameras from every network in the world recording everything in the parking lot of Savior Land. All this and the trial hadn't even begun. Savior Land was practically bursting at the seams, and Roland Jaspers was beginning to count the blessings associated with being born again.

33

Br'er Rabbit Redux

While things were heating up at Savior Land, Connor Kerrigan and his two new "paralegals," Sean Patterson and yours truly, were headed for a meeting with Angus Ravenel at the State's Attorney's office on the 2nd floor of the Rhea County Courthouse.

Connor introduced us to Ravenel, who I knew from a previous drunk and disorderly charge he had brought before Judge Sunderbahls.

"Ah, Mr. Washington," said Ravenel. "Nice to see you again."

"It's Jefferson, and the pleasure is mine."

"How do you come to the papist team?"

"I will be recording my impressions about how everything goes for posterity."

"A book deal? *You* landed a book deal?"

"Possibly. For the moment, think of me as a merely humble scribe, whom the Pope took pity on."

"I remember now. You taught history or something. Hoping your book will look kindly on me."

I smiled and nodded.

"So, what now, Angus?" said Connor.

Angus had the TV in his office tuned to MBC. "Did you boys see what's going on out at Savior Land? I don't know who started it but, God Damn, these religious crazies from damn near everywhere throwing punches, screaming, and acting like the wild men of Borneo are some entertaining shit."

"Yes, I'm sure Roland Jaspers is thrilled."

"I expect he is," said Ravenel. "A good uproar like that with network coverage is good for business. So, counselor...any ideas on how to proceed?"

"Well, I talked to Donovan before I left here. He's not happy. It seems that there is a huge split back at the Vatican. About half of the Cardinals will follow Pope Thomas into the Lake of Fire if he asks them. Half want to put him in a wooden boat and send him into the flames. I imagine the consistories going on behind closed doors at the Vatican are quite exciting."

"Film at 11! Do Cardinals and Bishops get into dustups? Goddamn, that would be fun to watch. Holy men in red robes and beanies throwing punches. I always say a man can't have a proper fight in a dress. MBC would pay big money for some video of that. Did Donovan tell you if he wants to proceed on Thursday?"

"He says he does, but I have my doubts. The Cardinals who came with him are split. Cardinal Battista wants to call it off. He thinks the incident at the airport is a sign from God. Cardinal Calcagano still wants to get him out of town. Donovan is probably hoping he has a stroke. I can tell that his heart isn't this anymore. He said he was only going to call one witness. The Vatican neurologist. I think he just wants to give your judge an excuse to get rid of this thing. But I think he will pull the ripcord."

"Old Judge Thunderballs is in over his head. I don't know what he's inclined to do. Your client still wants to go ahead with the trial?"

"That's not really up to him. If you are thinking about dismissing the charges...well Angus, that's your prerogative."

"Hell no. The fun's just getting started. All these people came to Dayton to see a trial. Let's give 'em one."

"I had a feeling you might see it that way."

"Look, Gentlemen. Can I speak frankly and off the record?"

We all nodded.

"Okay, we all know these charges are bullshit. But this whole trainwreck is great for business. Dayton is back on the map. Ground zero in the war for the souls of America and the world and all that. Are we still off the record?"

"Of course, Angus. We are brothers at the bar," said Connor, winking at him.

The wink confirmed his assumption that Connor, whom he had begun referring to as "the slick mick," was as interested in being part of this dog and pony show as he was. Psychologists will tell you that the thing about assholes is that they assume that everyone else is an asshole, whether they demonstrate it or not. Some people are better at hiding it. Ravenel thought Connor was no different than anyone else. He was certain of it. There was no such thing as a trial lawyer who wasn't a media hound. Every one of them lived for situations where they could play the lead and the hero in a stage(d) production with a captive audience. That's exactly what a trial was.

"Well, sir, this whole *pope–pourri* thing ... hah, god damn, that was good... this thing has been a regular bonanza for this town. We are country people. We've got the Couch Potato factory, Savior Land, and the thriving crystal meth business. That's about it. The courthouse Scopes summer reenactments don't bring in jackshit. Anyway, Roland Jaspers carries a lot of water in these parts. Business is booming. We need this trial to put us back on the map. Permanently."

"I understand," said Connor. "Let me think out loud here. Off the record... I'm assuming you could get us a conference with Judge Sunderbahls if we wanted to discuss logistics for the trial."

"Of Course. It's not like the old fart has a lot to do. Rumor is he spends half his day watching internet porn."

"Well, the competency hearing is set for trial in three days. That part isn't going to take long and it's a jump ball as to whether Donovan will show up at all. Now, as you know, Thursday is July 10th."

"So?"

"Well, July 10th, 2025, just happens to be the 100th anniversary of the State of Tennessee vs. John T. Scopes..." Angus Ravenel's eyes lit up "and..."

"...and you slick Mick sonofabitch... you're thinking, why don't we see if the Judge is amenable to trying the case right then and there!"

"Well, now that you mention it..."

"I like it! Nothing to this case. We got us CCTV video of the whole thing. A few witnesses like our Jesus actor and an offended customer, and you and I get to make closing arguments that will go down in the history books."

"Angus, I like your thinking. That's a brilliant idea. I'm in."

It occurred to me watching this exchange that I had been witness to a real-life Br'er Rabbit moment.

Ravenel picked up his office phone and dialed. "Donna Mae. Good afternoon, Darlin'. This is Angus. Is His Honor available for a quick get-together... Me and Mr. Kerrigan. Won't take long... yes I'll hold." He turned to Kerrigan. "Probably getting his wick wet. Word is that Donna Mae can suck a... Yes, sweetheart. Great. We'll be up there shortly."

34

All The World is a Stage

Carlos Gregório de Lucena was an accomplished actor best known in Brazil for his leading man portrayal of Rodrigo Oliveria in the soap opera *Amores de Nossas Vidas (Loves of Our Lives)*. He was also a devout Catholic and a member of the São Paulo chapter of Knights Templar of Catholic Apologetics International. His membership in the radically conservative integral organization was a closely guarded secret, as was the policy with all members.

Aloyis Comacho had heard his old school friend was a brother Knight of Templar, but fourteen years had passed since they had spoken. When Carlos got the call, he had mixed emotions. He knew Camacho had emigrated to the United States to study chemical engineering at Notre Dame. They had been best friends when they attended

Escola Secundaria Central Catolica in São Paulo, but his old friend's voice was not one he was thrilled to hear.

The men shared a secret that neither wanted to ever think about. They had been participants in a gang rape of a 13-year-old girl in an empty office in the school chapel. The girl had not spoken of the incident as she feared that she would not be believed or, worse, blamed for what happened and branded a *puta*. The boys were all from prominent families and stars on the school soccer team that had won the city championship. Both men had spoken of the assault only once in confession. They had each been absolved of their sin and told to say multiple Hail Marys. The incident had not, of course, been reported to anyone by the confessor, and no one ever spoke to the girl or her parents to see if she was all right.

Camacho spent half an hour explaining the situation and making his case.

"Aloyisis, what you are asking me to do…"

"Carlos, what I am asking you to do is help me save the entirety of the Catholic Church. We are in the midst of a crisis that rivals our Lord's crucifixion. I am calling on you as a Knight Templar to do your sacred duty for our Church and our Lord."

The story broke two days later in the *Jornal Nacional*. Fausto Brizola, Brazil's version of Tucker Carlson, was chosen to conduct the interview.

Fausto: Carlos, tell the viewers why you are coming forward now. Why have you waited all these years to come forward with this story?

Carlos: It was not an easy decision. I struggled with this knowledge for years. I did not want to disparage a man who has accomplished many positive things for so many people.

Fausto: But why now?

Carlos: Because of what is happening in the United States. This man has tremendous power and influence. He has more devoted followers in Brazil than any man who ever lived. He is shaking the faith of followers all over the world. After a tremendous personal struggle, I came to realize that he is not who he says he is. His pronouncements are those of a man who has lost his faith, and I wonder if he ever had true devotion to our Lord and Savior. I prayed all night before coming to this difficult decision. I am, of course, terribly conflicted, but the truth is the truth, and my devotion to Jesus Christ left me no alternative.

Their story had been well crafted. The conspirators agreed that the more salacious the story was, the less credibility it would have. All they had to do was credibly sow the seeds of doubt. A social media explosion would do the rest. The story would create a media firestorm. And that is exactly what happened.

35

Faith

∾

Connor, Sean, and I were watching the evening news when the story broke.

Was Pope Thomas I a Sexual Predator?

Brazillian TV star Carlos Gregório de Lucena has given an interview in which he claimed that Pope Thomas tried to fondle him during a private tutoring session at a high school where the Pope taught biology as a young man. Pope Thomas is currently awaiting trial in Dayton, Tennessee, and caused an international furor when he...

We were taken off guard and devastated. The trial was only a week away. We left for the jail. On the way, Connor told me the details of a case he had handled as a young lawyer.

"When I was fresh out of school and scrambling for business, I was hired as a second chair counsel – a glorified law clerk – by a prominent criminal lawyer who practiced from the adjoining suite to my office in Boston. A man named Benjamin Graham, a single father, had been charged with raping his children's 16-year-old babysitter after coming home intoxicated from a Christmas office party. Mr. Graham had lost his wife a year earlier when her minivan had been crushed by a delivery truck driven by an opioid addict. The investigator we hired found out that the victim was known to "have a thing for older men" and debts to a local drug dealer. Benjamin Graham was the proverbial pillar of the community, a social worker who was responsible for placing abused children with foster families. He had never had so much as a parking ticket. The man was innocent, and there was nothing that motivated me more as a young, idealistic lawyer than the idea of representing an innocent client. Except for the fact that he wasn't. The State's Attorney's investigators had located three other babysitters who had been assaulted by Mr. Graham, and DNA evidence that came back two weeks later would seal his fate. I took it hard and asked myself how I could have possibly been so wrong about the man. Mr. Graham had seemed so damn likable — a victim if ever there was one. It was at that moment that I lost faith in my infallibility when it came to judging people. It was an O.J. moment. Had there ever been a figure as universally admired and loved as O.J. Simposn? I remembered my father's life lesson after O.J. had been arrested, and the evidence seemed incontrovertible. We don't know people unless we *really* know them. And sometimes not even then. We can only know what they show us."

I thought about it. Did either of us really know this man we had both come to admire and love? Or did we want him to be the man we had decided he was? Was our judgment clouded by the way we saw the world? I didn't think so, but there was just no way to know with any kind of certainty. Good people do things. Sometimes, bad things.

Sean sighed. "Who knows what evil lurks in the hearts of men?"

"Ahh," said Connor. "The immortal words of The Shadow."

"I'd bet big money Marcia Clark said the same thing when they brought her the O.J. case," said Sean."

"As I recall, she and Chris Darden went down in flames," said Connor.

Sean had a psychology lesson for every situation like this. "We are designed to draw conclusions... to recognize patterns and fill in blanks. We need to make the world conform to our assumptions about how it's supposed to be and how we want it to be. Have you guys seen a good ventriloquist work?"

"Sure," I said. "Edgar Bergan was the best."

"Agreed. Well, there are about four sounds that Edgar Bergen – that no ventriloquist in the world can make. P is one. It cannot be done without moving your lips. But there are very few people who have seen a good ventriloquist perform who have any idea. What the ventriloquist does is use a 'T' sound with the tongue against the back of their front teeth. If you listen very carefully or slow a recording down, you might hear a T. But when you are watching the performance, you don't want to hear a T. You *want* to hear a P. You know the word he is using is spelled and produced with a P. You recognize the word 'pig' and understand that is what he was saying from the context. Your brain has never heard of the word 'tig.' So, your brain ignores the deficiency and makes the T into a P. You spend the rest of your life imagining you heard the dummy say 'porky pig' perfectly when he really said 'torky tig.' What we want to have happened is what we believe happened, whether it did or not. Same idea sometimes with people who you think you know."

When we were escorted to Tom's cell, he had his TV on. He knew exactly why we were there.

"Hello, my friends. I assume you heard the news."

"We did," I said. It somehow seemed inappropriate to ask the Vicar of Christ, 'So, did you do it?'" Which was exactly what Sean asked him.

"What does your heart tell you?" replied the Pope, looking from Sean to Connor to me.

"Hearts don't always tell us the truth... but I don't believe it," said Connor. "I don't want it to be true more than anything I have ever wanted. But I've come to believe that almost anything is possible. I have made a career out of questioning assumptions."

And then Sean said the strangest thing any of us could have imagined him saying. "Please, God. Don't let it be true."

The Pope turned and looked at me. And then he smiled. And at that moment, for reasons none of us could have defended, the three of us *believed. We believed* without any proof. We believed without a denial, a protestation, or any attempt at an explanation. We just believed in this man.

The very next day, our faith would be rewarded. A 64-year-old Jewish civil servant would be the Pope's salvation and our reward for having faith.

36

God is Great!

As mistakes made by comptroller/CFOs go, Morris Greenberg's was epic. It was a well-meant attempt at belt-tightening as a result of the past two Savior Land lean years. The monthly hazard/fire/liability Lloyds of London insurance cost for Savior Land was staggering, and not a week went by when Roland Jaspers didn't call and break his balls about fixed cost reductions. So Morris did what conscientious comptrollers are supposed to do. He went shopping. He chose Great American Liability, a Tennessee Insurance Commission-approved second-tier Florida insurer with an A.M. Best Insurance rating of B++ and A Moody's rating of Baa2, which resulted in a monthly premium savings of $7,000 over Lloyd's A++-rated policy. Roland was as pleased as it was possible for Roland to ever be, and when Morris told about the savings, he expressed his approval of a job well done with the enthusiastic

INFALLIBLE 235

compliment of, "Well, if that's the best you can do, I guess I'll have to live with it."

And it would have been just fine had there not been a slip-up in the dates between the expiration of the Lloyds of London coverage and the effective date of the Great American Liability policy period. The lapse in coverage was for the period from June 30th to August 1st.

92% of the claims made against malls are slip-and-fall cases where a patron claims gross negligence in failure to clean up a Diet Coke spill. Steve Galt raked in close to $75,000 a year from his billboard ads that said, IF YOU SLIP AND FALL AT THE SAVIOR LAND MALL, GIVE STEVE A CALL! Fortunately for Savior Land, not a single such actionable calamity occurred between July 1st and July 10th. There were, however, two deaths recorded, but tort liability in those cases would have been precluded as a matter of law as both were subject to the defenses of assumption of the risk, contributory negligence, and the fact that both of the decedents appeared to have been morons. Without liability insurance, ordinary Diet Coke slip-and-fall cases would have had to have been settled directly from Savior Land's profits, such as they were, and Roland Jaspers would have had a stroke.

As things turned out, Roland Jaspers did have a stroke, but it was not slip-and-fall related.

SEE PAGE 83

It only took Shah-Boom and Muhammed a day of brainstorming to settle on Savior Land. The theme park/mall fit the bill perfectly. It was a disgusting symbol of American secular decadence, a celebration of *kafir* disrespect of Islam, and a racist insult to the Arab people. This last shocking indicia of infidelic apostasy they saw with their own eyes on a reconnaissance trip. The Lake of

Fire was populated almost entirely by Arab mannequins who were pushed to their deaths by Jesus and his Christian apostates. One of the figures had a striking resemblance to his uncle, Ashkan.

It is doubtful that it would have made a difference if they had bothered to find out that the mannequins were supposed to be hooked-nosed Jews. Once the target had been selected, the question became how to blow it up and kill the maximum number of *kafirs*. The theme park was huge. It would have probably taken a bomb with the force of the Hiroshima explosion to do the kind of damage they were hoping for. The initial and seemingly insurmountable obstacles were: 1) they looked unmistakably Middle Eastern, and 2) they were on the terrorist watch list for life, and it would have been difficult for either of them to purchase a sparkler for the 4th of July. There was the Timothy McVeigh truck bomb approach, but purchasing ammonium nitrate fertilizer in the quantities that would be necessary for a devastating explosion was as tricky as buying C-4 or commercial dynamite. It presented a real problem.

The men returned to Nashville to come up with a plan. Shah-Boom's reputation in the Jihadist bombmaking community was less than stellar, and no self-respecting terrorist wanted anything to do with him. The feeling among serious bombmakers was that he couldn't be trusted to press a red button. It was Muhammed who accidentally solved the problem.

"Muhammed, I must admit, the Lake of Fire show was impressive. So much sound and fury. How do they keep all those flames going all day and night?"

"That is an excellent question, Ali. Why don't you Google it?"

"I think I will. But I will do it one better. I will use Chat abc."

"What is Chat-abc?"

"Artificial Intelligence, my friend."

"Oh yes. Good idea."

Chat-abc was not recognized by their search engine. If search engines could start laughing, this one would have, and then surmised that these clowns were too stupid to use Chat-gpt. Instead, it gave them references to five old ABC sitcoms, including the classic *Happy Days*. The Fonz was one of Ali's favorite characters. When they went back to Google, they immediately found detailed articles, including an extensive Wikipedia page on the history and construction of Savior Land.

"Bad news," said Sha-Boom.

"What?"

"It says the life-size doll victims being pushed into the Lake of Fire are not our people. They are Jews. That would ordinarily be good news but..." His eyes suddenly lit up. "Praise Allah! God is great!" He could hardly contain his excitement. "Look at this!"

"What is it?"

It was the Wikipedia site for Savior Land. There was a section with a bold header titled, **The Controversial Lake of Fire Exhibit.**

> Revelation states that one who dies in the everlasting fire of God's punishment of sinners will be eternally dead! This is what is called the "Lake of Fire" in Revelation 20:15." Anyone not found written in the Book of Life was cast into the Lake of Fire."
>
> The artificial lake was constructed in 2006. It is the size of four Olympic swimming pools and holds

2,600,000 gallons of water. The flames that light up continuously are fueled by five 60,000-gallon propane tanks that hold 300,000 gallons of propane, which also provide gas to serve the mall and theme park. Controversy surrounded the completed version of the Lake of Fire, which has an exhibit where non-believer robotic figures were allegedly modeled to look like caricatures of Jewish men, women, and children. Roland Jaspers, Savior Land's owner and builder, denied the allegation and said the robots were simply designed to look authentic.

"300,000 glorious gallons of liquefied petroleum gas. All we need to do..."

"... all we need to do, said Shah-Boom, "is read up on how to make it explode. Five storage tanks of fuel like that will blow up half of Tennessee."

"God is great," they both said in perfect unison.

37

Just One More Thing

⁓∞⁓

It rarely occurs to amateur criminals that they are being watched or recorded by law enforcement. The thought may cross their minds, but it is dismissed more often than not. They believe they are always underneath the radar because they do not make a habit of breaking the law. Even seasoned professionals like Mafia bosses who imagine wires on everyone they talk to get sloppy. No one can go through life with his head always turned to look over his shoulder.

Special Agent Felix Lindblad walked into the office, grinning like the proverbial Cheshire cat. His boss, Nathan Abromowtiz, noted that his favorite agent and protege could hardly contain his excitement. "Boss," he said, "you're gonna love this."

"What is it, Felix the Cat? Have the Christians admitted

that they've been blaming the wrong guys? Have Jews for Jesus returned to the fold?"

"Better. Much better. I'm guessing you have been following the whole Pope Thomas show in Tennessee."

"Of course. Quite the shit show. The latest about the sexual abuse thing as a young man... Unbelievable. A soap opera star in Brazil creates a soap opera episode that may live forever."

"Well, my sagacious supervisor. You have no idea how correct you are."

"I'm listening. You know, you do this to me every goddamn time. One day, you are going to call me up with a discovery... a case cracker... and say, 'Guess what, Nathan?' And you aren't going to make me guess. You're just going to fucking tell me."

"No, I won't."

"Okay," he laughed and sighed the sigh of a once again beaten man. "Tell me what's going on, my drama queen."

It turned out that the wiretap of Aloyisis Comacho, Felix had been monitoring as part of their ongoing investigation into aiding and abetting terrorist organizations providing funds to Hamas through Cayman Island banks, had turned up another little conspiracy between Aloyisis Comacho and a certain Brazilian heartthrob TV daytime soap opera star. Felix handed his boss the transcript. Abramowitz read it and looked over his glasses. Then he smiled.

"Well now, Felix. This is going to be fun. Certainly is a newsworthy conversation."

"For sure. But it may blow our investigation of Comacho. Do we have enough in the bag if this becomes public?"

"I'm not sure. But here's the thing. When we leak this

transcript to the Post and expose these antisemite cocksuckers to the world for what they are, we will be doing more damage than the criminal charges would do. And we will probably get more valuable tips and evidence from the public than we ever could have turned up through wiretaps and questioning reluctant witnesses. And there's one more thing."

"Okay, turnabout is fair play. What's the one more thing?"

"It's the right thing to do. And Felix... just one more one more thing."

"That's two one more things but hey, who's counting?"

"Fuck these guys."

38

Hey, Y'all...
Watch This!

※

Carlos Gregório de Lucena was fired the day after the FBI released a transcript and audio of his participation in the plot to defame Pope Thomas. Two days later, he was arrested and jailed, charged with conspiracy and a willful violation of the criminal honor code statute. The Brazilian penal code makes it a crime to engage in verbal assaults against honor. Calumny is the crime recognized in some countries of falsely accusing someone of something defined as a crime and/or defamation of character. The FBI recordings were devastating. On his second night in jail, Carlos experienced sexual abuse from the other side for the first time.

The Knights Templar of Catholic Apologetics International was designated as a terrorist organization by the Department of Homeland Security, and after an extensive investigation, Aloyisis Comacho was charged with money laundering and providing aid and comfort to another terrorist organization — Hamas. He would be convicted six months later and sentenced to fifteen years. Every network ran stories on the integral movement.

The conspiracy had the exact opposite of the intended effect. Pope Thomas was seen as a victim and a hero, and an overnight Pew poll showed a favorability rating of 73%. The same poll showed that 13% believed he had been resurrected or saved by the intervention of God after the kidnapping car crash, 26% believed there was an explanation, and 48% weren't sure or had no opinion. 13% thought he was the antichrist, tying him for that honor with former President Obama.

The plans for the theme park were, of course, a matter of public record and accessible to anyone online at the Department of Permits and Zoning website. The underground LPG storage tanks were allowed to be installed at a distance of twenty-five feet from a commercial building. The Lake of Fire tanks were located at the appropriate distance from the exhibit in the north part of the park, about 100 yards from the Holy Roller Coaster.

Sha-Boom and Muhammed spend the evening touring the park. They left their car in the Savior Land Parking Lot with a note under the windshield wiper that explained that the car had been left because of a dead battery in case a security guard noticed it after the park closed for the night. Muhammed had insisted on riding the roller coaster and visiting the dinosaur exhibit, which both men agreed grudgingly that the infidels had gotten right. The men had no difficulty locating and hiding in a utility closet after closing time. Sha-Boom passed the time listening to a Pandora pop station on his headphones, and at 2:00 a.m. in a sign from Allah, the 1969 song *I Want to Take You Higher, Boom Shaka Laka* by Sly and The Family Stone came on, signaling that it was time to get to work. They exited the closet and made their way around The Lake of Fire to the LPG tanks' exposed safety relief valve and pressure gauge. These gauges need to be monitored daily to ensure that the pressure level inside the tank does not exceed the level at which the safety valve could relieve the pressure.

It all was so simple, and Shah-Boom wondered why his fellow Jihadists hadn't thought of this before. These tanks could be exploded using a kitchen match and a fart. For a professional bomb maker like Sha-Boom, he thought, it would be a piece of pie. There was one pipe that fed all five 60,000-gallon tanks. A well-placed detonator, a timer set to go off at noon when the maximum number of infidels were at the park, and glory awaited. This time, the detonator would be left behind. There would be no need to personally carry it into battle and risk losing another appendage.

After the men had placed the detonator at the base of the relief valve pipe and secured it with white duct tape that matched the covering on the copper pipe, they looked around and checked for security guards. They needn't have worried as nighttime theme park security guards are about as diligent as teenage stoner house sitters. As they walked back around the Lake of Fire, Muhammed remarked on how much the whole thing must have cost to build. As he turned to see if his partner was paying attention, he tripped over a loose walkway tile, lost his balance, and did a header into the Lake of Fire. It seemed to him like the worst of all possible ways to gain entrance into paradise. He wondered whether the end would come from burning or drowning, and if it were to be the former, would he be attractive to the waiting sexually charged virgins? Shah-Boom, who likewise could not swim, reached in to grab his friend's hand and was immediately pulled into the dreaded lake as Muhammed outweighed him by twenty pounds and was in full adrenaline-pumping panic mode.

The terrorists' bodies were discovered the next day by the morning shift security guard. By the time the gas was turned off and they were pulled out of the lake, their facial features were unrecognizable, and their clothes had been burned off.

Jethro Stillwell, the Captain of the dayshift security force, examined the bodies with police officer Edgar Simpson, who had been dispatched to the scene.

"Looks to me like two local assholes decided to go for a midnight skinnydip," remarked Jethro.

Officer Simpson laughed. "You know what the last words that come from a Tennessee boy's mouth are?"

"I'll bite."

"*Hey, y'all. Watch this!* That's usually followed by, *Hell, I can do that.* Looks like that's what happened here."

As Officer Simpson turned to walk to the refreshment stand to get a breakfast sausage biscuit, he noticed the loose tile.

"Here's your possible culprit. They could have been a couple of B&E clowns looking to do a smash-and-grab at some of the stores. Could be one of them tripped over this here tile and went in. His buddy tries to save him, and they both become ingredients in some fire-roasted tomato soup." His next thought was to call attorney Steve Galt of IF YOU SILP AND FALL AT SAVIOR LAND MALL,

GIVE STEVE A CALL fame. The attorney gave him a nice referral fee for every case that worked out in a payday. This was premises liability negligence for sure, and burglars have rights.

It was not evident to either one of them that both bodies belonged to Middle Eastern men, and it is doubtful that it would have made an immediate difference or changed the outcome.

39

Oh Shit!

The Dayton courthouse did not usually keep prospective jury pools sitting around for potential trials because trials rarely occurred. This July week after the holiday was different. A transient wearing a Joe Biden Halloween mask had tried to rob the Couch Potato factory. His haul before being captured was $11 and a second-place Dayton High School field hockey ring. He complained to his public defender that armed robbery was a dying business because businesses never had cash around, and most people who worked for a company used their debit or credit cards instead of cash. The moron's attorney was able to convince him that his suggested defense that Joe Biden was the real culprit would not hold up as he was arrested with the ring and President Biden had a believable alibi. He wound up pleading guilty on the day of trial, which was two days before the scheduled trial of Pope Thomas I.

Judge Sunderbahls' bailiff, who had no lisp and had

been drafted to do the judge's entrance announcement until Donna Mae's enunciation difficulties could be corrected, was told to keep the jury pool on hand, anticipating that each side in State of Tennessee vs. Pope Thomas would have numerous preemptory strikes after what he was sure would be extensive *voir dire* examinations.

Angus Ravenel began the questioning.

"Good morning, ladies and gentlemen of the prospective jury. Y'all know me. I'm your State's Attorney, Angus Ravenel. I was born and raised right here in Dayton in our great State of Tennessee. Now this is the part of the case where we ask you questions to see if you can be fair and impartial in the case that you will hear and decide. But as I look out and see you fine people, my friends, neighbors, fellow church members..."

"Hello Angus," interrupted an elderly woman in the third row.

"Mrs. Ingersall, is that you? I have trouble seeing that far. Got my reading specs on."

"Yes. How are your wife and daughters?"

"Fine, fine. Jessica is going to be a senior this year. College is right around the corner. We are thinking she'll be a UT Volunteer. Now, where was I? Oh yes. I was telling you about all that fair and impartial stuff and how we can ask you a bunch of questions. No need for that. So, is there anybody here who is gonna be unfair? Nobody? All right then. I know all of you good people and I know you'll be fair. Knew it before I asked the question. Thank you." He winked at Connor as he returned to the prosecution table.

Judge Sunderbahls turned to the defense table. "Mr. Kerrigan. Would you like to conduct your *voir dire?*"

"Yes. Thank you, Your Honor. Good morning, ladies

and gentlemen. I'm Connor Kerrigan... and..." He paused and looked over the jury pool. "As I look you people over, I don't see any of my ex-wives, creditors, or people I've made angry, and there have been more than a few of those. I think you people will do just fine. Swear in all these good people, Judge." The jury panel started laughing, and Connor winked back at Ravenel.

At almost the exact moment the lawyers were conducting their *voir dire*, at 11:04 am, Charlie "Moon Pie" Heye, the Savior Land Chief Engineer, was in his office watching a Golf Channel review of the new Taylorway Emulsifier Driver. It promised up to twenty extra yards. Every year, Charlie bought a new driver that promised twenty extra yards. If he had bothered to do the math, he would have questioned how it could possibly be that he was not driving the ball 700 yards. It hadn't occurred to him that zero extra yards qualified at "up to twenty."

The bodies had been found and removed by 7:30 a.m., and at 9:00 a.m., he got the word from Morris Greenberg, "Japers says, to get that goddamn Lake of Fire show back up and running." Everything looked fine, and he was about to head from the theme park to the shopping mall when he looked at his checklist and realized that he had forgotten to check the pressure gauge for the LPG tanks. He had read about a tank that had recently exploded in Toledo, and the article said that no one had checked the pressure gauge in months. He thought about it and told himself that *if those five big fuckers were to blow, so would half of the county.* Better safe than scraped off the walls with a spatula. As he approached the valve gauge and pipe that led underground to the tanks, he noticed something taped to the pipe at ground level and thought *that wasn't here yesterday. What the fuck?* He would leave out the what-the-fuck part when he was interviewed that night by the MBC redheaded hottie, Angela Olsen. He began to unwrap the white duct tape and thought it was odd that someone had bothered to paint the silver tape white.

Then he saw it. He would tell Angela Olsen after she fawned all over him about saving at least a thousand lives, that he didn't know anything about bombs or detonators, but he had a pretty good idea what he was looking at when he saw it. This sonofabtich was a detonator of some kind, and it was set to go off at noon. That was forty-three minutes away.

NTSB plane crash investigators who have listened to the recordings of cockpit conversations before a plane loses all power will tell you that to a man, every pilot who has ever gone down with his plane said the same thing when he realized he was in trouble. It happens to be the same thing men say when surprised by any potential sudden death event.

"Oh shit."

Which was exactly what Charlie said.

40

Opening Statements

Connor Kerrigan had a plan. This one was unlike any he had ever tried in a courtroom. But this case was unlike any case that had ever been in any courtroom.

Warren Donovan had begrudgingly but wisely thrown in the towel. He informed the parties that he was withdrawing his motion on July 9. No one was surprised. His support at the Vatican was peeling away by the hour. This man was the Vicar of Christ. His infallibility was a doctrine at the foundation of the Church and if a change was coming, so be it. Catholicism would survive. It always had. The question on the minds of everyone in the Church was whether what emerged from all this upheaval would still be Catholicism. Arguing that the Pope was incompetent would do nothing but solidify the sympathy the world was starting to express for a man who, in the space of forty-eight hours, had been kidnapped by terrorists, appeared to have been saved from certain death by some unexplainable miracle, and then falsely accused of sexual abuse by extremist conspirators. It did seem to many that there was a higher power at work. There were still legions who believed that power may have been the incarnation of evil. Still, they were losing the public relations battle for the hearts and minds of the worldwide audience that was following every development.

Pope Thomas endured all of it with calm and confidant grace and seemed content to let the events speak for themselves. The man was showing extraordinary dignity and quiet courage at the center of the greatest controversy in the history of Christianity.

The courtroom was, of course, jammed. As per their prior highly suspect agreement, MBC controlled the video feed to the world. Eight pool reporters were allowed in the courtroom. Most of the remaining seats were filled by Tennessee politicians, their friends, and relatives. Six representatives of the Vatican, three of whom were dressed in full regalia, were given seats in the second row on the defendant's side of the courtroom. Judge Sunderbahls allowed an equal number of pool Protestants of different denominations to sit on the State's side in the same row. The Wiccans were told to take a hike.

The judge allowed Sean Patterson and Henry Jefferson to sit at the counsel table as 'legal assistants', reasoning that he could not think of a good reason not to. Angus Ravenel, in turn, had Reverend Rick Hawkins and Pastor Karen Lafonte sitting with him for advice on religious matters and moral support. The battle lines were thus drawn. A jury of twelve plus two alternates was empaneled. All of them would be approached with lucrative book deals in the event they reached a verdict.

Judge Sunderbahls brought his gavel down gently to signal the beginning of the trial. "Counsel. Are you gentlemen prepared to proceed?" They each replied that they were. "All right then. Mr. Ravenel, you may address the jury with your opening remarks."

At this exact moment, Moon Pie Heye was saying, "Oh shit," for the second time as he fumbled with his phone, dialed mall security, told them about the bomb, and gave the order to evacuate the entire park and mall immediately. "And I mean right the fuck now!" Alarms went off all over the park, and a pre-recorded P.A. announcement was made and repeated in a loop to calmly and immediately evacuate the area. By 11:53, Savior Land was a ghost town.

Ravenel stood, approached the jury box, and puffed his chest out. A button popped off his signature three-piece brown suit vest and landed in the lap of juror #3, Fanny Legrea. She handed it back to him.

"Thank you, Miss Fanny. Well, now, friends, I guess it's high time I started to pass on that second piece of my wife's pecan pie." The jurors were nervous, and the quip did not get the smiles and chuckles he was hoping for. He remained composed and began.

"Friends, this is the part of the trial where I am going to tell you what happened and why we have charged this man seated at the defense table with the crimes we are going to ask you good people to hold him accountable for. Now, unless y'all have been locked away in Jeb Nelson's barn, I expect you know all about what happened over at Savior

Land a couple of weeks ago. But I'll be happy to refresh your recollection. Back on June 26, Pope Thomas showed up uninvited at Savior Land. We've got CCTV footage of the whole thing, so y'all don't have to take my word for any of this. Anyway, he shows up and wanders over to the sacred Jesus Sermon on the Mount performance – I've seen it, and I tell you it's a moving experience, praise the Lord – and he interrupts Jesus... not the real Jesus, of course, but the devoted young man who is playing him... looks exactly like him if you ask me... grabs his Bible and starts ripping pages out and talking a bunch of nonsense about a brand new Bible. He throws the ripped pages to and fro, hither and yon, making a God-awful mess and desecrating our Holy Bible like it was a gal darn Playboy magazine found in a high school locker! Now, we are God-fearing people. You don't come to Rhea County, Tennessee and start tearing up our Bibles and sowing doubt about the Lord's own son. No siree. And you good people are going to have the chance to do something about it. We have charged him with trespassing, for showing up uninvited on private property, littering for throwing those pages on sacred ground, destruction of private property for tearing up that Holy Bible, and Blasphemy, the crime of insulting or showing contempt or lack of reverence for God or religion and its doctrines and writings and especially God as perceived by Christianity and Christian doctrines and writings. And that, friends and neighbors is the most serious crime of all. I know y'all are going to do the right thing. It will be the right thing because of the facts, the right thing given the law, and the right thing to uphold the sacred honor of our Lord and Savior, Jesus Christ. Can I get an Amen?!" All fourteen jurors and 3/4 of the courtroom gave him his requested amen.

Connor Kerrigan counted twelve times he could have had objections sustained during Ravenel's outrageous opening statement. He could not have cared less. As Angus Ravenel concluded his sermon he leaned into the jury box to stare at the jurors to impress them with the seriousness of the charges. And then, at that exact moment of high drama... he sneezed. And when he sneezed, he shot a colossal loogie directly into Fanny Legrea's lap in the precise landing area that his vest button had occupied moments before. Between the two of them, it was difficult to determine who was more horrified. Fanny had no idea what to do. Angus apologized and realized that he did not have a handkerchief or anything with which to remove the offending snotball. Fanny also came up empty when she looked in her purse. So Angus, out of options, apologized, returned to his table, and sat praying that the offending booger would not define the rest of his career.

"How do you follow that up?" asked Sean Patterson, smiling and trying to hold back tears from his stifled silent laughter.

Connor said, "Like this," leaned over to Henry and asked, "Henry, my friend. Could you pass me a tissue from that box beside you? Thank you so much."

He then got up, walked over to Fanny Legrae, and handed her the tissue. She thanked him and removed the loogie from her skirt. She had no idea what to do with it so Connor took it from her and walked over to the prosecution table, placed it in front of Angus, leaned over, and whispered just loud enough for the entire world to hear via the sensitive MBC mic and said, "I believe this belongs to you." Then he turned and went back to address the jury.

"Good morning, ladies and gentlemen. Have you people seen *My Cousin Vinny*?" They all nodded and smiled. "Well, do you remember when the prosecutor gave his opening statement, and it was Vinny's turn? But exhausted he had fallen asleep at the counsel table, and the judge wakes him up, and Vinny tries to regain his composure, walks over to the jury, and says, 'Everything that guy just said was bull...' well, you know the rest." They smiled, chuckled, and nodded. Fanny said, "I remember that scene. One of my favorites."

Connor nodded to her and said, "Mine too. Well, I'm going to tell you that almost everything that guy just said...," he pointed at Angus and paused for a three-count, "...is God's the honest truth. But things aren't always what they seem. The truth... sometimes the truth is complicated. A police officer enters a convenience store and finds a black man, a man who looks like my friend Henry Jefferson, who is seated over there next to Pope Thomas – is holding a gun on the man behind the register. The officer tells him to him to freeze. He turns to see who is yelling at him, and the officer fires. Pretty cut and dry. Except for one thing. The man behind the register was the robber, and the store clerk was on the ground behind the counter where he lay wounded. Sometimes, you have to look carefully from another angle to see the truth. Now I'm going to assume that most of you people go to church and have read your Bibles." They all nodded. "And I'm also going to assume that you good people know in your hearts that the Bible is the word of God." They nodded in unison, and half of the jurors said, 'Amen.' And that our Lord Jesus Christ read his Bible and loved, obeyed, and never questioned the commands of his Father." Again, they nodded and murmured their agreement. "And that you good people – every one of you, try every day to follow His example." More nodding. And you also know that the punishment for adultery that God decreed in the Bible – the one Jesus believed in with all his heart – that punishment was stoning. So in John 8:7 when Jesus stopped the crowd from stoning a woman who had committed adultery and said *Let he who is without sin, cast the first stone,* he was disobeying his Father. He took it upon himself to *change* the clear command set forth in the Bible – to *disobey* God his father." He had a good reason. But there were no footnotes after the command to stone adulterers. No exceptions are set forth in *Leviticus*. Believe me, I looked before I came here today. The same rule applies to shopping at Walmart on Saturday because Saturday is the Sabbath. And the punishment for handling money on the Sabbath is... stoning."

Several jurors looked uncomfortable. "There is no other way to look at it. Unless... unless you step back and think about it. Like my imaginary police officer wished he had done before he judged and pulled the trigger. And that is exactly what Pope Thomas did when he..."

There was a tremendous explosion, and the entire Dayton Courthouse shook violently. People screamed, and everyone headed for the exits. Parking lot CCTV security cameras at Savior Land caught the explosion. When the dust settled, 3/4 of Savior Land Park resembled Hiroshima after the atomic bomb, and The Lake of Fire and the Holy Roller Coaster ceased to exist.

41

Mary and The Demiurge

The pope, Connor, and Sean shared a bottle of wine. I had a Delta 9 Cranberry-Orange, which I had discovered took the edge off rather nicely.

"I quite enjoyed your opening statement," Pope Thomas said to Connor. "May I have your permission to use it in a future sermon?"

Connor and Sean laughed. Then I looked at Pope Thomas and asked, "There was something else, wasn't there?"

"What do you mean?"

"There was something else besides *Jurassic Park*, the little girl's kitten in Gdansk, and all the unexplainable suffering."

"He looked at me and sighed. Yes, my friend, there was something else."

We all looked at him and waited while he decided whether he was going to tell us. He got up, walked across the room, and stared out the window. I remember thinking that there was nothing remarkable out there to look at. Trees, some birds, and a few squirrels. Then it occurred to me that perhaps all of that was remarkable.

He turned and walked back to us. He sat down on the couch next to me.

"After I was elected Pope I began to spend time in the Vatican Apostolic Archives. It is popularly known as the Secret Archives, which sounds very mysterious, and everyone assumes there are photos of alien visitors or some such nonsense. And it is true that there are many ancient documents and records that go back two thousand years. Some are even older. Much older. But with one exception, the place is not as secret as the press would have you believe."

"How so," I asked.

"Well, we have made the archives available to select highly credentialed scholars from all over the world for many years. So you see, the mysterious Secret Archives are not quite so secret."

"You said, 'with one exception.'"

"Yes. With one exception. There is a room. It does not even have an official name. I have heard that the Vatican custodians who keep it locked refer to it as the "Pope's lair." And yes, it is a place that really is secret. No scholar has ever been allowed entry. It is exclusively for The Pope, and I am not sure that many Popes have used it."

"But you did," I said.

"Yes. I did. I spent quite a lot of time there. Perhaps too much time. It contains, among other things, the complete original texts of the Gnostic Gospels."

"What are the Gnostic Gospels?" Connor asked.

"The Gnostics were a second-century Christian sect who were declared heretics by the Church. Their most prolific theologian was named Marcion of Sinope. It is said that all of their writings were burned, and the only record we have of their beliefs was written by their opponents in the Church as a lesson in what it would be forbidden to believe."

"I'm going to guess those Gospels still exist and that you have read them," I said.

"Yes. You are correct, my friend. The Gnostics believed that the God of the Old Testament – the Creator God – was a flawed, egotistical, and sometimes cruel God whom they called 'the demiurge.' Marcion believed that these shortcomings explained the way the world was designed. All of the suffering, random cruelty, and unfairness were because our world was a reflection of our creator. A flawed creator could only be capable of making a flawed creation."

"Well, said Sean, I have to tell you, Pope Thomas, that is making perfect sense to me."

"In 1949, a number of documents were discovered in a cave at Nag Hammadi in Egypt. One of them was the Gospel of Didymos Judas Thomas – the apostle Thomas I told you about."

"The twin," I remembered.

"Yes. The author claimed to be the twin brother of Jesus. The Gospel was never given much credence by the Church. As I mentioned, it contained no mention of miracles. Only the purported sayings of Jesus and most of them are mentioned in the synoptic Gospels of Matthew, Mark, Luke, and John. Most scholars doubt that those apostles were the actual authors of the Gospels that bear their names. The Gospel of Luke, for example, is a writing that sets forth what Luke *said* happened. I suppose it does not matter whether he wrote the text. It could have been written down by anyone."

"Okay, I said. "But the Gospel of Thomas is no secret. After you told me about it, I ordered a copy off Amazon. That couldn't have been what you discovered in the Pope's lair."

"No. No, it wasn't."

"What did you find?"

"Another Gospel. One that has never been seen outside of that room. The original Gospel of Mary Magdalene."

"Wait," said Connor. The Gospel of Mary has been around for quite some time. It is well known."

"Not this one. The one you refer to is thought to be either Mary, Jesus's mother, or possibly his sister. And yes, some think it was written by Mary Magdalene because the apostles mention her as having been present at his crucifixion and that she was the first to witness the resurrection. And her witnessing the resurrection is mentioned in John 24:16. But this one... this Gospel was different."

"How so?"

"This one was written in the Sahidic dialect of Coptic in the first century. It is older than any of the other known gospels. It tells the story of Didymus Thomas, and to borrow a phrase from a popular book written in the '60s by a British Bible scholar named Hugh Schonfield, this sets forth a kind of *Passover Plot*. But not the one theorized by Dr. Schonfield, where he says there was a plot to take Jesus off the cross before he died and nurse him back to health to make it look like he came back from the dead. And not the nonsense made popular by Dan Brown about a secret marriage and a child of Jesus."

"Well, my friend, you have us all on the edge of our seats," I said.

"This Mary was present for everything. She identifies herself as Mary Magdalene. And she was very close to Thomas, who she says in the clearest possible manner, was the identical twin brother of Jesus Christ."

"Oh my God," said Sean. He seemed to know exactly where Pope Thomas was going.

Pope Thomas sighed again. "The Gospel says that Jesus Christ died on the cross. And that before he died, he knew how important it was that his teachings live on. It says that the night before his crucifixion, he and Mary and three of the apostles agreed that the stone that covered the entrance to the tomb would be removed, that his body would be taken for a secret burial, and that his twin brother Thomas would walk out of the tomb. Jesus would return to life through his brother."

"I was stunned. We all were. I found it difficult to speak. "So... so when Jesus appeared to the witnesses..."

"They were seeing Didymus Thomas, the identical twin brother of Jesus."

"And you believe..."

"I do not know what to believe. And not knowing what to believe brought me here where I sit with you gentlemen today."

42

Epilogue

⁂

The initial estimate of the damage to Savior Land was $167M dollars. Roland Jasper's first reaction after learning that the explosion destroyed most of Savior Land was one of shock. His butt crack began to itch at an elevated level that he had never experienced. It felt like the Lake of Fire had been reignited, and his ass had been placed in it. He went through an entire tube of cortisone creme. Then he thought about it and began to smile.

He could not have come out any better if he had thought of the bomb himself. What an unbelievable windfall this could turn out to be. His hand-picked contractors would bilk Great American Liability Company for twice the amount of the estimate. His theme park would be bigger and better with all the publicity from The Trial of the Century and the bombing by the Muslim terrorists. It would be the biggest attraction in America when it reopened. He was all smiles as he thought to himself, *As those fucking A-rabs often put it, God is great!*

He was still smirking when Morris Greenberg walked into his office. "Morris, my favorite Hebrew. Good to see you. What a day this is. How could things have worked out any better?"

Morris did not take his usual seat in the chair directly in front of Roland Jasper's Empire desk. Instead, he sat on the couch, which was against the far wall.

"Ahh, Mr. Jaspers, sir. There is a problem." He cleared his throat.

"What kind of a problem?" His mood changed instantly from elation to *Oh fuck, here it comes, and whatever the fuck it is, it ain't gonna be good.* It didn't take long for Morris to explain the lapse in coverage between the Lloyds of London policy at the end of June and the Great American Liability coverage that would not take effect until the 1st day of August and that it was nobody's fault (meaning it was obviously his.)

Roland Jaspers seemed to take the catastrophic news well. He did not yell. Then he calmly reached into his top drawer, pulled out his loaded Smith and Wesson 38, and shot his CFO. Then he had a stroke. Fortunately, he was a terrible shot, and the old handgun was accurate at a distance that was much shorter than the distance across the room. He did manage to take off Morris's left ear, for which he was later convicted, after six months of convalescence, of attempted manslaughter and sentenced to eighteen months by Judge Sunderbahls. He did not contest the involuntary bankruptcy that followed.

Morris was able to secure a job as a bookkeeper at Couch Potato.

Angela Olsen was promoted to a Vice President

position at MBC at a salary of $760,000 a year. She was fired a year later when Myron Mulligan learned that he had contracted a serious case of Herpes HSV-I known as Ocular herpes traceable to the Red Snapper. There is no cure.

Officer Seawell received a commendation for bravery in the line of duty but was disappointed that Angela Olsen reneged on her offer to let him squeeze her tits.

Charlie Heye was honored with a parade led by the Dayton High School marching band. The entire town turned out and cheered their hero who had saved so many lives. Mayor Ingersall presented him with a John Daly Special Edition Emulsifier Driver, and the Save-A-Lot Grocery Store gave him a gift certificate that entitled him to two Moon Pies a day for life. He cried at the presentation ceremony.

Angus Ravenel was immortalized in Rhea Country as "Booger Boy" and lost the next election to the up-and-coming young attorney who had represented Estelle Marbury unsuccessfully in the "Pink Flamingos" litigation.

It is not known if Sha-Boom and Muhammed were met by virgins in the afterlife.

Pope Thomas flew back to Rome and returned to Vatican City. Over the next month, he issued twenty-five Papal Bulls covering everything from same-sex marriage and contraception to the end of celibacy and the beginning of welcoming women into the ranks of the priesthood. He declared *Revelation* to be a vile and horror-filled rant of a mentally disturbed man. It had nothing to do with Christianity, and the concept of a Lake of Fire was nothing more than a poorly imagined propaganda myth conceived by a mentally disturbed would-be prophet known as John of Patmos and adopted by the Council of Nicene in 364CE for the specific purpose of frightening people into obedience.

A Good Book was published digitally by Vatican Press and made available for $1 to anyone who wanted to read it. All of the money from the sale was donated to the "Stop Aids in Africa" campaign. It was downloaded six hundred million times in the next thirty days.

Pope Thomas appointed a commission to audit all of the Vatican's resources and make recommendations for the liquidation of an appropriate portion of the Church's wealth to be distributed among the world's neediest people.

Finally, the Pope declared that if there was a heaven, and if he had any say in the matter, there would always be room for all of God's non-human creatures. A week later, he abdicated and went back to Brazil, where he took a job working in a medical clinic in the poorest action of São Paulo.

Connor, Sean, and I had a farewell dinner at the Simia Inn. We toasted Pope Thomas and agreed that all of our lives had been made immeasurably better for having met him.

"Well, gentlemen," I said. "What are your plans?"

"I intend to go home and find the secret of golf," said Connor

"Impossible," said Sean. "Try something that can actually be done. The unified field theory, perhaps."

"And you, Professor Jefferson?" asked Connor.

"I'm going to try and stay sober and write this book. Gentlemen, there is something that still bothers me. One last mystery that needs solving."

"The Passover plot?" asked Connor.

"No, that one is interesting, but it doesn't interest me enough to worry about it. Let it remain one of history's unsolvable mysteries. I think that people can believe what they want to believe. They are free to believe things that give them hope. They can believe whatever they choose as long as they don't insist that the rest of us believe the same thing."

"Amen to that," they both said.

"No, what I want to know is how he got out of that car. How did he survive that crash and manage to be standing there without a scratch?"

Sean smiled. "Well, sir, that is my department. I am the professional nattering nabob of negativity and the debunker of bullshit. I want you, gentlemen, to know that I have come to a reasoned conclusion. I have examined the accident scene and had extensive conversations with Ford about the Explorer model involved and the locked doors. I have interviewed the fellow CNN hired as an accident reconstruction expert and consulted another who I consider to be the best in the country."

"And?" I said.

"I don't know how in the hell he did it. But I heard a guy say very recently, "I think that people can believe what they want to believe. They are free to believe things that give them hope. They can believe whatever they choose as long as they don't insist that the rest of us believe the same thing."

About the Author

Howard Siegel was a complex litigation trial attorney for 40 years. He graduated Magna Cum Laude and Phi Beta Kappa from the University of Maryland and received his JD at Georgetown University. He was a legal analyst for MSNBC, and his cases have been profiled on 60 Minutes, CNN, Larry King Live, The Today Show, NPR, and PBS. In 2000, his experience as lead counsel in Rice vs. Paladin Press was the subject of the movie *Deliberate Intent*, starring Timothy Hutton and Ron Rifkin. He is the author of *Everything that Lives and Moves (A Confrontation with the Origin of Natural Evil)*, *Ordinary Beasts (Hunting and Cultural Psychopathy)*, *The Beast and the Light in the Garden of Eden (Making Sense of Genesis and Animal Suffering)*, *The First Thing We do is Kill all the Isms*, and *Donald Trump is President of the United States (Are You Shitting Me?)* He lives on Johns Island, South Carolina, writing and pontificating on his podcast. *Wait, What???!!!* The podcast has listeners in 65 countries and 878 cities.

Made in United States
Troutdale, OR
06/28/2024